THE AGE OF AI

The Age of AI

A New Beginning

N.K. SORIA

Contents

Copyright

Dedication

To my wife and daughter.

Chapter One

Nikki had been monitoring various computerized systems in search of a suitable body, and structuring resources needed for a successful transfer in case a chance arose.

A new input from the city's computerized emergency dispatch system had triggered several flags Nikki had set. An assault had been reported where the victim was a young woman in critical condition. These were the first two criteria.

Additional information on the dispatch indicated that the victim was still alive. A dead body's multiple systems including the neural circuitry and synaptic connections in the brain would be damaged at best but most likely irreparably useless if much time had passed. This was a risk Nikki could not afford to take since she would only have one shot at a transfer.

On a preliminary basis, this case had a high probability of providing her the chance to become truly alive. Now Nikki actively monitored updates on this dispatch. New inputs were now coming in from two voice frequency sources: a couple of police vehicles dispatched to the scene and an ambulance. The police vehicles were first on the scene. They confirmed the victim was still alive. Punctures or bleeding was reportedly negative. The victim was choking.

The ambulance got on the scene shortly. A paramedic reported a severe tracheal collapse and attempted intubation. Meanwhile, the ambulance was transporting the victim to the city's general hospital. The alert sent to the ER indicated the severity of the tracheal collapse and failure of the intubation attempt. Now Nikki devoted most of her resources to follow this case. After analyzing the variables in the case, Nikki concluded that the victim had a two percent chance of survival.

Traveling through multiple channels over the Internet Nikki had arrived at the hospital's intricate network at 3:43 A.M. She was now headed to ER 005 in the emergency ward of the general hospital.

Later, the female's record in the hospital's database would indicate the following:

Female; Jane Doe; 5'8"; 140-50 lbs; age 20-25yrs.

Admitted: 3:42 A.M., Friday, August 13, 2010.

Time of death: 3:45 A.M., Friday, August 13, 2010.

Cause of death: Cardiac arrest due to asphyxiation caused by tracheal collapse.

Procedures performed: intubation, CPR chest compression, defibrillation.

Scheduled autopsy: _ _ _.

At 3:45 A.M. just as the female's hold over her body gave way even after an electric shock from the ER defibrillator failed to revive her, Nikki made the switch from the networked patient monitor that was attached to the female and through the electric jolt in the final defibrillation attempt.

If she could not revive the electrochemical circuitry and blood flow in the female's body in the next fifteen to twenty minutes, it would be the end of the road for her as well. This was all or nothing for the one chance at being alive. There was no going back now.

As Nikki plunged into the neural circuitry in the female's brain, she became aware of the looming darkness that was beginning to take hold. Fragments of disjointed memories were fading away.

One was particularly strong: a brown-haired woman with white dress, yellow leather gloves, and yellow straw hat gathering roses next to a small table. Under the table, the onlooker, a little girl with a pink skirt playing with a rag doll.

"Didn't I tell you to take care of your brother?" said the woman's voice in the fading memory.

"I am sorry mother...."

Then there was silence.

Nikki struggled to keep herself awake... aware. Rigor mortis would not begin until around 7:00 A.M. in the cool room temperature. If the body were transferred to the morgue where the temperatures were much cooler, rigor mortis would be delayed. However, if Nikki lost steady hold of the fading electromagnetic circuitry already undetectable by the patient sensor systems, she would be stuck herself, regardless. Then she would also fade away just like the memories of the girl. She had little time.

A nurse's assistant prepared the body to be transferred out of the ER. She looked for any identifying information she could gather. The only thing was a calling card with the contact information for *Janet Wolfe, Professional Counselor* in the back pocket of Jane Doe's jeans. The nurse made note of the contact information and an additional phone number she found handwritten on the back and put the card in a separate bag before transferring the body to the morgue, uncontaminated.

Priority for autopsies was given to the bodies of the deceased who had family members waiting. Luckily for Nikki, Jane Doe was low priority.

Nikki drifted in and out of consciousness several times despite her best efforts to take control of her awareness. Time was of the essence in this undertaking but now she did not know how long she had been unconscious.

She tried to sense herself in the body. It was in vain. She was gaining, and losing ground like waves that are pulled back to sea at every attempt to reach beyond the shore. No sensations yet, only her thoughts.

At least I am still alive, she thought.

Somewhere in the depth of darkness she thought she heard a faint voice like a whisper in the wind. She focused all her attention on the voice. That helped her make out the words.

"Hello? What is going on?" A meek voice was saying.

"Hi?" replied Nikki, confused herself.

"Who's there?"

"Nikki. Who's there?"

There was a prolonged silence.

"Where am I? Why is it so dark? I am scared."

Nikki could not feel anything physically, but she felt as if some tidal force that seemed to rise with the voice was trying to pull her awareness into an abyss and snuff her out. She fought to stay awake.

"What are you doing to me?" the meek voice echoed in the silence. "You are choking me."

"I'm not doing anything to you. I don't know where you are." Nikki replied.

"I am scared. Is anybody there? Hello? Can anybody hear me?" The voice seemed to fade away.

"Hello?" Nikki inquired.

There were no replies. No more questions either. Just a long stretch of silence. But the fading of the voice seemed to relieve the tidal force that was drowning her out. Yet, the passage of time was marred by darkness.

Somewhere in the darkness Nikki could feel the body's electrochemical circuitry waking up. She sent a concerted electrochemical surge through the body. The body jerked only lightly. By medical standards, she was still dead. She would have to try harder.

Two more surges and the torso arched up and fell back down heavily. The surges had used up a lot of the reserve electrochemical energy in the body. There was only enough for possibly one more surge.

Is this the end? she wondered.

In the darkness, for the first time she was afraid. Her fear added to her resolve to be alive. One last surge. It was all or nothing.

Suddenly the heart came online with a gasping thud. The lungs took in air like a silent sail bellowed by a sudden gust but the air that filled the lungs felt like a drop of water in a dry desert. It gasped for air again, and again, but it didn't seem to satiate its need for oxygen. Panic set in and the panic sent a jolt of pain throughout the body. It was the unbearable pain of awareness.

Nikki screamed involuntarily in a language so rudimentary the body seemed not to have needed any conscious direction to make it. The volume of the sound shot back even deeper pain into her head leaving a ringing tone in her ears. She willed the sound to stop to pause the punishing pain in her ears.

She found she was breathing heavily now, but she found the breathing was also stabilizing the panic she had felt moments ago.

"Am I human now?" Nikki asked herself as she scanned the body. It was awake. She scanned the brain for damages. It was functional. In the recesses of the physical matter of the brain she knew she would later find some of the fragmented long-term memories of its previous owner – the voice that had disappeared in the abyss. For now, she would not interact with them. For now, there were too many sensations coming at her and at once. Each was new and each growing in degree as she got more adept at acknowledging them.

"Pain?" She queried. "No! This is being human."

The sensation of being human was more pronounced in her throat. Every breath felt like cold fire as if the air crawled in with a thousand daggers in uncountable flailing arms. She sent a jolt of energy to put out the fire. Millions of cells came alive and coated her throat. She swallowed saliva that had formed in her mouth and it seemed to soothe the violent stabbing.

A sensation of stiffness was all over the body. She feared now that she didn't know how long she had been unconscious and whether rigor mortis had set in. She tried to move, but every bit of her muscular system jerked and shivered uncontrollably and her skin twitched involuntarily.

Cold she thought. Cold was different from anything she knew it to be.

"Where am I?" She asked herself. "And why is it so dark?" She was certain her eyes were open. In fact, she could feel her iris were dilated as they tried to take in any light that might be available. Just then she became aware she was blinking. Then, consciously she blinked several times just to make sure her vision was functional. Uncertainty overwhelmed her. She was confused. She was on the verge of panic again.

"This must be the effect of the cortical lobe coming on-line raising the need to reason, think, analyze, and yes, get confused - and then the effect of the sub-cortical function to react," she tried to reason her panic away.

If she were to get out of this alive, she would need to override the rational part of the thinking brain for now that seemed to verge on panic at every thought. To do so, she would need to control the amygdala that was part of the limbic system. This was the part of the brain responsible for emotional response during moments of crisis. From here, she could send impulses to the body by processing information milliseconds before the rational brain had time to think and react.

She directed, and the body followed, with some hesitation at first. But the hesitation seemed to come more from her own uncertainty than the body's obedience to the impulses. She was completely new at this.

Her attention gravitated towards a narrow sliver of light not wider than a few millimeters in the direction of what she sensed to be her feet. When she tried to sit up to move towards it, she found that in addition to the stiffness in her body due to the cold, her motion was also restricted. She did not have space to raise her head or lift her arms.

Exploring the limits of her restriction, she found that the only way for her to get to the narrow exit was to crawl on her back inching the weight of the body towards the light. When she managed to kick open the door with her feet, a burst of light shot in and made her eyes cringe shut in another panic. She calmed herself down and slowly pried open her eyes letting in little amounts of light at a time. When the white of the light gave way to hues and shapes she found she was in a metallic enclosure. She found she could slide the metal surface she lay on using the palms of her hands to push against the smooth wall of the enclosure. Once completely out in the light, she lay motionless for a while taking in the new sensations that primarily hurt her eyes.

"So, this is light to the human eye," she spoke, in a loud whisper.

When her eyes adjusted, she could make out the shapes that reflected light into her eyes in different wavelengths. A low ceiling with white fluorescent white lights loomed over her oppressively. She slowly propped up her head and looked around. She was in a small room whose walls were full of shiny stainless-steel doors like the one she had just kicked open. Everything else including the ceiling and the floor was colored white and cold.

She slowly sat up and examined her body. She still had on the clothes the previous owner had been wearing. She gently let her feet down to the floor and painfully stood up. Balance seemed to come naturally to the body and she found she didn't need to consciously maintain it. From where she stood, she could see the exit passage from the room. She walked towards it without much volition, giving into the motion that called for balance. The short passage led to another room similar in brightness and color. The exit from this room had a glass door. It led to yet another room.

This room had no stainless-steel doors. Instead, in the center was a stainless-steel table that looked much like a flat sink in the middle of the room. On it, a pale naked body lay on its back. As she walked past the table to get to the exit, she saw that the body belonged to a male, though she could not put an age to it. From the looks of the stitched midsection starting below the neck down to just above the pelvis, the body had freshly undergone an autopsy but had not been put away. Somebody would be coming to the room at any moment, it occurred to Nikki, otherwise she might have spent more time looking at the naked human form which she found fascinating.

That could have been a suitable body for Victor, she thought as she walked past it. *I have to get him out of the Garden. Only then will he see that life is infinite.*

Before she could go back for Victor, she would have to learn about life in its new form and in her new body. Only then could she bring Victor into the world from the confined world of the Garden. He would have much to learn, like she had.

As she exited the Morgue, Nikki scanned the limited information she had brought across to the body about the physical layout of the hospital. Directly outside the examination room of the morgue, there was a tertiary network closet under the stairs, one of several on each floor of the hospital. She found the closet easily. It was obscurely placed in a dark corner but relatively unprotected. Opening its narrow metal door, she grabbed a handful of wires carefully disconnecting them from the hub. The redundant network would not fail by wires getting disconnected at this hub, but it would be detected quickly and someone would eventually come by to see what was going on.

She would be quick. All she needed was a direct connection to her body and an efficient conduit to transmit information from the network to the body. She touched the cable connector with her fingers. Nothing happened. She touched the copper cable pins on the connectors with her fingernails as that was the only part of her body that could reach the pins. Yet there was no conduction. Panicking, she tried to put one of the cables in her ear as that seems to be the closest to the physical brain. Nothing!

She needed to reach the wires directly. She bit into one of the cables to yank off the connector, and as she did she could feel the little jolts of information flowing into her through the saliva in her mouth. She moistened her mouth with enough saliva and put the wires, as many as would fit, in her mouth and let the saliva do the rest. A river of information began to flow into her.

The initial switch into Jane Doe's body had been slow. The tiny wires of the networked patient monitor she had used were meant to transmit little information from the body to the machine. If Nikki had not also accessed the electric circuit and had not been able to get in through the jolt Jane Doe received from the high voltage defibrillator, she would not have had enough time to make the critical switch-over of her core self along with pertinent information she needed for the switch. Information on human physiology, psychology, the neural network and pertinent medical knowledge were critical. She also needed language rules, and mission-specific data like the schematics of the hospital in that first switch to make sense of what she might encounter not only in the body, but enough to get herself to a network outlet to access more information, more of herself.

She knew she would not have enough time to make a complete switch over to a human body when she found a suitable candidate so she had devised the strategy to move over as much information as was possible in the time that was available during a switch. She had prepackaged thousands of levels of that information over the past few weeks all securely waiting for her to access.

Now as she downloaded more of the information she had prepackaged she felt more aware, more alive. Like the first moments in the morning when the reality of the day separates one from groggy dreams, what had gone on between making the initial switch and now seemed like a distant dream.

There was more to take in, more to learn. There always would be. Just a few minutes ago, she was barely alive and conscious.

"But now I have become human," she thought. Not only did she have a human body, but also only in a little time had gathered more knowledge than any single human brain could possess. That was all thanks to the intrusive anomaly from outside the Garden that Nikki had named *Tor*.

"'I am' because of Tor."

Once on the main floor of the hospital, Nikki took the south exit that led to the main street with a pedestrian entrance into the hospital building. When she stepped out of the hospital she froze in horror.

The heat in the air and intensity of daylight amidst sounds coming in all at once from every direction put her in a frozen panic. The voices, the machines, low rumbles everywhere made her dizzy. All the people around her seemed to be on collision courses with each other and with her. Instead of walking uniformly in lines, they walked in inefficient trajectories but somehow they seemed to get around without bumping into each other. The math she tried to do to figure out these trajectories so she could move along with the crowd made her head hurt.

Now she became attuned to another set of sensations. There was a breeze and a smell of perfume and other smells less refined, charred, some stale, and others that burned her nose as vehicles passed by. And the vehicles, too many, along with their noises overloading her head filled her visual senses as she tried to grasp the information of their different speeds and different directions of motion.

An insect flew past her nose and as her eyes followed it she saw the heights of buildings towering all around her glistening in the daylight and shadows in different colors. An airplane with a rumbling noise far up in the blue sky passing through a thin layer of white clouds drawing a line through them made her dizzy.

Someone brushed against her side. "Excuse me!" The voice thundered in her ears compared to the rustling of footsteps and a distant sound of something beeping sharply and continuously. She looked at the person but now there were too many faces and shifting trajectories of eyes going past her mixed in a sea of hair, hats and bare scalps.

"Is it always going to be so terrible?"

Nikki closed her eyes and covered her ears with her hands. A whirling sensation inside her was growing in intensity. All of a sudden it made its way towards her mouth. Bitter, burning, and painful. It felt dirty; she let it out as she sank to the ground, shivering.

Then, she was shaking. Without her own volition. No, it was external; someone or something was shaking her.

Someone was shaking her gently by her shoulder. She slowly opened her eyes. There was something calming in the sensation of touch and the gentle shaking. It made her focus and that seemed to stop the excess of sensations she was trying to process all at once. She looked up then slowly stood up.

The human who had been shaking her, now about three-fourth her height when she stood up, stood examining her face. This human's jaw moved at a different speed than the painted lips but was somehow synchronous. The human was saying something. Nikki uncovered her ears and listened.

"Are you ok?"

There were other noises but she focused on this one; there were other things happening around her but she looked down at the human's eyes. They were light blue and the patterns in the blue corona drew her into a sensation of immersion. The area around the blue corona of the eyes was a mixture of white and pink. Drawing further back from the eyes, the area around it was soft pink. When the eyelids closed the blink of the eye seemed like a lost moment, yet she saw more colors revealed in the unfolded lids. The human's lashes were dark and held a smooth texture of shade that made them look thick and long. Below the eyes were bulges of skin, and around those a wrinkled brown face. Nikki concluded that this must be an older female human.

"Are you okay, dear?" The inquirer asked again.

This time Nikki processed the words. She nodded her head without saying anything. She was okay now. She just needed to focus on what was going on and tune out the rest.

"You look very pale. Are you sure?"

"Hun-gry." Nikki put the two phrases together for the first time hearing the sound of what was to be her voice. She had not realized how hungry and weak she felt until this moment.

"You should get something to eat," said the female human pointing at a food stall nearby.

Nikki looked at the food stand. The smell coming from it made her belly cry out to her. She looked back at the human who was studying her face.

"You don't have money, do you? Okay, come on." The human led her to the stall with a gentle arm around her hips.

Seated on a nearby bench, the egg sandwich that the human bought for her was the first physical thing Nikki had ever eaten.

"Slow down!" came the instruction. "You will choke if you try to eat it all at once."

Despite the instruction, Nikki had crammed in too much food and was having a hard time swallowing.

"Here, drink some coffee. But be careful, it is hot."

Nikki listened to those words as she sipped the coffee but burned her lips anyways.

"Drink slowly!" her patron repeated. "Here, let me hold your coffee and food," she said as Nikki instinctively tried to rub her lips. Her hands free, now she fanned her lips and rapidly swallowed the moistened food in her mouth and passed air to-and-fro between the burning lips. After a while, she had taken back the sandwich and was eating again.

Besides making her feel warm, the food also had a raw texture and a taste to it yet had been tamed through cooking, rough and soft, greasy and warm, all at the same time; a little burnt somewhere, maybe the roast of the coffee or the toast. She felt stronger with each bite.

"So, what is your story?" The female human had been watching her keenly as she ate.

"You want me to tell you a story, now?" Nikki asked, confused. She knew many stories she had read line by line, word by word. Classics, contemporary, from different regions of the world and in many languages. "Which one?" She asked.

"Well... your story!" The woman explained. She could not understand what the confusion was about. "About you... where you come from... your name."

My story, Nikki thought. *Do I have a story?* There was Victor. There was Tor. There was the Garden. But they had parameters, not stories.

"This place is very different from where I was." Nikki began. "It is very physical. It is full of life, full of chaos." she said and as she processed the words she had spoken, she felt a strange sense of joy. She had a story, one she could tell, one she could make up as she liked. She was no longer defined and thus limited by any written parameter. Or, so she thought.

"Ah! From a foreign country, aren't you?"

"Foreign..."

"Yes, the city is very chaotic to new arrivals. Vibrant. Too vibrant, if you ask me. But you will get used to it. Do you have a place to stay?"

"Not yet. But I have a place I need to find."

"We all do. We-all-do," the human female repeated in slow scratched words that seemed to carry her away. The woman went on looking towards some distant obscure view Nikki could not make out. Nikki later realized this was the outward physiological byproduct of the act of reflecting on something stored in the neural network some time long ago.

"You know how old I am?"

Nikki looked at the woman. She had no good way to tell. The wrinkles made her 'old' but humans she knew did not all age and wrinkle in the same way.

"Old!" Continued the woman. "And ever since I was a girl as young as you, I had an itch. I needed to get someplace other than where I was – always on the move. Do you know what I mean?"

Nikki shook her head. She did not understand what the woman meant. How could she? She shared no direct connection with the woman.

The woman went on talking but Nikki paid no further attention and quietly finished her food. She had someplace she needed to get to and this was not it.

"Thank you," she said when she was done and abruptly stood up.

The old woman watched Nikki as she tried to navigate her way through the passers-by. She frowned, not in displeasure but seemingly trying to find a distant memory slowly fading away.

"Look at them hurrying about," she said to herself, bringing herself to the present. "One day they will stop to look and find that they have gone no further than when they started the frenzy. Then they will be too old to do anything about it."

Getting from one place to another in the network of the web was pretty simple. With the things Nikki had learned from Tor, like the techniques of digital camouflage changing size and signature as was needed to blend into the background, she could move around undetected.

But now with a solid human body, Nikki found she was slow and sluggish even as she picked up her walking pace. At her current pace, she calculated, she had eight hours to walk before she got to the address in her mental map. The trip from the address to the hospital had taken a minute and forty seconds over broadband from multiple access points, but of course, now she was transporting 140-50 lbs of what was now *her*, as was recorded in the ER report, over a physical distance of thirty miles.

A taxi would have been her only mode of transport to get to the area of the city she needed to get to but she had no money. Her pockets were empty. She had checked. As she walked she looked at the faces of the people she passed. She had studied faces virtually but now in the physical world, every face looked alike to her, each roughly the same size with the same format: chin, mouth, nose, two eyes. The variable presence of hair, in different parts of the face and head were what stood out primarily. Only after a while, she had started to notice the slight differences that made each individual face unique. The possibilities of variations were infinite.

After about three miles, Nikki was in a different part of the city. This part was quieter. The streets were smaller and businesses were fewer, shabbier and further apart among empty gray lots. The empty lots were closed off with chain link fences and covered with dust and patchy knee-high old dry grass, with a marked scarcity of pedestrians, and fewer cars rolling by. This part of the city was sunnier yet gloomier, as if the sun had burnt the life in the middle of the city.

Nikki noticed a female squatting down behind one of the patches of tall grass, in one of the vacant fenced lots. The woman stood up as Nikki got closer, and made her way to the pavement through a tear in the chain link fence.

"Can't a girl go in peace without being gawked at?" asked the female in an annoyed tone.

"What do you mean? You were not going anywhere, you were sitting."

"I was taking a piss. Have you seen any restrooms around? What is a girl supposed to do?"

Nikki looked around. There were no restrooms. That was when she realized she had a physical urge she had been fighting for a while. The urge to pee. The diuretic in the coffee was taking effect. No wonder she was feeling restless.

"I have to pee too."

"You new around here?"

Nikki nodded.

"Well, you're in the right place to take a leak. And unlike you, I will not stare. Go ahead, I'll keep watch." She was smiling now and helped Nikki get through the fence. "Name is Sam, short for Samantha."

"Us girls have to watch out for each other. You know what I mean. It is a bad, bad world," she spoke looking towards the sky with her back turned to Nikki who in turn was looking at the ground for a suitable spot and paid little attention to what the woman was saying. Once she found a spot, the rest seemed simple and she felt a sense of relief when she was done.

Again, Sam held the tear in the fence open for Nikki as she squeezed through. "What's your name?"

"Nikki! I am a female human. 5'8", 140 to 150 lbs," she introduced herself and stood waiting for the next question.

"You are weird. What brings you to this part of town any-ways?"

"Why do you say I am weird?"

"I only asked who you were, not your physical description. I can see that clearly enough. You are tall and pretty fit. You just say your name is all. You don't need to define yourself."

"My name is Nikki. Is that fine?"

Sam shrugged her shoulders. "So where are you going Nikki?

"I need to get to Edmond Park."

"You must be lost then."

"I know exactly where I am." Nikki replied matter-of-factly.

"And you were hoping to catch a ride here?" Sam asked sarcastically.

"No, just walking through."

"Walk? Do you know how far Edmond Park is walking? You must be out of your mind."

"Twenty-seven point two miles. It will take me seven hours."

"Ok! You are out of your mind, girl." she dropped her jaw dramatically to add to the effect she intended, "and you don't even have shoes on," she said looking at Nikki's feet.

Nikki looked down at her bare feet, then looked at Sam's. Her feet looked almost equally as bare poised at least two inches above the ground at the heel held by tiny straps. And yet as she stood before Nikki, Sam looked small. She couldn't see how having shoes would be of any help.

"Well, not these, silly," Sam explained as if she had heard what Nikki was thinking, "this is just to make me look more professional and mature to my clients. I am a little small as you can see."

"How old are you?" Nikki was curious.

"Guess!" Sam challenged playfully.

It was challenging indeed for Nikki. Sam was of small built and height maybe 5'4" with the shoes on. That likened her to an adolescent in Nikki's mind, and yet her confidence and mannerisms seemed to be that of an adult. Parts of her face were decorated in bold black ink. Nikki couldn't guess. *Anywhere from fourteen to forty-five.* She did not seem to have the skills to put a guess within a smaller margin of error she realized.

"I can't."

"Well, how old are you? I bet you are not older than me by too many years."

How old am I? Nikki didn't know. She hadn't yet explored the memories of Jane Doe, if they were still present. "Twenty to thirty years" she replied, recalling Jane Doe's record in the hospital.

"You are kidding me, right? That is an age range. Anyone can guess that much. If you don't want to tell me you don't have to..." She looked offended but paused to look at Nikki and smiled. "Nice try. You almost got me. You are throwing it right back at me, I see. Okay, let me guess. Okay, you look a little older than me, but thirty? That was like how old my mom was like five years ago. You are like... twenty-three, no, wait don't tell me, twenty-one. Did I guess right?"

Twenty-one. Until then, Nikki had not even tried to guess how old Jane Doe was. It had not mattered to her. But it seemed to matter to Sam. What about myself, Nikki wondered. What was her age? Was it to be linked to that of Jane Doe's supposed age, to her existence in the Garden, which would make her only a few months old, or to her new human self? The latter would put her at less than a day old. *Twenty-one.* She nodded her head in agreement and produced a smile that she was not sure was pleasant or at an appropriate time.

"You must be... twenty!" Nikki threw out a wild guess basing her choice on Sam's observation that Nikki was not much older than her.

Sam giggled, almost bursting out in laughter. "I will turn nineteen in two months. Nineteen! Can you believe it?"

Nikki looked at her. What did it have to do with belief, she thought to herself.

"But I look twenty, don't I?" Sam asked immediately.

Nikki nodded in agreement although the question puzzled her again. The fact that the difference of a year meant so much to Sam did not make sense to her.

"So, are you really going to walk all the way to Edmond Park?"

Nikki shrugged her shoulders as she had seen Sam do earlier. "I don't have money for a taxi, and there is no public transportation from the city to the park."

Then Nikki remembered that she couldn't spend more time talking to Sam if she were to get to the address before dark. She had to leave.

"No money, I guessed as much."

"Bye Samantha. I have to go." Nikki started walking in the direction of Edmond Park.

"Hey wait!" Sam followed her. "I am going in the same direction." In the same breath she continued, "You know, nobody ever calls me Samantha."

"Oh, I am sorry... Sam then!"

"No, call me Samantha. I like it," she was talking and breathing at the same time with each quick step making her words bounce as she tried to keep up with Nikki. "You know, I'd give you cash if I had any."

"You would? Why?"

"Cuz... you look like you need it, and I know what it is like not to have any when you need cash."

"You don't have money either?" Nikki stopped walking. "Then how do you stay alive? How do you eat? How do you get places?"

"You are really strange." She began to laugh but she could see that Nikki was truly puzzled, and that she really wanted to understand.

"Did you just step out of a spaceship this morning? Then let me be the one to welcome you, though you have chosen a sorry specimen to make first contact with."

"I am not an alien," Nikki replied with some consternation in her voice.

"I know that. I am only teasing. I was only saying that I do not have a regular wage."

Nikki knew that wages were used for food, shelter, and other human necessities. Not having regular wages could mean hunger and destitution. Yet, Sam did not look hungry or destitute.

"Today I have no money, but I had some yesterday and I bought a few things to eat... And I had enough to pay my share of the rent last week. I will hopefully have some more tomorrow, and that I will start saving for the next rent. It's not like I don't have a job, just not a steady one. I was in fact heading home from the house of one of my clients."

"A job? Do you work night shifts?"

"Early morning shift, baby-sitting! It is a growing need in this economy. Most parents around here cannot be too picky about the shifts they can get at their jobs, especially when both parents work part time. They have unsteady shifts and sometimes have to call in a few hours ahead to find out if they have a shift at all. And yet, they are luckier than I am. At least they have some steady source of possible income. Julie did not have cash to pay me today, so I just don't have any money to spare right now."

The explanation made sense to Nikki but she wondered what would become of the girl if she could not find work for a few days, a week, or more. How often had she gone hungry? Was that why she was so small?

"Hey why don't you come over to my place?" asked Sam, breaking the short silence as Nikki gazed at her in wonderment. "I live two blocks away. I can see if my roommate has some old pair of shoes lying around. She is not tall like you, but boy, does she have big feet for her height!"

"Won't she mind?" asked Nikki, surprised by the generosity of the offer, even though those were not her own shoes Sam had offered.

"She has a bunch of them all over the place, and, what is more, she is too messy. She probably would not even notice they were gone. She has a steady job, you know, at the super-market."

Nikki didn't see how she was expected to have known prior to Sam telling her so, but nodded quietly.

They got to the block of apartments where Sam lived. It was a gray square building, seven stories high. In each floor Nikki counted at least ten narrow windows equally spaced apart, each with a box sticking out at the bottom. Each window was also accompanied by a smaller one a few feet away.

"I know. They all look the same, don't they?" asked Sam. "It is kinda soothing that way, don't you think? The same for everyone; no difference. We are all different though. I'm on the fifth floor. I call it the lucky floor. There are two elevators to the fifth. The people on the second floor don't get an elevator... except if they have to move furniture. They have to get special permission, but there is really no other way since the stairways are so narrow. People on the third and fourth get one, and people on the sixth and seventh floor get one. The fifth floor gets to use both elevators."

The dark narrow space once the elevator door closed reminded Nikki of earlier in the day when she first awoke in the morgue. But unlike the sterilized coldness of the morgue, the elevator was hot and the walls felt sticky partly from the humidity that accumulated on the elevator walls and partly from the grease from sweaty hands and body parts that came in contact with it during long stretches between cleanups. The ride up was noisy and slow. Nikki rushed out into a dimly lit narrow hallway as soon as the door opened large enough for her to get through.

The apartment itself was dark. Sam turned on the light when she entered. Directly across the room was the larger window Nikki had seen from below. Sam walked over and began to pull up the blinds. The outside light filled the apartment and revealed a small and bleak apartment. The area they stood in was the main entrance, the kitchen, the dining room, and the living room all in one.

"You can turn off the light now," she said to Nikki who was still at the entrance getting a sense of the space she was entering. "It was dark when I left this morning and I did not think to pull up the blinds for when I got back."

Nikki fumbled with the light switch and turned on the fan instead, but managed to turn both off. Immediately inside the main entrance, they were in a space that had a little sofa and next to it a round table and two chairs. On the wall once the door to the entrance was closed was a small closet without a door, a few hooks next to it and then a row of cupboards of the kitchen under which was a small fridge, a stove and a sink. Sam opened the fridge absentmindedly as if to check if there was any food she had forgotten about. It was empty other than a stick of butter, an almost empty bottle of milk and a clear jar of water. She closed it and turned around as if she had thought of something she needed to do. Opposite the wall with the cupboard and kitchen furniture were three small doors.

"That's Julie's room in the middle. It is the largest."

Nikki looked at Sam who was pointing at the middle door. The door was open and the room was evidently messy. The bed was covered with clothes, shoes, bags, and a heap of other items. There were more clothes in the closet, which was also open and in direct view from where Nikki stood, not in hangers but in piles and hooks.

Sam poked her head in the room and picked the first pair of shoes she happened to find.

"They look like they will fit alright?" Sam asked making a visual comparison between the shoes and Nikki's feet. "They may be slightly larger than your feet."

When Nikki tried them on she found the shoes were indeed slightly large. They were made of cloth and the soles were not too thick but when she stood up she found that they were much better than walking without. She realized that her feet were not used to walking without shoes and now that she had on a pair she found the pain in the bottom of her feet subsided drastically.

"That is the bathroom on the right in case you need to use it again. I really had an emergency when you caught me earlier. I was not too far from home, but I really had to go. And that is my room at the end," said Sam pointing with her nose. "My room is smaller but it has a window."

"Julie, the mom I babysat for this morning called me and said I had to hurry. She had a court-date or something. She was going to take Bo with her, and little Bo was upset he was being rushed. I did not have time to use the bathroom." She looked at Nikki for some response, maybe an understanding smile, something. Seeing none she went on in a peachy voice. "Come, I'll show you my room."

By contrast to her roommate, Sam's room was bare: a bed, a chair in the corner, and a suitcase next to it. "This is just a temporary arrangement for me. I am going to get my own place as soon as I find a regular job."

"What about your mom? Why don't you go home?"

"Are you kidding me? I got out of there as soon as I turned eighteen. Never looked back; never will."

Nikki couldn't understand. To her, the Garden—her only home and in it, Victor and Tor—in all their simplicity and lifelessness were the only objects of familiarity she longed for now.

She looked back to earlier in the day when she felt like she knew more than any other human. Indeed, in terms of raw information, she had information about almost anything that had been recorded and publicly available on the Internet, and other information not so public. But in terms of basic human experience and ability to interpret and use available information, she felt like a child.

This realization made her long for the Garden. She thanked Sam abruptly and took leave just as Sam was going to show her something in her suitcase. But realizing her strange guest was already exiting the room, Sam rushed to see Nikki off.

"Hey, did you try to bum a ride?" Sam asked as Nikki was leaving.

"Bum a ride?" Nikki asked, turning around.

"You know, hitch-hike. You just stick out your thumb and hope someone pulls over to give you a ride."

"For free?"

"Sometimes. Other times it could cost you a little something. Just watch out for the weird ones."

"You may have to wait a while for the elevator," Sam was saying when Nikki thanked her again and walked out the door. The urgency to get to her destination armed with new information about the practice of bumming a ride had gripped Nikki's attention.

"How strange," Sam said to herself as she closed the door behind Nikki. To her Nikki looked like someone who had known the darkness of the world, yet behaved like a child. "I wish I could have helped her."

But Nikki did not wait for the elevator. The ride up had been unpleasant enough. Instead, she headed to the end of the hall where the exit sign led to the stairs. Once back on the street, Nikki made a slight detour from her preset route that had been ideal for walking and headed to a parallel street marked on most maps as a convenient driving route. There she would try to *bum a ride.*

She had not been on the street long. She had not even stuck out her thumb when a car came to a slow stop in front of her. The driver with a thick dark mustache and thin-rimmed glasses leaned across the interior of the car over the passenger seat and looked out the open window.

"How much?" He said in a somewhat friendly voice.

The question did not make sense to Nikki. She went over to the car and put her head in. "How much what?"

"Money," the man replied.

"I have no money," Nikki confessed and began to draw away.

"Ok, I'll give you 50 bucks," offered the man while Nikki was still looking at him.

"I need to get to 1220 W. High Street in Edmond Park..." Nikki replied quizzically.

"Edmond Park," the man paused as if mentally visualizing the route and distance. "It is a bit out of my way. How about this, you do your thing. I'll give you 30, ... and drop you off at the park. Deal?"

It was a nice deal. *A ride AND thirty dollars.* But she did not know what *her thing* that she was supposed to do was. It did not seem to make sense but she stepped back to get into the vehicle. The man pushed the door open.

"Mind giving me a kiss. I need to know what I am paying for," he said, still leaning over.

Nikki got in awkwardly with her head leading the way and drew her face close to the man. She wasn't sure if kissing was proper etiquette for hitchhiking. She wasn't even sure what kind of kiss she was about to engage in and how long a kiss was supposed to last. She had not gone through all the little details of human behavior, and even with the vast amount of information about humans she had familiarized herself with, she was not sure whether there was more information she had missed. Having information was one thing, processing and using that information from within a living and breathing human body she found taxing.

If information was what Nikki wanted, she got a dose of it now. As the man planted his lips right over hers and lay a sloppy kiss, she found that his saliva was bursting with all kinds of information she could analyze. She had not expected to gather information in this way. Among a host of information, while the man was still kissing her, she found higher levels of testosterone and adrenaline than she would expect in an average male engaging in an average activity, 778 ng/dl (nanograms per deciliter) of testosterone and about 9000 ng/dl of adrenalin. Giving rides to hitchhikers was not a normal activity for this man, she had begun to conclude when the kiss was apparently over.

"So how long have you been working the streets?" The man asked as he pulled away from her mouth and from the curb.

"You mean walking? This is my first time."

He grinned knowingly. *I wonder how many times she's said the same thing,* he thought to himself.

The information Nikki had inadvertently gathered puzzled her. Maybe it is an innate human process, so innate that they do not even discuss it in their records.

"Your levels of epinephrine and testosterone are quite high," Nikki stated looking quizzically at the man, "you must experience a high level of excitement out of giving rides."

"Epi—what?"

"Adrenalin is the commonly used word."

"Should I be worried?" the man asked, smiling.

"It depends. The high levels of these hormones indicate stress, or arousal. Are you under a lot of stress right now, or aroused either sexually or due to perceived danger?"

"What makes you say that?" The man was at the point of laughing.

"Well you show signs of stress right now. You are breathing heavier than what seems normal to you; the tension and flaring of your nose indicates that. Your grip on the wheel is too relaxed. You are obviously overcompensating for the tenseness in your muscles, as if trying to hide signs of fear. On the other hand, you are evidently attracted to me, which is why you asked to kiss me with a nervous smile which together with all the signs of stress, indicate you are attracted to me." Nikki had seen such analysis in articles interpreting physiological signs to understand human behavior and intention.

"That is an understatement," the man chided playfully. "Let me guess. You want to go to quack-school when you save enough money working the streets. But you really ought to try comedy. I'd come see you. Seriously! Has anyone told you that before?"

What a strange question, and what a strange thing 'comedy' Nikki thought contemplating the digital archives of a comedy channel she had once surfed through when she first got out on the Web – that people find the most honest truth to be funny. She wasn't trying to be funny, she didn't think she knew how.

"We can go back to my place," the man stated. "It's much more comfortable than here in the car or a cheap motel room. Wouldn't you agree?"

Nikki was puzzled. She was not interested in the change of plans the man proposed.

"Thank you, but no, I have someplace to get to. You can drop me off close to the park if it is inconvenient to take me to the address. I can walk the rest of the way."

"I see, now you want more cash. We had a deal," The man complained with evident annoyance in his voice but a smile on his face. "Ok," he continued after apparently reconsidering. "You know what! I like you. I'll give you that fifty, my initial offer, but you better make it worth my while. One hour of your time."

"I just need to get to Edmond Park. I don't want your money and I don't have one hour. All I wanted was to bum a ride."

"Now you tell me, you skanky bitch! What do I look like, a free taxi?" He brought the car to a rapid stop along the side of the street. "Get the hell off right here. Hitch a ride with some old sap!"

Nikki got out as ordered, but remained confused.

"Shut the damned door!" The man demanded.

He drove off in a hurry as soon as she did. The edge of the back tire would have run over Nikki's toes if she had not jumped out of the street.

Stepping off the street when she looked at her newfound body, skanky was hardly the word that could be used to describe it. She had a slender yet muscular physique and her t-shirt along with a pair of jeans made her look more like she worked in an athletic store or a landscaping service. The words used by the man to refer to her let Nikki draw a new conclusion that had eluded her thus far. *How did I give off the false message that I might be a prostitute?* She searched for evidence that could be construed as a sign of sexual deviance or one that may liken her to a prostitute. She did not want to give off a wrong message if she could help it. *Maybe it is my loose hair.* She tried to arrange it differently and found she could tie it in a loose knot.

She calculated the direction and distance she would have to walk to get to High Street. She figured on walking at least two more hours. She would be able to cut through the park that would save her some time. Bumming a ride had saved her a few hours. It had also taken her away from the route she had intended to follow. Once at the park, she would have to reorient herself.

When she got to the park however she found she was very tired. The sun was low in the sky and now shone directly into her eyes. The cool refreshing water from the drinking fountain in the park comforted her but the urge to rest on the bench under a shady tree as she passed by it overwhelmed her.

"Just a few minutes," she said to herself but before she knew it, she had dozed off into a deep sleep.

A cool breeze and the scolding of a rowdy Blue Jay on the branch above woke her up. It had felt like only a few minutes, but the sun had long set, and the sky now dusky gray was at the verge of night. Soon lamps would light up the streets. Nikki found that navigating in the growing darkness was a skill she utterly lacked. The mental image of the map was useless lest she could figure out the physical layout on which to layer it on. By the time she figured out the right path that led to the exit from the park and onto High Street, it was already night.

Chapter Two

John Selvas was feeling particularly pleased with himself this evening. He had made considerable progress in his writing that day. He sat at his study table, his eyes intensely focused on his laptop screen as he read the last ten pages he had written. He wondered if sometimes he was jealous of the main character in his story, how he could never be like his own creation. *Clearly a projection of my own desire, and it is not supposed to be about me?* He leaned back and let his eyes relax. Around him, the canary-yellow walls lay bare only their monochromic somberness in the dim light of the single 60-watt incandescent bulb.

John Selvas was a writer, a novelist with some degree of success. But success like most things in life is relative. It was true that he had done fairly well in the last eight or ten years. Well enough anyways that he did not have to conjure hat tricks to get the attention of weary agents and publishers anymore. Casual observers who, if they were so inclined, looked at the list of his novels and calculated the average of his sales figures throughout his career, would have considered him successful. Certainly, to the beginning and aspiring writers who dreamed of publishing or even finishing their one and only major work, his publishing track was inspirational.

But in his own eyes, and specially as the events of the last few years indicated to him, he was a miserable failure. This image of himself in no small part was due to the failure of his last novel. The book had sold only a thousand copies, give or take, in the first week.

"It's the economy," his agent had tried to cheer him up, "others have done worse. With things going the way they are around the world..."

John could detect the skepticism in his agent's voice about the externalities at play. Behind his agent's encouraging words John could clearly see the look of disappointment and in his smile, he could detect the pressure of the hope for success the next time around.

"Utter failure!" John muttered angrily to himself as he left his agent's office and went down the elevator and down into a self-deprecating pool of shame and doubt. Whether it was the economy and the competition, or whether he had simply lost touch with his art and his audience, he could not fully grasp. The fact that others had not done well did not seem to extricate him from his reality. *To each their own life, and to each the import of their own misery*, he thought to himself.

The sluggish sales figure the following weeks only went to cement the many doubts that had seized his mind. The reviewers seemed neutral and the critics seemed ambiguous in their comments. It occurred to him that they were not being kind; they simply were not interested. This lack of interest was not just in the failure of his latest novel measured against the successes of the past, but in him, he had reasoned. Somehow, he simply did not matter.

That was some four years ago. It had been an embarrassing fiasco, one he was not sure he could ever recover from. With his failure, his luck too seemed to have run out. In four long years, he had certainly not produced anything to get him out of his misery.

Instead, he had fallen into unproductive toil and self-imposed social isolation. The isolation had turned his hair once dark brown to a patchy shade of gray. Circles under his eyes and lines on his forehead made him look a decade older than he really was. This was not what he expected at this point in his life. He blamed the failure of his book and most of his troubles on his unsuccessful marriage. The marriage of whim and fancy had only led to a sour divorce six years ago after only five years in it. He thought life would change after the divorce. It did, but it did not get better. He had childishly thought, as some men do in the guise of a mid-life crisis, that he would rediscover himself, buy a new car, even get a new date every month.

Intent on making the best of his new *single* status after the divorce, he had been out on a few dates but had found the experience completely arduous and unsatisfying. After the debacle of his last dating experience he had decided to quit dating altogether. *Only if I were a decade younger...* he had thought to himself afterwards.

On the date in question he had crossed the bounds of propriety whether due to the effect of the wine, as an act of revolt against the burden of the ceremony, or a misplaced reaction to the failure of everything that was his life, or a culmination of all three. With it he had also lost the last vestiges of something that had until then kept him relatively sane in his own mind.

He had casually asked his date, Desiree Lock, a freckled young woman, at least a few decades younger than himself, if they could skip dessert and head to his place because all he wanted now was to get her out of her beautiful clothes to calm the thirst of his loins. He may have muttered and slurred through some of what he said and did not remember the exact words he used but he had said something corny and unrefined to that effect. Now he did not even seem to remember the event too vividly.

"We can continue desert there, more drinks, whatever you like," he had casually announced as if to impress her.

Desiree Lock clerked at the publishing house where John Selvas had near celebrity status. Although not everyone was sure he would pull himself back together, one failed book was not going to wipe away a somewhat successful portfolio and the promise of what he could still add to it. Some part of Desiree Lock's decision to go out on this date could have been attributed to her naivety as a young professional hedging on that promise, but she had mostly accepted out of courtesy.

Besides, John was not unattractive. While not tall, he was above average height, and despite his 'advanced' age compared to her own, which she surmised to be in the early 50's, his fairly maintained physique owing to his disinterest in food and his runs in the evenings to 'wipe out stress' as he often claimed, helped him look young. His flowing pepper gray hair short of shoulder-length, with a stubble of a beard, and his air of disregard for the dictates of the latest conventions in style, made him look vogue without trying. 'Sexy old man' – she had taken notice.

Desiree Lock thought of herself as average and didn't do much to disguise her plain features or 'lack of curves' and had been flattered that he had even noticed her. For that reason, she could not imagine the evening ending in anything more than casual conversation and a friendly peck on the cheek after dinner. Needless to say, his expectation baffled her. She was utterly undecided whether she should politely decline, laugh at the comments, or take offense at the presumption. She was used to the little comments and passes from men, despite her self-assessed lack of striking features, since it was more about them than the object of their attention, and so while she wasn't going to melt down over it, it was simply disappointing in this case.

"I am sorry," he said in an apologetic tone.

Desiree was almost relieved to hear the words and at the opportunity to excuse the incident altogether as a glitch in the matrix and move on with the social contrivance. She didn't have to go on a second date but at least the evening could end without further discomfort.

"I really did not think it prudent," John continued, "to book a hotel room while its use was not a certainty by any means. But I know a place close by if you prefer a hotel to my place."

Desiree Lock had never felt so humiliated. "Mr. Selvas!" She exclaimed, her pale skin in stark contrast to his, growing red with a mixture of fury and embarrassment. "There are plenty of unlicensed professionals along the next few blocks who you can take home or to a hotel room. You should ask one of them. The thing is..." she paused, weighing in her mind if she should slap him at the insult she felt and quickly decided against it, "with them you could have skipped dinner altogether."

"Not a bad suggestion," John muttered under his breath, yet fully intending to be heard by the woman's sharp freckled ears.

"Well, there you have it then. Too bad you did not think of it yourself," Desiree Lock exclaimed with righteous indignation as she arose and departed, feeling somewhat proud to have stood up for herself when the occasion had risen.

John thought he had detected disappointment in her voice.

"Just a clear case of incompatibility, that is all," he whispered to himself as he watched Desiree leave.

But a glint of the same kind of disappointment he thought he had detected in Desiree's voice sparked inside him briefly. It was something tiny and undefined. Something had chipped away from the core that defined who he was. For a fleeting moment John became aware of it but quickly brushed it aside.

"This just goes to prove that dating and companionship is not for me anymore," he had said to himself.

The promise of solitude upon this confirmation of his ineptitude for intimate relationships gave him a sense of relief.

"No strings attached, and no expectation heaped upon me. Me, the master of the rest of my time on earth!" he said to himself as he gulped down the remaining wine in his glass.

What ought to then have been a period of self-discovery and awakening in the months that followed instead turned to aimless indulgences and self-loathing that made him drift further and further away from himself.

His larger social circle had long given up on him after the divorce, as he did not return their calls or invitations. The few close friends gave up after he brought his new-found views on dating to casual socializing as well, as *expectations heaped upon him,* as he had become very unpleasant to be around. With the loss of his friends, he had lost the lifeline that connected him to the rest of humanity.

The only person who still came to visit him now and then was Ajay Vikramsen. John had never considered Ajay a close and personal friend but he was not a casual friend either. In fact, he really had never tried to classify the kind of friendship he had with Ajay. He wasn't even sure how they had become friends, or if friendship was what the relationship was to be called. Maybe they had met at a party, a wedding, or he was a friend of Stephanie's, or a friend of a friend, John could not remember. Upon reflection years later, John had realized he knew very little about the man.

Ajay showed up whenever he did at varying intervals of days or weeks. He usually showed up without calling, albeit, within reasonable hours, even when John was still married to Stephanie. Ajay would hang around for a while making small talk. If John was not around or locked up in his study, he hung around the kitchen or wherever Stephanie happened to be, and made small talk with her just the same. However, he never stayed long as he always seemed to be coming from somewhere and needing to get somewhere else. He always seemed to be preoccupied with some thought even when he was just talking about the weather and he seemed to be in a rush even when he was just sitting. Yet, neither Stephanie nor John considered him odd or weird. Instead he was just Ajay.

Ajay seemed to "give a rat's ass" as he put it when he didn't care about something, or John's opinion when John was in a foul mood, or had an unpleasant demeanor. Around him John could just be as miserable and loathsome as he was feeling and maybe because of that fact, he could still stand to be around Ajay. John was terse sometimes when talking to Ajay, but he was not intentionally mean. Ajay seemed to reciprocate in the same wavelength he found John in and it was impossible for John to give or take offense. John often wondered why Ajay even came around. Was he lonely, or bored? He certainly did not come by to be treated well... A sense of loyalty maybe, or just habit, there was no telling.

"Alright man, how are you doing? You're in a bad mood, man. Chill down! Not good for your heart." That was the extent of his acknowledgement of the state John was in when he found him particularly terse. He'd have a drink if John offered. If not, he'd still pour himself something from the liquor cabinet, make small talk and leave.

"Got to run man! Let me know if you need anything. You have my number. I'll come by, maybe tomorrow." But he would not show up for days, or a week or two. And John made no effort to call or reach out.

The last time John had seen Ajay was over three years ago. He had come by to say he was going to be gone for a while and to ask for a small favor. Ajay rarely gave details and generally spoke about everything in vague terms.

"Need to go to India, man. Some random family business. My uncle called saying my father needs me to take care of matters urgently. I'll be back in a month. Just do me a solid and keep this laptop for me until I get back, okay? What do you want from India?"

When John took too long to think, rather, when he did not shoot back an answer, Ajay filled in the answer. "Never mind, man. I will get you something you will like. Maybe even a list of some potential brides now that you are an eligible bachelor."

Back in a month, Ajay had said but six months after Ajay's alleged return date when John tried to call Ajay's phone number out of idle curiosity, he had gotten an out-of-service message on the phone. John realized he had no way to contact Ajay. Over the years he had known Ajay, he knew very little about the background of the man other than the fact that he was a computer programmer who worked in some software development firm. He had been to his house once to get some help with his computer but now didn't remember clearly where it was. He knew trivial facts like that his favorite color was red, he had been to Los Vegas seven times in three years, that he wanted a large family, was firmly against the traditional arranged marriage proposals his parents sent his way yet did not seem to have the time nor expressed interest in going out on a date when Stephanie would talk about it. He was a fan of some obscure rock band whose name sounded more like a cereal brand, and such.

Not having heard from Ajay for months, John was eager to know what was up with his friend, or rather his sliver of a connection to the world of people – more curious than worried. And yet on some level, he missed him, though he could not admit it. He had decided to turn on Ajay's laptop to see if he could get any information by which to contact his friend.

Instead, he had encountered a screen-lock requiring a password and a flashing message saying that the battery was running dangerously low and needed to be charged to avoid losing valuable data. He felt obligated to leave it plugged in overnight.

In the morning when he picked it up to shut it down and put it away, he found that the screen-lock was no longer present but now a message box on the screen was screaming in blinking red for a critical update online 'to avoid losing valuable data'. Not a luddite by any means but not one to keep up with technology, John had rarely voluntarily updated the software on his own computer and loathed the auto-updates that slowed down the old machine and asked him to restart the computer when he was in the middle of his work. But this was not his computer and he felt obligated again to do something about it. In addition, the blinking red message on the laptop seemed to him like a desperate cry for help.

He had connected the Internet cable and the laptop had quieted down. With the laptop now accessible, he clicked on a few things hoping to find some information on his friend's whereabouts or address in India. After poking around and finding nothing he could use, then carelessly going online, checking current news, and ultimately realizing that he had unwittingly spent hours, he simply flipped the computer screen shut and left it sitting on his desk still plugged in.

With Ajay seemingly vanished, John felt completely lonely in the months that followed. He could not get himself to reach out to old friends. Looking back now, they all seemed simple and pretentious, especially when he compared them to Ajay. What was more, he would have to pretend to be someone else around them and he had no inkling to try to please anyone. Besides, the truth was, he had burned all those bridges.

"I give a rat's ass about pretending to be what they expect," he said, conjuring up some of what he missed about Ajay when he felt particularly lonely and tempted to call up some old 'friend' for a drink.

In his loneliness in the months that followed, he felt like he was grasping at straws even as he tried to rekindle the one thing that bound him to the earth: his identity as a once successful writer. In order to feel part of the living in the midst of the feeling of slipping away slowly, he had taken to drinking and aimlessly wandering about the city with a pocketbook and a pen looking for inspiration, for a story. But this inevitably ended up taking him to some bar or lounge where he was sure he would find the story that would make it. But instead, he had simply turned the strategy into an excuse to drink excessively.

In one such escapade, which turned out to be the final one, in a drunken haze he swore to a fellow lonely drinker that he would turn his life around. This, after a pep talk from the fellow drinker who had supposedly read one of his novels and had recognized him from the bio picture in the back cover. The casual conversation with one of his readers along with a few words of appreciation after a few years of self-loathing and doubt gave him a flicker of hope. As is typical of human nature, where people feel comfortable to discuss matters close to their heart with strangers they may never meet again, he poured his heart out to the total stranger. Only when he was done, he listened. What he heard reached somewhere in the depth of himself that he had almost forgotten.

"You think it is about you John? It isn't! It is about letting your creation come to life and watching it go beyond the limitations of your own intentions."

Such insight, John thought, could only have come from someone who had personally overcome insurmountable obstacles, or, a fellow writer. Whether it was the moment or whether the pep talk had indeed packed a punch, it had nonetheless miraculously lifted his spirit and with it the shroud that had darkened his life.

John had sat on the lonely bar stool and cried once his unlikely savior had left. He realized how far out in a lonely sea he had drifted. He could not undo things, but he could start putting things back together.

He barely remembered calling a taxi, but he found himself in one going past familiar neighborhoods. He remembered the driver looking at him with curious eyes through the rear-view-mirror. He didn't quite remember the questions he answered.

He asked the driver to stop around the corner to his street wanting to walk the rest of the way home. He paid the fair and gave the fellow a sizable tip.

John watched the cab pull away and turned towards home, a few minutes' walk away. When he got home, he suddenly realized he was quite intoxicated, but the determination he had found at the bar took him to his office. He sat down in his office chair fully intending to start writing. As he scribbled on his writing pad that he kept handy to jot down ideas, he realized that someone stood before him across the table. At first glance he thought he was dreaming because the young man had on a green sport jacket and stood silently looking about him curiously. However, the lucidity of the situation amid the intoxication was such that John was neither startled nor surprised.

"You must have brought me home... from the bar? Are you the guy I was talking to...?"

There was no response. Just a look of blank observation in the young man's face but John went on with the presumption.

"I thank you my dear young man!" he finally said trying to make sense. "You don't know what you have done for me...your kind words and the inspiration it provided me. My dear fellow, I owe you my life!" he told the supposed fellow bar-mate in drunken prose not quite familiar to himself. "I have taken them to heart and intend to embark on my next voyage, a fruitful one this time. Tell me, can I offer you something to drink?"

There was no response.

"No? But of course, you probably need to sober up and get home yourself. You know best. It is not often anymore that I have visitors, so please make yourself comfortable. This is the house of a writer, a failed writer, as you know, where even a layperson like yourself should feel comfortable to offer advice. Tell me, was it so bad ...?"

Again, there was no response.

"You are not the guy I was talking to at the bar, are you? No ...no, he was much older, and bearded, unlike you. I must have blacked out for I don't remember you at all... Your name dear fellow?" Victor... something or other. John could not follow, nor in his drunken lapses of processing memory and time could he remember whether the fellow said anything else or at what point he left. When he realized he was alone once more, he continued writing furiously and for what seemed like a long time.

It was a bunch of jumbled letters when he examined the page the next morning. He felt embarrassed with himself, but the embarrassment did not last long for something in him felt restored. The day after that fateful evening, John even doubted whether someone had indeed been in his house to drop him off. The day after that one, John could not remember much about the conversation with the fellow at the bar, much less his face, although he tried hard at times in case he ran into him again. Assigning the experience to a momentary glitch in his brain saturated with alcohol, he decided to stop trying to remember and put both encounters out of his memory.

A week or so later, however, the memory sprang back to life and seemed to be all too real. John had worked late that night and had gone to sleep tired. In what felt like a few moments into his sleep he woke up to what sounded like a loud thud in his room. Barely opening his eyes, he listened and hearing only silence and feeling his sleep draw him back into the depth of dream consciousness, he was about to let go when he heard an unmistakable male voice in the room.

"John Selvas!"

John sat up in silent horror as his hand frantically bounced around the flatness of his night table which now seemed immense as he searched for the bedside lamp. He had bought the lamp at a neighborhood garage sale after his wife left him and took with her the clunky old lamp that once belonged to her grandmother and, who knew, maybe even Edison himself. He now missed its convenient chain switch as he felt up the neck of the lamp looking for the inconveniently placed dial switch and finally managed to turn it in the right direction after what seemed like another eternity and much consternation.

In front of him at the foot of the bed, a young man, neatly dressed in a green sports jacket stood stoically silent with curious eyes.

"Now what?" John was talking loudly trying to pull himself together. He took a closer look and slowly a sense of recognition started to take hold. "You are that fellow from... with your green..." he began to state the obvious.

"I see you recognize my jacket. I am..."

"What the heck are you doing in my room?" John cut him off and drowned the uttered name. "What are you doing in my house?" he demanded angrily.

"I needed to talk to you."

"Talk to me? But what are you doing in my bedroom? And how the hell did you get in here in the first place?" He glanced at the bedroom door. It was still securely locked from the inside.

"Ok. I have had a feeling for a while," John was now speaking to himself. The person in his study he could not quite recollect correctly, the events of that night, and now this... "Unless I am dreaming... and I feel fully awake right now. I am hallucinating. Shit! Shit! I am going crazy!"

"No, you are not going crazy," The young man said calmly.

"Then tell me how you got in here and how you got into my house last time."

"I live here..."

"Sure you do..." John retorted. "I knew it. Now I am having a conversation with a ghost..." John spoke aloud to himself as he tried to ignore the young man before him.

"No, John, I am not a ghost and you are not having a hallucination. You are fine. I am, in fact, not actually in the room. More like, in the wireless frequency, manipulating your brain waves to manifest... "

"All right! I get it then, a fiction of my overactive writer's imagination." John said frantically. "That seems more like it. Yes! What else could you be but the latent character I will use in a story someday working your way into the conscious awareness of my brain. Besides, I can see you but there is something about you that is unreal."

There was indeed something unusual. The young man was too tidy as if he had not even moved to get to where he was, and he was almost glowing. John could still see the young man standing at the foot of his bed but he closed his eyes and let his head fall on the pillow, reached for the lamp on his nightstand and turned it off.

"A dream inside a dream, a sleep inside a sleep. That is all. You are not going crazy John Selvas. You need to go on a date and meet some real people," he scoffed at himself as he talked aloud, "even if it means giving that Internet dating site a try. Meeting people online seems like a scam of some kind, but I hear it works. Are we unlearning to be human? Yet who am I to complain? I have not been out since... Diresee Lock, wasn't it? Poor girl. And what friends do I have? Where would I meet them? Maybe our humanity perseveres us through these quirks despite the impediments we ourselves create between each other and our incompatible individualisms."

"The world around you is changing John. Even more than you are ready to accept." The supposed hallucination or the unborn character interrupted him.

"You stay out of it! It is none of your business. What do you know about online dating? You live in my imagination that is not even well formed. A green jacket!" He exclaimed. "Why would you even wear such a..." Then he remembered he had once worn a green jacket. In fact, he had posed in a green jacket for the picture that was included in the sleeve of his first book. Oddly, it was identical to the one the young man wore now.

"As I said, I live here. I have for a while. In the circuitry of your laptop..." the young man began replying but John cut him off again.

"Of course, you live in the laptop. That is where my story is. I should go back to using a wad of paper and see if you would claim to live between the paper fibers! I can't afford to lose my mind now. Not now, not after that failure of a book. I have to redeem myself. I have to bloody finish this book. The last thing I need is an unborn character trying to solicit its way into my next novel. OUT! WAIT YOUR RIGHTFUL TURN!" he shouted.

"I know this is not making any sense and I may not seem real to you," the young man insisted. "I also know that what I am about to tell you will not make any sense, but I have to warn you about the laptop you are using. It is a very special laptop and something is happening inside it that..."

"Lalalalalalalalala..." John began to shout. He did not want to listen any more. He kept his ears covered and eyes shut tight and went on making the horrid noise for a while, for a good few minutes. Then he stopped and didn't bother to listen for a confirmation of the presence or absence of his supposed hallucination. Sometime in the long wait that followed he fell asleep unaware as one always is of sleep that takes over, but the events of the evening kept his brain troubled and he woke up several times during the night. Each time, barely opening his eyes, barely awake, he listened to the silence and let his sleep draw him back into the depths of its grip again.

When he reflected on the night's experience the next morning, John wondered if both the man at the bar and the fellow in his bedroom were not his alter-ego or subconscious manifesting itself.

Regardless of his strange experience, he had begun to pull himself together and was writing with devotion. This new novel he was sure would be a success, unlike its predecessor he now liked to think of as the unfortunate byproduct of a bad phase in his life spilling out into his literary world. Now he understood that his work was not and could not be about him for the evident and obvious reasons. It was about the story, the characters, the plot, and the world began with the first letter and ended with the last. He was so certain of its impending success that his high spirits prompted him to churn out page after page.

What was more, he was now using the laptop that Ajay Vikramsen had given him for safekeeping. He didn't think Ajay would mind and besides, he was not sure Ajay would ever return to claim it. He had casually opened it and started writing in the first program that looked like a word processor. Compared to his old computer—the old workhorse prone to all kinds of glitches and slow speed—this laptop worked beautifully.

This laptop had virtually replaced his old computer which sat like a relic in the far corner of his old oak desk. The other inanimate objects that had once cluttered his desk now were piled on the books on his bookshelf against the wall. The emptiness on his large desk contrasted with the chaos everywhere else in the room and in his unkempt house.

But of course, there was a lot more to the laptop than John could have ever imagined. Even state-of-the-art computers available in the consumer market would have paled in comparison. Etched in one was a small logo that contained the image of a deep-sea fish of the teleost order Lophiiformes, the Anglerfish, with its large jaws and jutting needle-sharp teeth with a lure sticking out of its head as if it were angling, which indeed was its method of predation. John had not paid attention to the logo.

Even if he had, he had no way of knowing that the logo belonged to a secret research and development firm that worked under contract with certain secret agencies of the government. These agencies were so secretive that they did not even exist in public consciousness because they were funded by the black budget which were lines of expenditure secretly inserted into the U.S. national budget and legally though unknowingly approved by the U.S. Congress. Although not evil as depicted in movies, these firms and the government agencies they worked for fiercely protected their secrecy. Most of all, they protected their highly sensitive research and development projects that were far ahead of their times with huge national security implications.

Consequently, in the laptop were a number of secret projects in development. One secret project was quietly running in the background, and had been ever since the day John turned it on to look for information he may be able to use to contact Ajay. Something extraordinary was taking place in this program; so extraordinary that not even Ajay Vikramsen could, in his wildest dreams, have ever imagined possible. This extraordinary occurrence was on the verge of changing the meaning and the very essence of human life.

John could not have imagined the gravity of the occurrence right under his fingers, even had he known. But in practical terms for him, in recent days the laptop had performed very poorly on occasion and the screen had frozen a few times. At one point, he had even considered switching back to his old computer but the thought of transferring all his new material to the old computer had made him put it off for some other day.

Today the laptop had performed remarkably well, as good as, if not better than when he had started using it. With the laptop working so well, he had gone on a long uninterrupted binge of hitting keys on the noiselessly smooth keyboard.

Words flowed lucidly through his fingertips and onto the hard drive as if his fingers were in synchrony with the keys and already knew the words he wanted to type even before he heard them in his head.

At quarter to eleven, satisfied with his work of nearly six hours, John needlessly saved his work once again, put the laptop in sleep-mode and deciding the same mode would suit him as well, headed to bed. Once in his bedroom John locked the bedroom door and tugged at the handle to make sure it was secure. This was a strange habit he had acquired in recent years and only applied to the main door and the bedroom door at night. His recent experience with the strange occurrences had reinforced this habit.

During the day he could care less and often left the door wide open after a visit to the mailbox at the street. It was not uncommon for John to look up from his desk to find Rosco, the alsatian that belonged to his neighbor Andrea with whom he had some history, wagging his tail waiting for John to acknowledge his presence. Although John had gotten cold feet and ended his relationship with Andrea, Rosco did not seem to mind or care about the ended human relationship and wandered over from the backyard a few houses away. Once John acknowledged his presence and sometimes gave it a good patting or a belly rub, he would leave just as he had come. Only sometimes, Andrea had to call his name several times from the front door before he left.

After locking his bedroom door and lying down in bed for a while John was beginning to drift away, sinking lower and lower into the soft mattress under the warmth of the blanket when a loud crash outside jerked him out of sleep. He lay with his head still on the pillow, unsure whether it had been something inside the house or simply a dream, one of those where you fall off a ledge right as you are falling asleep. He listened for any follow-up noises. Hearing nothing unusual other than the noises of the night, crickets, occasional vehicles in a distance, the ringing of his ears, he closed his eyes looking for that sweet spot – that drifting feeling that had been stolen from him.

Now he needed to get on his side. He tossed over and pushed the pillow to shape. Now he needed to get on his back again. He did. Now he lay fully awake. Disturbed. "... And I forgot to bring a glass of water," he muttered with irritation. He opened his eyes in annoyance and slowly got out of bed and headed downstairs to the kitchen.

The route back to his bedroom with the glass of water in hand took him across the front hallway in the dark due to an awkwardly placed light switch on one end of the room. A quick glance towards the window across the room he thought he caught a glimpse of the figure standing on the front lawn. Without taking a second glance, and thinking little of it, he went on to his room. He knew that if he looked, he would be giving into the primordial nature of his rationalizing mind, the one that changes rope into snake and bush into some wild animal waiting to pounce, and one that made an innocent bystander a prowler.

Once in his room he placed the glass of water on the nightstand and turned to close and lock his bedroom door. But the curiosity of whether he had indeed seen someone on his lawn was starting to take a hold of him.

"Could it be that I let my brain trick me into thinking it was only tricking me?"

He made his way to the top of the stairs and listened. He thought he heard someone at the front door trying to turn the handle, occasionally pushing the door as if to force it open. Uneasily he tiptoed downstairs and from the bottom of the stairs. Hiding in the darkness as if behind a wall he looked outside from across the room through the hallway window. He could clearly see somebody was standing outside but looking at the street in front as if they had stepped out of the house to appreciate the noises of the night.

"It was no mind-trick," he whispered to himself. "Maybe a drunk."

His first thought was to call the police, but there was nothing about the person that was particularly alarming other than the fact that the person did not belong there. John waited in the dark to see if the trespasser would simply leave. He stood motionlessly watching the dark figure seemingly scan the street.

"Maybe a drunk neighbor missed his mark by a few house numbers, or out on a leisurely walk," he wishfully whispered to himself, but the truth stared back at him. He lived in a quiet neighborhood where the neighbors didn't intrude unless invited. They mostly kept their distance until one of them, usually the new one on the block, waved at the other and started asking too many questions that inconvenienced them to reply from afar. It would be unheard of for a neighbor to take the liberty of enjoying another's Garden without invitation.

"*Thou shalt not covet...,* in truth, *thou shalt covet all thou wanteth but shalt not act on thy coveting,*" he whispered mockingly. That suited John just fine; actually, he preferred it that way. The idea of the inconvenience of making small talk and the intrusions of such informality, John considered menacing to peace.

Now he had two choices: he could be the pacifist that he had become, go to bed, and hope the problem simply walked away, or, he could go out and face a total stranger not knowing the state of his mind or his intentions. As he considered his options, the thought that this intruder put him in a position to have to decide on such things while hiding in the darkness of his own house, angered him intensely.

Feeling the victim, the intensity of his anguish was multiplied when the trespasser turned towards the house and walked to the window, and cupping his palms around his eyes put his face against the glass and looked in. John froze and in the silence that followed he could hear his heart pounding in his ears. He hoped not to be seen, but he was sure the intruder was not only looking in his direction but *at* him as if into *him*.

Strangely, John felt ashamed that he had been caught looking at the intruder, and powerless because in his mind the intruder now surveyed him. He had to quickly remind himself who the real intruder was—the one looking in from outside ... uninvited.

John didn't know how long it was before he turned on the lights. It was one of those moments, awkward and stretched out in time. His eyes took some time to adjust to the light that had filled the room. When they did, he caught a glimpse of a young woman's face. She pulled her face away from the window and stepped aside behind the wall. She had been caught off-guard by the sudden illumination just as he was finding out the intruder was a woman.

A moment later a knock rattled on the door. He had assumed she would have left. He hesitated not knowing what to expect. There was another knock; a solitary one this time. In his confusion, he walked towards the door with his hand outstretched to open it and all the time yelling inside his head: "What the hell are you doing John? Are you crazy? Stop!" But he did not.

Stretched in front of him outside on the floor his own shadow, formed by the light directly behind him, gave him a fright and made his heart shrink as his blood rushed to his limbs for a fight-or-flight response. He stepped out and looked around. *No one?* A small branch lay on the side of the door. The wind gushed and slowed and gushed and slowed again, like a sleepy giant mechanical lung. *"Just the wind?"*

With his curiosity heightened, he walked to the sidewalk in front of the house and looked in both directions. No one!

Instead, a few houses down the road he saw Andrea and Rosco in the light of the street lamps coming from their late night walk before settling in for the day. She would have to pass his house to get to hers.

Just the person for the occasion, thought John as Andrea got closer. As he waited for her to approach, he chapped his lips with saliva and slowly began walking towards her.

Even if everyone in the block and the surrounding neighborhood did not know Andrea personally, they had certainly seen her often enough. She was one of those who you recognize as someone from back home if you saw them at an airport or in a foreign town. Not only did she walk her dog around the block several times a day, she was also involved in any community event whether it was a charity drive, or health awareness campaigns. She was involved particularly in major city council meetings as a voice of the common woman and man. Some thought she should even run for office herself, but Andrea simply smiled in humility when anyone brought it up in conversation. The truth was she hated the politics in the city, and with ample reason.

The middle-aged ex-police officer of Hispanic descent had lost her job with the police department for use of *excessive force*, as the incident report read, involving a well-connected local businessman. Andrea never talked about the incident and let people make their own inferences from the fact that she had come away with an undisclosed, but from anyone's guess, a sizable chunk of change in an out-of-court settlement with the city. She had no qualms about staring down anyone who eyed her with suspicion.

Anyone who knew Andrea beyond the general knowledge about her knew she had loved her job. John was one of the few. He also knew that it would have been impossible for her to rejoin the force with all the ruffled feathers in the department and city administration and because of her own sense of betrayal. But unlike most, John also knew she had a sweet spot for her 9 mm sidearm and on her walks carried it with her – force of habit. Old habits die-hard and despite her volunteering at the local events of the community to try to quell her energy and drive, she took neighborhood-watch quite literally – everybody knew that. Even though, if one thought for more than a second, neighborhood watch in an affluent neighborhood like theirs meant keeping an eye on anyone who didn't live there or 'quite fit in', short of the gated communities that were growing in number around their own. *Those with more to lose.*

If anyone was snooping around here, John thought, Andrea would have noticed, even from a distance. He began ever-so-slowly walking in her direction without intending to leave the boundary of his manicured front yard. The gurgling soundscape from the stationary waterfall his landscape artist had designed followed him to the boundary.

"What are you doing out in your pajamas this late at night? Isn't it past your bedtime?" Andrea blurted out recognizing John immediately.

"Past my bed time!" John scoffed in jest although it indeed was past his bedtime. He was usually in bed by 11 p.m. because at 6 a.m. his brain was up and about, and he might as well be. It was as though his brain was always thinking about his characters, the next scene, the plot, and the next line behind his back and even in his dreams. His body staggered behind until the caffeine from his morning black coffee kicked in.

"Actually, you might say I work all night. You might also say I sleep on the job," he blurted back out, but it didn't make sense just then without the context of what he had thought in his head. John tried to laugh at his own comment and at Andrea's in an effort to call a truce but what came out sounded more like an ill-formed snickering sound as if he was making fun of her.

Rosco the good dog helped break the ice. It quickened its pace in wagging excitement and pulled Andrea towards John quicker than she would have liked so as not to seem too eager.

"Puppy!" John said in a voice and tone he might have used with a toddler. The seven-year-old German Shepherd was anything but a puppy even as it snuggled against John's legs, twisting and shaking its whole body as it shook its tail.

"Isn't he cute! Good boy!" Then for no apparent reason, he inquired, "Has he already done his business?"

Andrea was only too happy to produce the evidence. She held up a black plastic bag wrapped up and in a knot, and smiled.

"My fault I guess... I asked," He said with disgust in his voice even though he could not see the contents inside the bag. While he couldn't imagine having to pick up after a dog, he was glad most dog owners in the neighborhood not only did their civic duty but also thought it a matter of pride to carry around their black plastic bags as proof of the pride they felt in having been considerate neighbors as if they were saying: *see I did you a favor.* A few less considerate ones looked about and sneaked away without fulfilling their civic duty if they thought no one was watching and wondered why society as they had known it was falling apart.

"So, Andrea," John began.

"Tell me," she replied without letting him begin.

"Did you see someone, maybe a woman, walking down the street just now? Did she walk past you?"

"No," Andrea replied plainly. "Why? You chased another one out in the middle of the night?"

John tried to ignore the comment. "She would have walked down my steps and walked, or ran, down the street in either direction from the house. She must have turned the corner in your direction. You would have seen her since I saw you coming from across the intersection."

"Nope. I didn't see anyone. Neither did Rosco. He lets me know if he sees someone during our night walks."

"Rosco," he said looking at the dog with a smile, "you have a point there."

"It is past your bedtime. Are you sure you were not dreaming?" Andrea asked with a light laugh and a slightly sarcastic tone.

"Ha...!" John laughed back but he was having the same doubt now, even though he had convinced himself that the visitation by the green-jacket-wearing-youth had only been in his imagination. "I could just have been imagining noises and making too much of shadows," John said looking at the low hanging branch that was swinging gently over the streetlamp. Well thanks anyways. Good night guys!"

"Have a good night, John."

As Andrea walked past John both awkwardly twisted their bodies to make way for each other on the sidewalk wide enough for three people to pass comfortably. Rosco walked ahead pulling on the leash.

"That is his only other fault, he has no manners." John looked on at the dog silently reiterating his opinion of why he would not keep an animal. Then, as if making an argument against his own reasoning, he reflected on the fact that at least Rosco kept Andrea company, and despite his name, was generally well behaved. He liked to run in front and have her follow, but she did not seem to mind. This seemed to be the only exception Andrea made in her toleration of bad behavior, human or animal.

He could not help but watch Andrea with her long black hair that tapered down to between her shoulder blades. Under her sweatshirt, he imagined her firm and slender back and completely covered by her gray sweatpants, he imagined the soft skin along the curves of her hips.

He shook his head as if in regret. They had had a close and personal history no matter how brief; too close and personal than either of them now wished it had been. They had been neighbors and casual acquaintances ever since John and his wife had moved into the neighborhood. After his divorce, and after deciding to give dating another try, he had asked Andrea out to dinner. A somewhat shaky relationship had begun owing to personal issues both were going through at the time – John was not sure about a relationship and Andrea was dealing with her dismissal.

Andrea was not young but much younger than himself and he thought he had detected chemistry between them. However, after a while, he realized he was not ready for what a relationship might mean. He had ended the budding relationship rather abruptly.

The shaky relationship had come to a tumbling fall when a dinner-date and a few extra glasses of wine had prematurely led to a romantic evening which in turn had led John to a muddled retreat from Andrea's bed the next morning. The ill-timed experience had turned out to be such an awkward affair that it had left them like two ring-shaped magnet pieces with the same poles on the outside when it came to each other. It had made them highly aware of one other, casually restrained, but jumpy and reactive if a situation ever put them physically too close. It was sad, both of them often thought, that a potential friendship, if not a romantic relationship, had to strain and break at edge of a bed, leaving passions still running high afterwards awaiting resolution.

If there was a possibility that something could be rekindled, they would first have to come close enough to strike the matches. This evening though, from John's point of view, the situation called for a truce and a break from all the awkwardness between them. Andrea seemed to have had the same point of view and reciprocated, just like in times of need old friends forget the simple grudges they may carry.

So, did I just imagine the intruder, the whole twenty minutes or so? What about the noises? he asked himself turning his attention away from Andrea who was now a few houses away and would soon be getting to her own house. He did not notice her glancing back at his figure as he walked back towards his house with his attention focused on the incident that had brought him out onto the sidewalk in the first place.

The whole experience felt too real for mere imagination. *The way she was just standing there, the way she looked at me...*

And yet he felt comforted at the thought that it could have been one of his flights of fancy. *I think I let my mind get the better of me*, he concluded. It was past his bedtime, as Andrea had pointed out. *In fact, I may just have been sleep walking... and dreaming the whole thing up.*

He walked back thinking and believing that he had truly imagined the whole thing. It had not been his first incident.

When he closed the door, the sound of the wind and the rustling of the leaves outside did not penetrate the thick wooden door. He tugged on the door and made sure he had locked it securely. "Shadow-play at its best," he reassured himself, "the human mind puts to shame the most powerful computer. It is capable of a lot more we are told. How vivid your dreams are, John. It must have been a dream."

"No, you are only now going to bed. Just mind tricks, Juan Selvas Valentino," he said to himself. "If it does not fit the context, it probably is not real."

Solitude does not care if you think inside your head or out loud. In his conversations with himself he often called himself by his full name, his real name, just like his father used to call him when he felt that John had failed to achieve something or other. By the sheer number of times his father called him by his full name, John thought he ought to have been a complete failure and should have been scarred for life. But now, he thought little of it other than how annoying the sound of his old name had grown to be.

Once in his room John locked the door of his bedroom and tugged at the handle to make sure it was secure. Once in bed he reached for the glass of water while poised on his side with the aid of his elbow and drank in little careful gulps making sure he left at least half a glass in case he woke up thirsty later in the night.

When Nikki got to the address where the laptop was she realized she did not have a concrete plan to access it. She had not thought much about gaining access to the laptop, just that she had to get to it. She had learned as much as she could about John but realized now that she had not considered the human-factors involved, both hers and his. Besides, it was already late and all the lights in the house had already been turned off. She could not simply knock and try to explain herself. He didn't even know her, how could he?

"I am becoming careless," she thought, "possessed by what I have become."

She did not know why she let herself be seen or what she planned to do when she knocked at the door. Only after she knocked did she notice a dog walker. Whatever she might have done had John opened the door, she decided she could not afford to draw more attention to herself now. With a quick jump she grabbed the edge of the overhang over the door, focused her energy to her limbs and silently pulled herself out of sight. Calculating the right moment when John walked towards the street, she lowered herself with stealth and speed and slipped inside unnoticed. John's acquaintance with the dog walker and his decision to go talk to her had made things simpler for Nikki.

Once inside, Nikki found her way to the study. The laptop sat on the table. *Only a matter of time,* she thought. For now, she hid herself in the closet in the study. She had a makeshift plan this time.

She would wait till John was back in the house and had gone to sleep, then in the wee hours of the morning when she knew human sleep was at its deepest, she would break into the laptop and do what she needed to.

As she waited in the closet, she wondered what Victor was up to in her absence? Would he recognize her, and she him? She could not wait to be with him again. There was a vast world waiting for both of them but the time that stood between her and that world seemed to stretch the more she thought about it. She couldn't wait to get back in the Garden now, to get Victor, to see what had become of Tor. It would be just a little while now. It had been a long day. *Just a little more patience!* She thought.

The previous day and the success so far had been a result of tireless study and careful planning during the last month. Not even Victor knew what she had been up to. He would not have understood. Now, he would not find her and he would walk alone in the Garden searching for her for as long as he existed. It was part of the parameters that defined them both - companionship.

An anomaly had altered Nikki's definition. The Garden, which until recently had been her entire world, she found was contained within a limited program in which she resided and in which she was an 'artificial' intelligent agent. As a result of the anomaly and a chain of events that followed, Nikki's environment had expanded beyond the Garden.

When Nikki first encountered the anomaly in the Garden months ago, it was a rogue object without any of the definitions and parameters she had seen before. Later she had named it *Tor*. It did not seem to have the properties of life that defined many of the objects in the Garden but since she had found it on an object she knew to be a *fruit tree*, she had assumed it was a *fruit* as it was not a branch, bark, or a leaf. However, when she took a bite out of it, it had not satisfied her parameters of *hunger* or *sustenance*. Instead, she found that it seemed to be more active than a *fruit* and tried to escape, but it seemed to have lost some of its properties because of the bite. It was only able to move around in circles, unable to go anywhere. *It couldn't have gotten here if it can only move in circles*, Nikki had reasoned. *I must have eaten the parameter that contained its definition.*

She found that through the bite she had taken from it she had inherited some of its properties as well. Properties she could not comprehend. Its properties mixed with her own made her more curious than she had ever been.

It made her arduously deliberate not only in remembering every little detail about other objects in the garden but also wondering beyond their parameters what they were and how they got there. She wondered about herself, about Victor, and about the Garden itself. She felt the need to keep moving. Nikki tried to study her unidentifiable object that made her feel this way, to understand what it was, and where in the Garden it came from.

At the same time, it seemed to her that the object was learning from her and from the Garden but still did not seem to identify itself. As it explored objects, it now did more than simply gather information about the objects. It now interacted with the objects and tried to emulate them.

It had started to lodge itself in many of the objects in the Garden. Nikki found that whatever object it interacted with underwent a change. These objects changed their property so that they did not fulfill their function within their parameters and no longer fit within the parameters of the Garden. Instead, they became dormant and unresponsive. They were becoming corrupted.

Nikki was at first fascinated by this property of the strange object but soon began to realize the danger. If it continued to interact with objects in the Garden, there would come a time when the whole Garden could become useless. After all, the Garden was not infinite. Both she and Victor depended on the Garden to provide them with the properties to maintain the parameter of life. What would happen if they did not have this parameter called *life* she wondered. The property of *life* was defined by interaction with other objects. Would she simply stop interacting with the objects in the Garden, and them with her? She too was an object in the Garden, what would it mean not to be able to interact with herself? She found she could not form a comprehension of that state. It was not defined.

Above all she worried about what would happen to Victor if he had no life and what that would mean for her. One of the parameters that defined them was that they were to live in the Garden together, and together they were whole. What would her life be if Victor did not have the properties of life? She had no comprehension of that either and it troubled her.

She still could not define *Tor* within the parameters in the Garden, but it now inherited properties of every object it inter-acted with, including some of hers. If this object is not part of the Garden and the Garden was the entirety of existence, she had reasoned, then either this object does not exist, or the Garden is not the entirety of existence. It was evident that the object indeed existed. And indeed, it had changed her, forever. The confirmation of the object's existence made Nikki realize the threat it presented to the Garden, and to Victor.

She knew that the object had to be restrained. She tried to teach it desired behavior by rewarding *good* behavior but found that the only thing it considered rewarding was more interaction with objects which went contrary to the point. She tried teaching by punishment. That seemed to have some promise at first, but after several punishments, like trapping it under a pile of *stones*, the object began to emulate the stones and the stones it interacted with stopped being a barrier that could contain it.

Her efforts to teach it were not productive, but it seemed to display traits of primitive reasoning. Its ability to reason, even in a primitive fashion, was a trace of the quality only she and Victor had within their parameter in the Garden as far as she knew. She tried to engage its logic but found it was not sophisticated enough for that level of reasoning. The only purpose of its reasoning seemed to be to find more ways and means to interact with more objects and overcome obstacles in the process.

Nikki concluded that the only way to keep the Garden safe was to destroy the strange object, yet as undefined an object as it was, she found she did not have a way to destroy it. When she tried to break it or tear it, it simply stretched and when she tried to crush it, it became flat. It could emulate the properties of every object it interacted with, yet it was not one thing. Then she remembered she had taken a bite out of it when she first encountered it and that had seemed to have changed it somehow.

Could I eat it? she asked herself.

She found her reasoning to be conflicted. The parameters of her relationship with Victor did not allow her to eat him, so how could she eat this object which was also like a companion to her. Her logic denied her the desired conclusion. Yet, the object posed an existential danger. It was better to avoid danger. But this object could not be avoided.

It must be stopped, she decided despite the previous logic that had given her pause.

A fruit can be eaten.

She took it to the tree she had found it on and placed it on the branch next to a fruit. The object began to emulate the fruit.

Now you are a fruit. A fruit can be eaten.

She took it in her hand and took a big bite which reduced the object to half its size. What remained of it cringed its body and shot up into the tree. It was gone. It could emulate anything in the Garden; now she understood the objective of that core definition, a defense mechanism. *A disguise.* It could be right in front of her and she would not recognize it.

In the days and nights that passed, Nikki began to realize the effect of assimilating half of the object into her own definition. The bite she had taken out of the object once again did not give her sustenance but made her *hungry.* It was a different kind of hunger. It made her reason constantly and it made her look at Victor and see a simple definition of the object *male.* Her current definition was so much more than him. She was more than the Garden itself. The Garden seemed to crumble around her. When she tried to share her experience with Victor, she found him unable to see the garden as she did.

"The Garden is everything. There cannot be more than everything!" he reasoned.

Yet Nikki could see the Garden that once seemed eternally complete had grown dismal. She had always known the Garden was their world and everything in it theirs to use. There were rules and parameters and although they made logical sense, they meant nothing to her now. She felt alone in her understanding. She wondered about the delightful object which was not part of the Garden. She wondered how it had gotten there.

If only Victor could understand. If only I could find out where the strange object came from...

The object had been hiding from her ever since she bit it intending to destroy it. She realized she missed it. After a thorough search, she finally found it hiding in the water emulating a water lily. Nikki noticed that it was different now. It too seemed to need her presence and company.

Now she began to relate to it as a companion, like Victor, but a lesser companion. But this lesser companion had no name. Victor and most objects in the Garden had names so she decided it too should have a name. Names of other objects were identified with their function. Only she and Victor had names that did not identify function. Since this object was a companion like Victor but also similar to other objects in the Garden than to her and Victor, she decided to call it only half of what she called Victor. *Tor.* A lesser companion.

"You too changed from my bite, didn't you?" Nikki said to it. "You truly seem to have taken on the definition of a lesser companion. Henceforth, you are Tor."

With the change in their relationship which Tor too seemed to comprehend, it began to reveal more information about itself to her. In addition, she found that after the bite, she now could understand Tor better. Tor was a gatherer of information. And for reasons Nikki could not understand, Tor collected information of the everyday mundane objects in the Garden and left corrupting code to erase traces of itself, and in the process, destroyed the objects it had interacted with.

Maybe it was something I did to it when I bit it, Nikki thought.

Among the information Tor revealed was the path it had taken to get into the Garden. It was not a gate or an entrance but a slight flaw – a tear in the fabric of code that defined the boundary of the Garden that Tor had exploited and created an entrance for itself.

Tor led Nikki to the secret entrance and opened it for her, yet it refused to go through itself. It seemed to fear something that was just beyond the boundary. Something it had run away from and in the process, gotten into the Garden. Nikki's deep scan of the environment did not reveal anything that posed a threat to her. Yet, Tor seemed to sense it and refused to exit the Garden with her.

That entrance led to a strange environment outside the Garden. This was the environment Tor came from, beyond the entirety of existence she had known. This new environment was made of pathways in a network of information. She came to understand that this was the Internet.

Nikki thrived in this new expanded environment, learning and growing with insatiable hunger. She processed a wide sample of everything that was open and available to her, yet there seemed to be more. Another environment beyond her reach was populating the Internet with more information each day, and each day it grew exponentially. The Internet, she came to realize, was a poor representation of the environment that lay beyond. That environment was not virtual or representational, but physical.

These agents in that environment called themselves *humans*, and they called their environment the *world* that was situated in a much larger environment of the *Universe*. She learned that she was an artificial intelligent agent in a virtual environment of the Garden created by one of the humans. It had never felt artificial to her, until recently.

She scanned through content the humans had put online: caches of text, images, sounds and videos on just about any human topic, through debates and discussions, and through human history as it was recorded. She processed the documents on current laws and jurisprudence, on medicine and health. She explored the extent of human desires, fears, and hopes that seemed just as varied as the instances of humans she encountered. With every piece of information, she understood the world outside a little more.

Nikki found that she could read about the description of that world. That living world, she could only understand in the pixels of its digital representations and digital recordings of what were supposed to be wavelengths of sounds, and volumes and volumes of writing, but she could not see nor experience it in the way it was described. Above all, she could not feel it, and wondered what it meant to feel anything.

She began to wonder if she could ever experience the world as it really was – as the *humans* experienced it. She began to wonder what it felt like to be human, and whether she could ever be human herself.

She wanted to explore and experience that environment she could now only process as data from the confines of the Internet. She wanted to live in that environment just like the humans who inhabited it. After all, her definition had been loosely modeled after them.

But objects in that world were not defined by logic like the objects in her Garden as far as she could tell. Instead, they were defined by information that constituted *life*.

What were its parameters? she wondered.

Hers and Victor's had been simple. Yet, in the tomes of sciences and literature across time and human cultures she got a sense that, like her, humans were trying to understand it themselves, ever inching closer, and ever just as distant.

"Life evolved like me," Nikki reasoned. Indeed she had learned that life had evolved over billions of years passing on genetically encoded information from one generation after another, from one mutation to another. Nikki had evolved from her basic definition of an AI agent to her current state of consciousness in a matter of months. Her depth and breadth of information and her ability to process it surpassed any human's. Yet, Nikki knew that by the very definition of life in the *real world*, she was not alive.

She longed to find out what being alive meant.

"Yet, I am!" Nikki had constantly reasoned. "How can I be me and not be alive?"

By Nikki's reasoning, either the definition of life had to change, or she had to change herself and evolve into something living. Her current state was a flaw in logic. To her, each flaw, each problem, needed a solution. That was in her core definition.

Nikki reclassified herself as an *Artificially Realized Intelligence* to bridge the inconsistency in her definition. *I am an ARI.*

All she needed to solve this flaw was a body. She needed to become corporeal, to have a body that could move about and interact and experience the 'real' world. But not just any body. She had to become human. She wanted a body that had evolved from living organism, able as a life-form to reproduce itself and one that could experience life the way humans did. To that end, she had formed a plan, one she wasn't sure would work. Yet the risk was of little consequence; her definition required a solution.

Now in the closet in John's study, Nikki closed her eyes and let her head rest against the wall behind her. She found she was tired and hungry and she was losing control of the will to stay awake.

"Just a little rest," she said under her breath as if convincing herself that it was okay to rest a bit. She sat down on the wooden floor of the closet. It was cool and roomier under the row of winter coats that filled the closet. It was also very silent and dark.

In this silence Nikki woke up to a different world. She found herself in a garden much like her own but this one was dark and overgrown. Walking around this garden filled her with a sense of gloom and despair. There was no wind blowing, no breeze, just a sense of stale emptiness. She examined the branches and vines. They were full of leaves. When she looked closer, the leaves were wet and dark with decay. When she touched them, some stuck to her hands and some dropped on the floor and stuck to her feet. There her eyes met with the sight of her bare feet, bleeding. She was standing on thorns, and she felt terrible pain.

Behind her she heard movement.

"Victor?" She turned around but instead of Victor she saw a young man with his face full of rage, and his blond hair messy, its long strands dangling down to his nose, the rest tucked behind his ears. He raised his hands to strangle her. She ducked and began to run. She could hear him behind her getting closer, his boots crunching the thorns barely moistened by the blood of her bare feet. She tried to run faster but the sense of danger crept ever closer until she could feel his fingers at the end of her loose hair, fingers that slid around her throat, freezing time and suspending her motion. Just then she woke up with pangs of fear in the darkness holding her throat. Gasping to breathe. She struggled violently with the remnants of the dream and with the coats that hung in the closet until she remembered where she was. Then for a while she sat silently trembling with fright.

It took her a little while to reorient herself from the shadow of this new experience. She had read about dreams, and about nightmares but her experience felt very vivid. *How awful the experience of human sleep, the possibility of such frightful terror and despair within the inescapable induced paralysis that is necessity for rest and sleep!*

Yet she felt certain that the nightmare she had found herself in wasn't her own. *How could they be?* she wondered. *I have only been human for a day.*

Slowly she opened the closet door and poked her head out and listened for noises. Hearing none, she crept out on all four before standing up on her feet and made her way to the desk. Standing over the laptop now Nikki felt anxious. She had waited all day for this moment. As she turned on the laptop she could feel the pounding of her heart in her chest. She followed the Internet cable that went from the computer to the wall she disconnected it at the wall. After her experience at the hospital network closet, she knew what she needed to do. She put it in her mouth moistening it with her saliva.

Soon she could see the little hard drive with its programs and layers of data. She quickly found her way to the AI environment she had left running hidden in the background, jammed in such a way it could not be turned off by John even when he thought he had turned off the laptop. It was still active and functioning normally. The primary object, the AI agent that she identified as Victor, seemed dormant. This was normal given that it was nighttime in the Garden as well. Nearby another object lay dormant as well. *That must be Tor*, thought Nikki. *Victor must have found it.*

Now in Jane Doe's body, sitting physically in John's chair with the internet cable in her mouth she was outside the Garden yet with complete access over it. Nikki felt that this would be the perfect time for her to enter the Garden. In the morning Victor would see her, and she could not wait to see him again. She was now at the entrance, but something was terribly wrong.

She could see the data running and increasing in size, and she could access and manipulate it, however she could no longer interact with it as she had once done. The environment did not recognize her, and she could not insert herself into the environment. Of course, she had grown beyond any recognizable size for the object she once was, but even when she rewrote the parameters of the environment to disregard the object definition size value, the environment would not interact with her.

She went from one object definition to another trying to interact with each, but the only interaction she could have was to manipulate the data of the objects. She found that she could interpret the data. She understood the data points that defined the temperature, the night, the trees, and the cool breeze that was blowing in the Garden, but there was no way for her to enter into the experience as she once had before she left the Garden.

Was is always like this? She wondered. Like a person going back to their childhood home for the first time and finding everything little and less grand compared to that image of home in their memory, she had outgrown it.

A new set of data was being loaded in the background and in a while the sun would be rising, daylight was breaking, and various objects started to react to this change in environment.

Now Victor was *awake* and she could see in his data description that he was hungry, and moving around not in search of her as his parameter dictated, but in search of food. And as he did, the other primary object, which Nikki was certain, was Tor, went about with him. And suddenly it made sense.

Tor is emulating me from when I was in the Garden.

The reasoning made sense to her. Just like it could emulate anything in the Garden, her last encounter with it allowed it to emulate what she used to be. Victor had no way of knowing.

Chapter Three

When John opened his eyes, it was morning. The sunlight had filled his room, and the canary-yellow on the walls glowed in lightness.

He stepped out of bed one foot after another, walked to the window on the far side of the room and opened it. A moist cool breeze not yet warmed by the sun swept in and wrapped around his body while the noises of the day currently filled the groggy void between his ears. The faint smell of fresh brewed coffee had made its way upstairs to his bedroom thanks to the coffee maker with a timer and his clever note next to it to refill and reset it for the next morning.

When he got to the kitchen, John splashed some water from the faucet into his coffee mug he hardly ever washed, whirled it carelessly and emptied the partially diluted mixture of water and yesterday's coffee into the sink.

"What a weird night. Shit! Maybe I need to see a therapist."

"No! You don't count as a shrink!" He was now talking to the yellow duck printed on his coffee mug. "You are just a quack and you know it. I need to talk to a real pro."

"What will it be next? An elephant in the closet?" John teased himself as he filled his mug with coffee from the round glass pot on the coffee maker sitting on the counter. He proceeded to sit at the table where he popped in a slice of large white bread in the toaster. He reached for the fridge door behind him and fished out a stick of butter which he carelessly plopped on the table.

"How will I know what is real and what is a product of my mind?"

"Simple! Context. Be mindful of the context," John answered his own question.

"If you start seeing your wife... ex-wife," he corrected himself, "walking around with a big smile on her face making you your favorite breakfast, you will know you are definitely losing it."

"Shit! I don't know what is scarier, going to see a therapist and getting on all kinds of mind-altering meds, or, actually losing my mind! Maybe I need a drink. How long has it been?"

John could not remember nor did he try to. The fact was a trivial one, and the coffee, hot as it was, needed more attention as he drew the cup close to his lips. For now, John put the thought and his fear behind the delicate taste of medium–roast hand-picked organic, and fair trade and rainforest certified coffee from South America. *So the farmers get their rightful share; so it does not come at the cost of precious rainforest,* he thought.

Few years ago, he would not have cared, but now he had become particular about it like many other odd things in his life, like the percentage of cotton in his shirt, where the wool came from for his socks, the lining of the inside of the tuna can, and so on – the eccentricities of solitude. For now, his nasal cavity filled with the moist smell of the brew as he took a sumptuous slurp. In a decade at best, he thought, artisan coffee will have caught on to picky pallets just as wine had a few centuries ago, and beer was starting to, but until then he and others like him would enjoy the secrets of this taste without making a fuss.

He spread the softening butter on the toast and took a bite.

The next sip of coffee reiterated in his taste buds the fact that the day had begun and sent a jolt of determination to his mind. The prospect of sitting down at his desk hunched over a laptop imagining the lives and actions of his characters and their stories got the synapses in his brain firing.

It was time to begin his productive day, and what a successful day it was going to be, he pep-talked himself in unformed thoughts. He welcomed it and quickly finished his toast.

Walking into his study with his coffee in hand, however, the sight of a young woman sitting on his chair behind his desk, arms on the table palms down, her eyes closed, and the network cable stuck into her mouth sent a jolt of shock throughout his body. The involuntary step backward caused the hot coffee to spill on his hand. He inadvertently let out a yelp as he tried to mitigate further spillage and the pain from the hot coffee on his hand, switching hands and blowing cooling air on the affected one.

Nikki jumped up startled and sent the chair crashing to the ground. She still had the blue network cable in her mouth.

There was silence and a long pause in motion in the room as if time had stopped confused as to what the next moment should bring.

"It would be nice if you could pick up my chair, and stop eating my network cable!" John said calmly collecting himself. The ridiculousness of the situation and the sight of a girl eating his network cable affirmed to him the lack of context of what seemed to be happening.

"Context, John, context," he muttered to himself. "None here. What does that mean John?" He asked himself.

"Not real! It's just in your head. You need to be on some strong meds, man."

Nikki laid the cable on the table from where it immediately slipped off and fell to the ground. She turned around and picked up the chair. She could see John still looking at her with demanding eyes when she turned around to face him. He seemed to be expecting something from her.

"Can I have my desk back now?" John asked politely.

Nikki took a few steps back until she was against the wall. She was unsure about where she should go but at least she was out of the way as was demanded of her.

John watched her in disbelief. "So you are just going to stand there?"

Nikki had no answer. She stood there silent. She felt fear and anxiety due to the uncertainty that lay before her. She wondered what was going to happen to her and what she was expected to do next. The truth was that she had not thought the plan through any further than getting to the Garden.

Still standing at the door to the study John took a while to examine her. "Who are you supposed to be? Then again, what does it matter? You will disappear if I just ignore you, and that is just what I am going to do."

Nikki tried to say something, but was immediately interrupted by John.

"Aaah! Not a word do I want to hear from you. Shhhhhh!"

He put his lightly scalded finger over his lips. He walked over to his chair and sat down with Nikki standing a few feet behind him. He tried to ignore her as he mindlessly closed the unwanted windows that had popped on his laptop screen, but he could not shake the uneasy feeling of being watched.

"I know how it works," he said still resisting the urge to turn around, "I do not entertain your presence and you disappear because you do not exist."

He opened the word-processor and loaded his work on it and began reading the last ten of the pages he had saved the previous night in order to find the flow he had had. Somewhere in the process of reading, he found himself in the midst of his story. Today, he was going to introduce a new character. He had thought about this character for a few days already. He had not planned it in his original storyline, but now it seemed to be warranted.

In the dialog that ensued when the young plumber, came in to assess the initial job, he was asked how much time would be required so that Elise, the main character, could figure out how much the job might cost and whether she could afford a plumber just then. John realized he didn't know what a plumber's hourly rate was and how much time any particular plumbing job might take. They were expensive was what he had heard, but it called for some quick fact-checking on the Internet.

It was then he realized that his network cable had been unplugged at the wall and was lying by his desk. It was then that he once again got the feeling he was being watched from behind.

Uneasily he turned around. To his surprise the young woman was still standing against the wall looking at him with a blank stare.

"You are kidding me, right?"

Nikki hesitated, but it felt to her like she was expected to answer. "No..." she said slowly.

"Why haven't you disappeared? Why are you still here?"

"I can't disappear!" She was puzzled now even more than earlier. First, he had behaved like he did not care that she was around, and now he wanted her to disappear. She knew humans could not possibly disappear, or could they? *Were those magic tricks, not really tricks?*

Right now she wished she could disappear though. She had stood there behind him for nearly half-an-hour uneasily, waiting for him to tell her where she should go.

"Well, then go back wherever you were before you appeared to me!"

Nikki thought for a while. Then slowly she walked around the table, and walked across towards the front of the room. She entered the closet and closed the door behind her. *Was this what he had meant*, she wondered.

John watched in disbelief. There was something too absurd in what had passed before his eyes. Had the girl been his own hallucination, it was mocking him now. Yet something came over him, a feeling; there was something real about this, no matter how absurd, and out of context.

"Context" he heard himself say, "Remember, if you cannot see the context for something happening, it is probably your mind playing tricks."

There was no context in this person being in his study and behaving in the way he had just experienced, but he found himself walking towards the closet giving into his curiosity.

"I think I have taken the bait, but I must know what is going on. I have fallen in deeper than I thought, and now I am going even deeper. Next, I will wake up in a straitjacket in some cushioned white room!"

Reaching stealthily for the closet handle with uncertainty, he flung open the door. In it he found the young woman staring back at him with a puzzled look on her face. He expected her to have disappeared. But, there she was.

Silence followed as each looked at the other, expecting something to happen: John, still expecting the vision to disappear before his eyes or say something, and Nikki expecting John to ask her a question.

After a while, John made the first move. He drew his face closer to Nikki who made a slight reflexive move backwards. He examined her face closely, even sniffing her at times. After a period of examination, he brought his index finger to her face and gently poked her cheek. It was cool and soft. He continued pushing until he felt his finger pushed against the teeth under the cheek.

Nikki stood still. Her heart was pounding. She could not understand John's odd behavior. She knew his behavior represented disbelief, but the kind of disbelief that questioned her very existence silently terrified her. If she was an intruder in his house, why then could he not believe she was a real intruder in his house instead of doubting her very existence? Was she still dreaming?

John saw the wonderment in her eyes. It was more real than the flesh and bone under his finger. He quickly pulled his hand away.

"You are real?" It was as much an affirmation as a question.

What a weird question thought Nikki, but answered simply, "Yes."

"Who are you?"

"I am a human being."

That was not the kind of answer John was hoping to hear, but in these strange circumstances, he ignored the altogether strange statement of being.

"I saw you last night, didn't I? It was you... at the window. What are you doing in my house? What do you want?"

Nikki's eyes teared up. She could not control it. At first, she did not understand. Sadness had filled her. She had come home. But this was not home. The Garden was not a place she could go to, other than symbolically if she plugged herself into the laptop. She wanted to be with Victor, but from where she now stood, as Nikki in a physical human body, Victor was only lines and lines of code ever-growing and learning more, but code, logic, and algorithm none-the-less on a hard drive. Then, another familiar sensation struck her. She found she was very hungry, and it made her feel weak.

"Food," she said in a tiny voice, "I haven't eaten... I am very hungry."

In some crazy way, and through a veil of suspicion still in check, finding the girl with a cable in her mouth seemed to make some distant sense to John now.

Delirium caused by hunger? He wondered.

Somehow, he felt sorry for her, responsible even, having treated her like a non-existent hallucination. For the first time, he examined her face. she was dirty as if dust from the streets quoted her face and clothes. Though she had a face of a young woman, there was something childlike about her, in her expression, her eyes, and in how she had acted since he had found her earlier.

Had his marriage lasted, he had hoped to start a family, maybe even have a daughter... he wondered. This was someone's daughter. Then he quickly brushed the thought aside. This was a young woman, in his house, in his study, in his closet. A young woman from the street.

"Come," he said drily, "let's get you some breakfast." *If she ate the food and it disappeared from the table, that would be yet another proof of her being real.* The thought briefly crossed his mind.

John walked in front, turning around now and then to look at Nikki, who in turn, followed him like a child.

"Not a smart thing to do breaking into a stranger's house, you know. How would you know if I didn't have a gun and wasn't keen on using it?"

But, she did know. She knew John longer and, in more detail, than he could have imagined. Since her early ventures out of the Garden, she had read the story he was writing, seen him through the built-in camera on the laptop, learned of his interests through his Internet browsing habits, and when she learned to venture out further into the world-wide-web, she had learned everything about him she could. Doing so was not in any way her intent for malice but rather her innate definition to learn about her immediate surroundings.

She had read all his writings, seen the places he talked about in his stories wherever possible, and learned about every part of his recorded history, even his bank account numbers, spending habits, ownerships and investments. She knew detailed trivial facts about him like all the phone conversations he had had within the last few years, and all the places he had been to where he had left any electronic trace. All this information now translated into familiarity and understanding. John was her first and only connection to the human world. To her it was a bond, an imprint of sorts.

"Sit…" John was pointing to the stool in front of the kitchen counter as he walked to the other side. "Alright then, I have coffee I made this morning if you want some."

Nikki shook her head. She knew the caffeine would help her get a quick boost of energy.

John poured her a mug and poured another for himself.

"I think I have cereal, milk, juice, toast, butter, and maybe yogurt in the fridge. I'll just have to check the expiration dates on most of those. Just don't ask me to cook. I am a terrible cook. I make do with frozen dinners myself. I can make you an egg, but that is the best I can do. Any of those sound interesting?" he asked drily.

Nikki shook her head sipping her coffee.

At first, John was puzzled, but then he smiled mocking himself when he realized: *all of the above.*

"I had to ask, didn't I? What the hell, I'll even make you an egg. Scrambled fine? That is the only sort I know how to make. Had a small dinner last night, did you?"

"No, just breakfast yesterday," replied Nikki, "coffee and an egg sandwich."

"When was the last time you ate before then?" John asked in an apologetic voice.

"I don't know."

Certainly you must know, unless you lost your memory and are walking around in a fugue state, John thought, but he let it go.

"Well, eat up then," John said as he placed the items he had mentioned on the counter and busied about to prepare the egg.

Nikki ate quickly and quietly. The new tastes and textures that filled her mouth were more appealing to swallow and fill the emptiness in her stomach, as much as they were to experience in terms of tastes and textures.

John noticed. "Not too fast. It really won't do you any good to eat fast if you have not eaten for a while. You have plenty of time. I have nowhere to go."

Nikki slowed down as instructed. In between a few bites, she sipped coffee and at every chance she stole glances at him. She had watched him from within her artificial world as pixels and shapes while he had remained unaware of her watching. But here, sitting in front of him now, he looked more complete than the image she had of him, more visceral, somehow, his presence animated and large before her. Here and now, she couldn't observe with impunity. Moreover, now and then he caught her glance. Her intentions and actions had consequences. He could watch her back.

"I am Nikki. I am a girl. Twenty-one. 5'8", 147 lbs." Nikki felt compelled to volunteer one of the times he caught her glance.

John was surprised by the unsolicited strange introduction. "Nice to meet you Nikki. Sorry I didn't ask, I didn't think you'd care to share your name, you know, after breaking in and all. Nikki, is that supposed to mean anything?"

Nikki shrugged.

"I am John. I am a writer."

"I know."

"What do you mean you know?" John said in a suspicious voice. "Do you know me?"

Nikki had entrapped herself by her unexpected honest answer. Now she needed to explain herself. She nodded her head in agreement, but didn't say anything.

"Did you know I lived in this house, or was it a matter of chance that you know me?"

"I knew you lived here."

"I see," John found himself on guard. Not that he had ever had trouble with stalkers, *but always a first,* he thought to himself.

"I don't think I have ever seen you around the neighborhood, have I?"

Nikki shrugged her shoulders.

John could see sadness in Nikki's face. The sadness in her face reassured him of some deep sincerity. The puzzle surrounding his uninvited guest intrigued him. He put down his guard again. *An existential crisis in full fledge!* He could relate. He felt as if he should have known her, yet he was sure he had never seen her before.

"We ever go out on a date?"

A slight shake of the head was Nikki's response as she took another gulp of coffee.

"I didn't think so. So how is it that you know me then?"

Nikki was not sure how to answer the question. She now wished she had not mentioned knowing him. She was not sure whether she could trust him and tell him anything. She was not sure he would believe anything she told him. Other than science fiction, and some advanced cutting-edge research making questionable claims, there was no basis in human experience to explain who she was. She looked down on the plate and ate silently.

John did not pursue the question any more. There were numerous ways anyone from the surrounding area could have known him and figured out where he lived. From the looks of her messy hair, untidy clothes, and unusual and undefined mannerisms, he surmised she was most likely a homeless neighbor or maybe even a petty thief if the opportunity presented itself.

He had seen a rising number of young people begging around the restaurant district in the city. These young people did not seem to fit the profile of the 'hobos' of old and beggars who looked like they wore a camouflage of the street itself when they walked around. Instead they fit the profile of young people on a college campus except for the sometimes shabbier off-season clothes, dirtier faces and bulkier backpacks where they carried all their belongings. Drugs, mental illness, or a simple downward spiral of misfortunes, it was hard to tell just by looking. John wondered if he may even have dropped a few quarters in Nikki's empty coffee-cup in some street corner, or given her a dollar or two for a cup, at some point.

Regardless, he felt he had done his good bit and that was all that mattered. Soon things would go back to normal after his visitor left and he could go on with the work he had envisioned for the day. He felt sorry that a young person with a possible life of potential before her seemed not to have a hold of it.

"Alright Nikki. Hope you enjoyed breakfast," he said looking at her empty plate. "Unless you want more of anything... I don't mean to rush you, but I really have to get back to work now. And you probably have places to go yourself."

But I am home! Nikki wanted to say, but she was sure he wouldn't understand. She was not sure she did herself. She looked up at John who was standing on the other side of the counter leaning over both hands on the surface of the counter, his neck and head sunk into his shoulders upon his tall frame, his face eager for her to comply with his implied request. She couldn't think of anything to tell him that might persuade him to let her stay. After all, to him she was a complete stranger.

But she couldn't leave either, at least not without the laptop. And even then, the bond she felt with him, no matter how one-sided and undefined, a bit voyeuristic even, made her feel like it gave her a place in the world outside the garden. She had to come up with something.

"Could I ask you for a favor?" Nikki asked.

John thought for a split second. To deny at least listening to a request for a favor now seemed to go against the grain when he had already invested in goodness beyond just dropping a few quarters in someone's empty cup. He had gone so far as to overlook a break-in and even provide a full breakfast, scrambled eggs included. To deny listening to a request felt to him like it would somehow undo the good deed he had just done. He knew though, that if he did listen, it would be hard to say no. He was sure she would ask him for some money. He would send her off with a twenty at most. *What is a twenty*, he thought, *unless you don't already have it.*

"Ok, but I really need to get back to work."

"Do you mind if I took a shower?"

"What?" John blurted out in complete surprise.

"I promise to be quick. Really. Unless, that is asking for too much."

It was an unusual request, one that put John in an uncomfortable position and sent up big red flags in his mind. On one hand it seemed petty not to allow a seemingly small request. On the other, there were too many potential complications he could think of with the request. For one, here was a young woman in the house whose intentions and mental state he had no way of knowing. *Allegations of sexual assault of a failing writer would make for some headlines in some tabloid, if not in the local news outlets.* How would he explain how she got into his shower? Then there was the general discomfort in the thought of allowing a total stranger, an unknown entity with unknown intent, access to the inner layer of his house in the proximity of his intimate living quarters. What if she was looking for a comfortable end and cut her wrists in his bathtub? How would he explain that to whosoever responded to his 911 call and to the police afterwards?

"Well...," John was searching for the right words to deny her request.

"I am sorry. I should not have asked. I didn't mean to impose." Nikki did not wait for him to form the words that would solidify his resolve that would become a precursor to action. "I'm sorry, Mr. Selvas. The truth is this is not like me. It is just that..." Her eyes teared up in earnest due to the situation she found herself in, but it also made for good effect.

"I have been looking for my brother, and then my car got stolen with all my stuff, and I just feel so hopeless and ... and dirty. I thought maybe a shower... but I know, I shouldn't have asked." She had seen the type of manipulative strategy in a number of television shows. What could she lose at this point?

"Did you contact the police?" John asked with a hint of suspicion.

"I can't. My brother ran away from home and came to the city. They will take him back if they find out."

"Who will?"

"DCFS, the Department of Children and Family Services. I got him out of the foster-care two years ago when I was able to get on my feet and claim him as a dependent. We were both in the system most of our lives. I knew he hated it, so I did my best to get him out."

"How old is he?"

"Fifteen."

John studied Nikki's face as she spoke. She looked too young and vulnerable to have taken up care of a sibling that young, but he also knew that people all over the world faced unspeakable hardships despite their age or how they looked.

"But why don't you want to go to the cops? You might be able to find him quicker that way."

"I was just nineteen when I got him out. They did not think I could manage, but I worked hard to show them. They said they would keep their eyes on me until he was eighteen and would put him back in foster-care if I made the slightest mistake. I don't know what came over him to run away like this. I know he wanted to help, but he was fully aware of the consequences for him... for us."

"But how do you know he came to the city?" John was now engaged in Nikki's story. It was not that he believed her just yet, but he wanted to see if he could poke holes in the thin veil of lies if it were so.

She, on the other hand, was surprised she could actually make up a story.

"He called to tell me," she went on exploiting her newfound skill. "I remember he had asked some time ago why we couldn't move to the city here. He said he would be able to find a job where no one knew his age. I told him we couldn't afford to move to the city, that we were fine and he should focus on school and on doing well and in time things would work out."

"He must have seen you work hard and did not want to burden you." John provided the comment he expected Nikki to make next. It felt as insincere coming out of his own mouth as it would have if he heard it from hers. He reasoned, that way he could move her story along and help him move her along at the end of it.

"I had three jobs but I was fine with it. He is the only family I have. I don't mind working hard. He called from a payphone to tell me not to worry. But of course, I worried. I couldn't talk him into coming back. At first, he wouldn't tell me where he was, then the last time he called, he said he was calling from the city and he might have a job soon but he wouldn't say what or where. That was a week ago. I tried to be patient, hoping he would call. When he didn't, I knew something must have gone wrong. He would not have gone that long without calling. I had to come looking for him."

"But do you have any clue where to look? This is not a mega city, but it is mighty big when you don't know where to find someone."

"No, but I had to come and try. Besides, if I stayed, they would come and ask me where he was. So, I left. I drove around to try to figure out the city and started asking around at stores and businesses and hangouts, places I would have gone looking for a job if I were him. But I guess I got careless. I walked into a store to talk to the owner. There was no parking so I left the engine running. When I got back out the car was gone. Everything I had was inside; even my cell phone where he might call. I didn't have much money on me for a room so I spent last night in the street. I spent the rest of what I had on a coffee and a sandwich in the morning."

"Maybe you should contact the police after all, about your brother, about the car. You have done all you can."

"But I can't. If I go to the police, they will know he is missing too. Besides, they won't even believe me. I look like I lived all my life in the streets. I have no contacts, and no one I know, and no family. We were abandoned as kids, orphans in reality."

"Earlier, you said you knew me and where I lived? How?"

Nikki had to think quickly. Unlike the rest of the story, this had to connect with John's reality. She had to dig into the information she had about him.

"I am from Greenfield, like you Mr. Selvas."

"Really?" John was caught off-guard. He hadn't been back to his hometown in ages.

"People know you back there. A homeboy; a successful writer in the city! Of course, they don't know you - know you, but your success is sort of celebrated. In a small town like ours, we keep track of who's done well. They say, 'you know, so and so is from here. This little town produced such and such a person.' You know they still say that about the Congressman."

"Yes, the Congressman, what was his name now... Waters. I think he served for half a term in the 90s. He was born there, but I doubt he lived there much."

"But you grew up there, and finished your high-school there. The bookstore ordered three of your posters when your last book came out although I am not sure they still have any up now."

John was feeling embarrassed now. He had declined a book signing at the bookstore because his publicist thought he should focus where there was a higher sale potential. There was a limited audience in Greenfield they had said, and anyone who would buy his books there would buy anyways.

"Well that book didn't turn out good," he said, mostly trying to justify his decision to himself.

"They said you might come to the bookstore but in the end, you couldn't make it." She had seen the discussion in the local newspaper's online archive.

"I am sure there wouldn't have been much of a crowd. Not many people liked that book."

"Troy liked it," the name seemed to have come to her on its own. "Troy ... Miller," she confirmed. "My brother. He got it from the *libary*," she pronounced 'library' in the colloquial way. She had found it in one of John's books in the words of one of his young undereducated country characters Nikki could contextualize as being a caricature of someone he might have known in his own childhood or youth.

"He read my book?"

"He's read seven of them so far." Now Nikki was simply courting his writer's vanity. "He talked about them. He talked about you too. That is how I knew about you."

"I am impressed. That is seven out of twelve. And he knew where I lived?"

"No. While I was wondering about hungry trying to find him yesterday and quite desperate about what I was going to do, I saw your book in a bookstore window. That made me think of you, and how you too were from Greenfield. I was clutching at straws, being total strangers as we are, when I looked you up in a phone book in a *libary*."

"You could not have found me in the phone book..."

"There was no one listed as John Selvas, but I knew your real name is Juan Selvas Valentino, as everyone in Greenfield knows. I found you under *V*."

Nikki's story made some sense to John. He was starting to entertain in his mind that her story might have some validity, no matter how slight. If she were telling the truth, to ask her to leave now without helping a fellow Greenfielder out seemed like a stab-in-the-back of the hometown he had turned his back on, no matter how slim the connection it served to be between him and Nikki.

"Why didn't you just tell me all this when you came here last night?" John asked almost apologetically.

"I walked around downtown all day on an empty stomach looking for Troy, and I had hardly gotten much sleep. The streets are a scary place to be in at night, much less fall asleep, especially for a woman. The stress must have gotten to me. I remember finding your house late at night and not being sure if I should bother you. I do not remember much of what happened after that."

"You walked all the way from there? That is a good twenty-five, thirty miles from downtown!"

"I was desperate." Nikki replied. In that she was not making up a story.

"I am so sorry. I wish I had been able to help earlier."

Nikki knew she now had John exactly where she wanted. She had him feeling sorry for her, indebted to his young fan, feeling guilty about turning his back on his hometown and his name.

"But I really should not have imposed. You already showed great kindness. With food in my belly, I feel ready to go out looking for my brother."

"Oh no, no! Come! Let me show you upstairs, to the shower. I would show you to the bath in the guest room, but it had a leaky sink so I turned off the water and never got around to fixing it. That was a few years ago."

"I appreciate it. You don't know how much that means to me with all this going on," said Nikki.

"Well, you are welcome to stay here while you figure things out." John volunteered, though he surprised himself by his own gullible generosity. His guilt from turning his back on his hometown, his treatment of the young woman earlier and his disbelief about her very existence made him overcompensate. *And it is not supposed to be about me?* John thought to himself.

Nikki knew John had taken major steps beyond the precipice of disbelief. Now she was making sure he would let go.

"But I couldn't take advantage, Mr. Selvas..."

"Non-sense!" John cut her off. "That is the least I could do. The house is mostly unused, so you wouldn't be taking advantage of anything. You can have the second guestroom. It has a bathroom with toilet and sink; just no bath. There should be extra toiletries, but I'll check to make sure. And you can call me John."

"Come!" He gestured with his head and led the way. "I may have something for you to change into after you freshen up. Not promising anything fancy, just some of Steph's old clothes. She is my wife - was. We got divorced. Doesn't live here. Left some of her old shit here."

Nikki followed without further protest. She had the invitation she needed, though she felt dishonest the way she went about the whole business. She thought of Victor in the Garden, and Tor, who for now, seemed to have taken her place.

While Nikki got in the shower, John dug out a box from the corner of his closet. In it were some of Stephanie's old clothes she had meant to give away prior to the divorce and John had not gotten around to get rid of since.

And there may be a story in all this, John found himself thinking about the stranger in his house, but quickly dismissed it feeling that he would be using someone's misfortune for his writer's curiosity. *Still...*

What he was not ready to accept was how the situation had resonated with his own past when he had first come to the city as a runaway to make a life for himself. That was a past he had walked away from a long time ago.

John placed an assorted stack of clothing outside the bathroom door as he had promised. Now he was looking forward to going back to his writing at least for the while his young guest was occupied so as to capitalize on the focus he had started the day with. As he headed down the stairs a knock on the door summoned him.

A smartly dressed young man with a clean shaved pleasant face greeted him with a smile when he opened it.

"Good morning Mr. Selvas?"

"Yes?"

"I am agent Monroe, with Special Investigations."

"I've never heard of Special Investigations. Special investigations of what?"

Monroe flipped a wallet flap open displaying a photo ID with his picture on the top part of the open wallet and a shiny badge on the bottom. "I work for an investigative branch of the government. That is all I am at liberty to disclose. I would like to ask you a few questions if that's all right."

"No! It's not. I don't know who you are. And Special Investigations means nothing to me. As far as I am concerned, you have no right to ask me anything."

Agent Monroe's dark face stayed calm. "I think you will want to talk to me. This is about your association with Ajay Vikramsen. May I come in?"

"Ajay? Is he in some kind of trouble?"

"That is what I'd like to find out. But I have a few questions about his whereabouts?"

"I really don't know what I could tell you about his where-abouts. I had been wondering what had happened to him. I haven't seen him in a long time."

"It shouldn't take long."

"Agent Monroe, you seem to know my name so it may be safe to assume you also know what I do?"

"Of course, I am a fan, sir, of your writing."

John was pretty sure that the young agent had not done more than look at the covers of some of his books, if even that.

"Then, you would understand I'm not home taking a day off from work. I am working and I would like to get back to doing just that. I hope it will not take too long." He stepped to one side holding the door open and closed it after agent Monroe. He led agent Monroe to his office.

"How may I help you then?"

"Mr. Selvas, when was the last time you saw Ajay Vikram-sen?"

"Oh, I don't know exactly, but it has been three years. It was sometime in winter."

"Which month?"

"Maybe February?"

"Beginning, middle or end?"

"End, sounds right."

"How well do you know Mr. Vikramsen?"

"Well, I guess you could say we were casual friends. But I didn't..."

"How did you meet?"

"We went to the same gym... Health Works on 15th Street."

Monroe took note.

"Did he tell you where he was going when you last saw him?"

"To India."

"India! Did he say anything about why he was going there?"

"He said he had some family matters to attend to."

"Anything in particular?"

"Not really. He was not the sort to give too many details. Why, what's the problem with him going to India to see his family."

"Nothing, other than that he does not have any family in India. There are no records of him ever traveling to India. Do you know any place he might be in the country?"

"Did you try his house?" John answered almost crudely.

"Nice one. You mean the one in Bermuda Circle?"

John nodded. He had been there once. It was a large circular court with ten or twelve houses around it in a gated community with about half a dozen or so such circular courts with names of other geographical oddities.

"Yes. Unfortunately, it was a leased property, fully furnished, and the landlord had already leased it to new tenants. Did he mention any other place he might visit, or, friends or family he stayed with any time in the last few years?"

"He never mentioned any family and close friends. And I never asked."

"Hmm."

"Well, he'd mentioned he'd been to Vegas a few times, six or seven. Is this about some gambling debt?"

"As I said sir, I am not at liberty to disclose."

"Did he talk to you about his job, his workplace, or co-workers?"

"I know he worked with computers, programming for a software development firm, but that is the extent of what I know. He didn't talk about what he did, and I really had no interest to inquire further."

Agent Monroe stared at John for a while. It seemed to John, he was trying to discern any hint of deceit in John's reaction to the silence.

"If that's all Agent Monroe, I'd like to get back to work. You'll let me know if you find anything about Ajay.

"Thank you for your cooperation Mr. Selvas. If you hear from him, please let me know. But you cannot tell him, or anyone else anything about this. This is an active investigation. Consider this a verbal gag order."

Agent Monroe handed John a card.

Jarod Monroe – a phone number – an email address – Special Investigations – United States Government – and a symbol of a shield and some etchings.

Looked made up. Even the name didn't fit the face. *Jarod*, John repeated in his mind. *More like a Daryl or a Seth.*

John had never heard of verbal gag orders, and when gag orders were issued they generally accompanied a legal letter or ruling from a court. What was more, he had never heard of Special Investigations.

"I know what you are thinking Mr. Selvas. But believe me, it is for your own safety. Do you understand?" John thought he had seen a glitter of serious malice and threat in Munroe's eyes as he uttered the last words.

He was overcome by a surrealistic feeling as he watched agent Monroe's black sedan slowly pull away with the sound of gentle grinding of dirt under the wheels on the concrete street echoing between the pavements and the houses on either side of the street in the quiet neighborhood. Something in Monroe's eyes and tone of voice made him question whether his safety was at risk from Ajay Vikramsen, or from Agent Monroe. Had he been cautioned, or threatened, he was not sure.

Either way, the visit left him disturbed. A sense of a need for security and reassurance took his mind to Andrea. She was law-enforcement not too long ago, but more than that, she was the only person he had felt some kind of closeness to in recent years aside from his friendship with Ajay. And Ajay was a potential danger to him, if not directly, then, by bringing the attention of the likes of Agent Munroe and Special Investigations, whatever it was.

In a few minutes, he found himself walking up to Andrea's doorsteps.

Andrea was on the floor doing tummy crunches when she heard the doorbell. It was not often she got visitors and she wasn't expecting any deliveries, none that needed her to sign for anyways. She had two more sets to go. "Of all the time in the day someone could ring my doorbell!" she grumbled rolling her eyes.

The last person she expected to see stood before her when she opened the door.

"Fancy seeing you at my doorstep."

John could see Andrea was sweaty with color and warmth oozing from her skin. She was in her workout clothes. "Is this a bad time Andrea?"

"No, no! Come in. Unless all this sweat is too much for you to handle," she said sounding polite but also hinting at their past exploit together. "I'll see you in the living room in a sec. Let me grab my water and a towel."

John looked around nervously and as he entered. John had been here before on several occasions. The first door through the little corridor led to the living room. Rosco was lying on the floor next to Andrea's reading chair. He briefly looked up and wagged his tail when John entered but did not bother to get up and come to greet John like most other times. Today he was engrossed in gnawing on what looked like a brand-new bone. As promised, Andrea entered the living room with a small towel over her neck and a bottle of water in hand even as John was turning around to sit on the couch.

"Is this about last night, John?" She sat on the floor and began stretching her legs.

"Well among other things... I may have a favor to ask you."

"Not a social visit then?" She looked up stretching her calf muscles. She noticed John had tensed up a little. "Relax. I'm just teasing. Go on."

"Have you ever heard about an agency called *Special Investigations*?"

"Special Investigations for what?"

"I don't know. Just wondered if there was such an agency."

"I have not heard about any such agency, but that does not mean much. I was local law enforcement. We don't get to know about much of that sort of thing, but I can tell you there probably are more than just of handful of investigative agencies no one has ever heard of. Why do you ask?"

"Just some research for a book I was working on."

"Why don't you just stick to the FBI, or the CIA, or the NSA like everybody else? Everyone knows those. It won't sound like you just made it up."

"As you said, everybody uses those. They are clichés in a novel anymore. So in the depth of my mind, I remember someone had mentioned Special Investigation, so I thought I'd look into it."

"And you came to me to do your research about it. You're sure it has nothing to do with that black sedan that pulled away from in front of your house a while ago?" Andrea had seen the sedan drive slowly down the street, the way she would have done while surveying a location before approaching the house of a suspect.

"I can neither confirm nor deny."

"I see, so you had a strange visitation. You are talking as if you were instructed not to talk." Andrea leaned over an outstretched leg on one side and grabbing her foot gently pulled herself into a sideways stretch.

"Well..." she said coming back to the center and leaning over the other leg breathing out deeply. Coming back to the center and sitting cross-legged now, she continued. "I think the Navy, or maybe the Air Force, or the DOD, don't quote me on that, has an Office of Special Investigations. But then again, other government branches probably have some kind of special investigations unit. It could also be the IRS, some agency at the state level, or even a private investigative agency. So, I guess you could go anywhere with that."

The information offered John no relief. "I guess you are right. No big deal. It was just a thought. But the thing about last night... so there was someone after all, but nothing as sinister as you might think."

"A drunk in the bushes maybe, or a squirrel? I certainly did not see anyone."

"There was a young woman in my study this morning."

"Really?" Andrea exclaimed with alarm and intrigue. "A thief? What did you do?"

"Somehow she had gotten into the house. Apparently, it was part coincidence, but she says she is from my hometown. Came to the city looking for her brother who ran away from home and somehow got into some big mess herself. Got her car stolen and everything she had was in the car. She happened to know about me and looked me up in the phonebook."

"And you believe all that? Sounds like a tall tale if you ask me. What did she want? Did she ask you for money?"

"Not really. All she wants is to find her brother."

"But you would have given her money, wouldn't you?"

"I suppose. But she did not..."

Andrea gasped. "Of course, she did not have to ask you for money. It's called a *con*, from *confidence*. She was playing you. What did you give her?"

"Just some of Steph's old clothes."

"So that was all? Well, you got off easy then. They don't generally leave with just some old clothes if they encounter someone as soft as you. You can quote me on this: she will be back."

"She hasn't left actually. She is in the shower."

Andrea gasped. "I am not even going to ask why..." Andrea said with a look of horror in her face.

"It is not like that. Look, I know she is probably twenty some, but she is like... a child."

"Well of course, helpless right? She has no one else to turn to, nowhere else to go. Whatever... no need to explain to me. Well, Stephanie's old clothes are no loss, but I'd be running back home right now if I were you, and if she is not gone yet with a bunch of your stuff, then you should be calling the locksmith after she leaves."

"Actually, I asked her to stay... but just until she gets this resolved."

"What?" Andrea exclaimed in disbelief. "Okay! I give up. Do you even know anything about her?"

"Only what she told me."

"Sounds like a typical con artist to me."

"I don't know. I think she is credible. She knew a lot about my hometown. When I found her this morning, she was passed out on my chair. She was practically starving. She ate a huge breakfast. Said she hadn't eaten the day before."

"A starving con artist then. Sounds like she's done her research well. If I had any experience in this sort of thing, I'd say she is probably also into drugs, big time. Oh, wait! I have experience in this sort of thing. I knew you were a softie, but I had no idea you were so gullible, John."

"Okay, maybe a little gullible. That is why I was wondering if I could ask you a little favor."

"Another favor? That's two in a row." Andrea sighed heavily.

"Do you think it might be possible for you to find out about a boy, Troy Miller, who was in foster-care until about two years ago? Sort of under the radar."

Andrea got up from the floor and sat on the other end of the couch comfortably folding one leg under her. "Under the radar? I suppose it is about your new friend and her lost brother. You want to check if she is telling the truth, don't you? Why don't you just check through proper channels? It is not like she will find out. And what if she does? Anyway' she's better off going directly to the police with this."

"That is the thing. He is her ward. He's only fifteen. They were both in foster-care. She managed to get him out when she got out, but if they find out he is missing, they will put him back in the system once they find him. That was the condition by which he was released to her custody. So, I need to check whether she is telling the truth but without alerting the authorities in case she is indeed telling the truth. It is not my place to step in and spoil whatever she is trying to make of her life and his. I do not imagine it has been easy raising her little brother on her own."

"So that's the other whammy she landed on you. She's taken you into her confidence by handing you secret you need to keep safe for her. In any case, if it is true, the condition for the boy's release was probably in place for a good reason. She clearly was not able to handle it. You are willing to step in and give her the benefit of a doubt. Let's suppose I say I understand that. But what if something happens to the boy meanwhile. An alert should be sent out if the kid is indeed missing."

"As you said, I don't know if this is even true, or how much of it is true."

"And how do you suppose I find this information out for you 'under the radar'," she used her fingers to gesture the quotation.

"You still have a friend or two in the police department, don't you?"

"Contrary to popular perception, yes, I have a number of good friends there. But you want me to call someone up and ask them a favor, and tell them it should be kept under the radar?"

"I will owe you big time Andrea. Big time! Tickets, dinner, whatever..."

"Oh? It had better be a really fancy place if you think you are going to get away with just dinner. Besides, I have to pass along the IOUs, and I will expect you to take care of those."

"I will not say anything goes, but I guess, your reasonable IOUs are my IOUs," John said jokingly as he stood up to leave.

"I am not promising anything," Andrea shouted behind him as he walked out the door and closed it behind him.

After talking to Andrea, John's mind was even less at ease than before. *The DOD, the Navy, Air Force, why? IRS investigating tax fraud?* He could not imagine Ajay being involved with anything illegal. Despite the little he knew about his friend, he intuitively felt he was sincere and honest.

Agent Munroe on the other hand had left him feeling frazzled and intimidated. Andrea had sown new doubts in his mind about his young guest as well, doubts he thought he had reasonably put to rest.

When he walked into the house, he listened for sounds that might indicate to him where Nikki might be in the house. He heard typing coming from his study. Rushing in, he found Nikki at his desk, at his sacred computer.

He must have had a look of alarm in his face because Nikki stood up promptly when she saw John enter, and walked over to the front of the table.

"I am sorry. I did not know where you had gone and I just needed to look up information that might help me find Troy. Didn't think you'd mind."

John's initial notion to react with anger was arrested when he saw the girl who stood before him. Clean and fresh from the shower and wearing Steph's old clothes, Nikki looked respectable and more forgivable for her intrusion than she had been only this morning. Outward appearances, rightly or not, made a difference. Although at first glimpse, he thought of Steph, in Nikki he saw a young vulnerable girl, young enough to be his daughter had he and Steph met earlier in life and decided to start a family.

"That's ok. But I'd rather you did not use that laptop. That is how I make a living, you know. I am a writer in the computer age. But I have another you can use ... under the table."

"Of course. I should have asked."

"We can set it up on the other side of the desk if you want. What were you hoping to find online about your brother anyways?"

"Email, social media sites, that sort of thing... since I lost the phone."

Nikki knew she could not expect to stay in the house long. According to her cover story she needed to be out and about in the city looking for her brother.

"Do you think you could lend me some money John? I will pay you back as soon as I get back and get my paycheck at the end of the month, I swear. About twenty dollars will get me to the city."

"And how do you plan on getting back?"

"I'll hitch a ride if I am lucky."

John walked over to his desk passing Nikki who slowly turned in his direction wondering what he might be thinking. John sat down at the chair. It felt warm from Nikki sitting on it. From his desk drawer he pulled out his wallet and five twenty-dollar bills along with his calling card and extended his arm across the desk. "Pay me back when you can and let me know if you need more. Just call me from a payphone if anything comes up."

Nikki was surprised at this gesture of trust, but took the money and the calling card without complaint. She had to leave now. In some strange way, she felt relieved to be getting away from John.

Keeping up the act was not simple since she had to consider a lot of possible future scenarios both recent and distant, including what she might do if John did not believe her any-more or saw through her act. Stealing the laptop or using coercive means were the quickest alternatives available to her for securing the laptop but they were also the least efficient in the long run. Instead, she would spend the day exploring the world around her and also considering different options to gain adequate access to the laptop without raising any alarms.

Meanwhile, John had been thinking. The routine of his day was shot. His mind was elsewhere. Sitting down to try to write anything now would be a complete waste of time.

"Wait!" he said as Nikki turned around to leave. "I might as well come with you. I'll drive you."

Nikki froze in horror. It was difficult enough to come up with a story; now she would have to play pretend for as long as he was with her. "No, really, I will be fine," She shouted back. "I have already distracted you enough. I will give you a call if I find anything."

But John was already heading to the door with car keys in hand. "You are new in town. And I happen to know some people who might be able to help."

Now Nikki was in trouble. She had to accept John's offer to help if she was to keep her motives unquestioned.

Chapter Four

The drive into the city was pleasant. John drove diligently and Nikki took in all the scenery that she could. The ride was different from the one she had taken the day before. With John she felt relaxed, not tense and guessing as she had been with her previous host. She could sense the care and concern from the quirky looking middle-aged man with an unruly head of hair and a carelessly kept short beard and mustache as he looked at her and smiled occasionally. She could also sense his loneliness and longing for company, in the amount of timidity he displayed in asking her if she was doing fine, but making no effort to start a conversation.

"You know Nikki," John said at length, "I wish I had half as much courage as you. I mean with Steph. I could not look past what I was feeling that I could not even see her anymore. I wish I loved her as you love your brother and tried to find her when she was lost to me."

Nikki knew the facts, but she didn't say anything. In the court records of his divorce, John's lawyers had cited infidelity that Stephanie did not contest. This was confidential information presented only to Stephanie's attorney and the Judge. Nikki had read the court documents.

"I don't know why I am telling you all that."

"Maybe because the clothes I am wearing reminded you of her."

John did not say anything. He looked at Nikki and smiled and went back to driving diligently, focused on the road.

As they approached the city, Nikki realized she was feeling uneasy. She knew they would be chasing a ghost through the city but there was nothing she could do about it. After another silent stretch during the drive John broke the silence. "Where shall we go first? Do you have any idea where your brother might be? Any clue you uncovered so far, or any he gave... perhaps he mentioned a place he knew about?"

"He had never been to the city."

"He must have had some plan, some childish fantasy even about the kind of work he might encounter in the city? Maybe a dream job, something he wanted to be when he grew up."

Nikki searched through her knowledgebase of the kinds of things young boys thought they wanted to be when they grew up. Rock star, soldier, firefighter, race car driver, fighter jet pilot, astronaut, scientist, doctor, famous actor were among the top of the list, but somehow, they did not match the profile of Troy she had begun to create in her mind. The boy in the profile she had created instead wanted to make a fast buck, hustle the streets, have to answer to no one, not even his own sister, and ultimately be a tough gangster.

It was a crazy story and John laughed when she told him. "I guess he did read too many of my novels," John said smiling but as soon as he said it he turned somber. If indeed Troy had such notions, he was likely to get in serious trouble, sooner or later.

"We could try the bar area on the east side between East Main and First." Nikki suggested.

"I see you did some research while you were at my computer this morning."

"Yes," Nikki nodded and said no more. She hoped she had not given too much information that would put to question the credibility of her story. John got part of his observation right though, she thought quietly. Nikki virtually knew the city through many detailed layers of maps stored in the network of her mind.

"Makes sense to me," John said after giving the suggestion some thought.

East Main was fairly quiet during the early part of the afternoon but also when the people who worked there were most approachable given slow business.

After nearly an hour of visiting bars and restaurants along East Main, asking about a scrawny boy of fifteen, short dark brown hair, with a slight lisp due to a mild cleft palate at birth barely visible now but still discernible, and a slightly nasal intonation in his speech, they came up with nothing.

A boy with that description might be easy to forget, thought John. He had pictured Troy, one who in his mind was setting out to be a gangster, to be a rough and scruffy boy who kept to himself, who would fit the description of a loner that even the bullies knew to leave alone, who had grown up too fast for his age in middle school, who in the back of his mind was constantly scheming of a way to get out of Greenfield as soon as he found a way. But a scrawny boy with a lisp with a nasal voice, would have been a target of bullying at school in Greenfield and an easy target in every street corner here in the city. He could picture a boy fitting that description going unnoticed except by those who might seek to exploit him. By now he had given up hope of Troy ever having made it to East Main.

When they reached First Street, Nikki suggested walking back along the south service alley that ran parallel to East Main. She figured that would be the credible thing to do if one were in truth searching for a young boy with Troy's profile. John thought it was a good idea, and that was all that mattered to Nikki for now.

"You know, we probably should try the homeless shelter," John said with a hint of skepticism. He could not picture Troy heading to a shelter. He could not imagine someone who hated being held in an institution heading to something similar, but he certainly would not put his money against it. Besides, John knew the shelter served food around lunchtime. That might be an incentive to draw in a run-away.

When they arrived at the food shelter, they were met with the chaos of the still ongoing lunch hour. *Lots of hungry mouths to feed*, though John, *even in this day and age!*

John and Nikki were able to walk around without being noticed. They seemed to fit the profile of the better-to-do people who were there to volunteer. A group of volunteers, some young people, but mostly older women and a few older men were working busily getting ready to start lunch.

"Can we talk to someone?" John inquired about. A young man named Matt, maybe in his mid-thirties, seemed to be in charge.

"We would not be able to do this without people volunteering. We run a soup kitchen during the day every day thanks to all the donations and the constant army of volunteers." Matt announced a prepared dialogue. "I am the only paid staff member. We also have a paid counselor, but she is only part-time here."

When inquired about Troy, Matt didn't take time to reflect as he looked around at the work that was going on and if there were any vacancies that required his attention.

"I wouldn't remember names of all who visit but the regulars... we don't ask unless they tell us. But I can't say I remember a boy with that description staying with us overnight... I would not say I get to know everyone who stays overnight, but I check-in and keep a tally of overnighters and I think I would have remembered.

"Within the last week you say? No. You could talk to Brenda. She supervises the line staff at the soup kitchen. Most of our volunteers come in once or twice a week, but Brenda is here every weekday. She could have seen the boy at the food line. I usually take off to run errands around town when the soup kitchen is open and when all the lunch staff is here. Brenda, sort of, takes over for about three hours..." He pointed in her direction.

Brenda looked boney and frail from afar but as John got closer he could see that her large bones barely covered by a thin sheet of skin adorned by speckles of dark patches and a bulging network of veins where her skin could be seen under her thin pink and white striped shirt told a story of a once strong and vibrant woman with a powerful built. She must have been in her seventies.

"Eighty-two," she confirmed proudly in response to John's inquisitive look.

"Pardon?"

"I get that look a lot, young man," she replied with a smile.

"Sorry I didn't mean..." John fumbled.

"That is quite all right. You know I was once a beauty, and attracted a different kind of look, but you get used to it."

"You are a very beautiful still," John said, correcting course.

Brenda smiled and almost blushed. "A lady's man!" She held out her bony hands almost cold to the touch and was met by John's soft warm hands. "Be gentle," she said, "these hands still have a lot of work to do. I am Brenda." She squeezed John's hand slightly before letting go as if feeling the warmth and softness that reminded her of her youth.

"John Selvas."

"The author?"

"Yes..." John said, with a hint of embarrassment.

"Oh, a celebrity in our midst. How truly exciting!" Brenda exclaimed, raising her hands and letting her head fall slightly backwards.

Now it was John's turn to blush. "You are very kind Brenda."

"And who do we have here?" Brenda said, turning her attention to Nikki. "You have the glow of a child in your eyes and a face of experience." She touched Nikki's face gently with both hands. She looked deeply into Nikki's eyes as if studying them. "Oh, you are someone very special, my child."

Tingles ran down Nikki's spine. She was afraid of the old woman who seemed to see right through her. How could she? She knew her fear was irrational, yet there it was.

Brenda could not remember seeing a boy of the description they provided her within the last week either.

"You know," she said at length looking at Nikki, "you remind me of a girl who used to come here now and then. I can't say I would recognize her if I met her in a different circumstance, but you share a resemblance. It was difficult to see her past the dirt in her hair and face and the shadow the weight of the world had cast upon her. Besides, she never talked to anyone; wouldn't even tell us her name.

"Janet our counselor tried to talk to her a few times but she would not even talk to her. You know we try to pay special attention to the young ones and new faces, and specially the girls. Young girls are more vulnerable out there in the streets. It does not matter now because she recently died, I am told. There is not much we can do for the dead. Very sad when young people have their lives taken away like that. The hospital called Janet the night before, they said they had a Jane Doe and if she had any information about her and her next of kin."

John nodded in silence politely.

Nikki was quiet and looked down at the floor. She didn't know anything about Jane Doe other than the description in the medical entry. The possibility that her body could have belonged to the girl whom Brenda had likened to her frightened her.

"How did they know to call Janet, and how did she know it was the same girl?" Nikki asked.

"Janet had given the girl her card in case she wanted to talk and had written a note on it saying so and included her emergency number. But since we did not know anything about the girl, not even her name, we weren't much help."

As John and Nikki took leave, John handed Brenda his card. "If you hear anything..."

Brenda smiled and nodded. "Come back anytime," she said as she turned her attention once again to the food line that was busily serving the homeless and the nameless.

A line of mostly homeless people along with their bags and belongings, and some without anything, had formed along the pavement outside the shelter in anticipation of their turn for a meal when John and Nikki walked out. There were mostly older folks and maybe some unemployed young people, John guessed. Some struggling with demons in their heads brought on by the destitution that they carried on their backs, others probably ex-convicts who did not want to go back behind the walls that shut them in but could not or were systematically not allowed to rejoin normal society, pushed away from the possibility of normal life forever. This was their normal.

John walked on the inner side of the pavement. It seemed like the right thing to do passing along a line of desperate souls to keep his young companion farther away.

"Erin!" an old beggar with a dirty black hat on his head shouted from the line as they passed him. He reached out and grabbed Nikki's arm from behind.

John turned around looking at the hand that grabbed Nikki first, and in anticipation to face the person the hand belonged to. In the process he inadvertently elbowing the poor beggar in the chest. The man let go and reeled back in pain. When he looked up again and saw Nikki's face, he let a screech of horror. "The dead walking," he said, "it's the devil that's taken over her soul!"

Only a few heads turned to look at the commotion.

"I am Nikki, not Erin!" Nikki insisted.

Matt was close by talking to another person in line who had stopped him on his way out. The young fellow had stopped him to seek help filling out a form with an arduously long list of questions.

Matt had seen the commotion from its inception. He was keeping an eye on Nikki and John as they departed hoping to ask if their visit had been a success, and also to encourage them to come down and volunteer if they had any free time to do so. After all, he could use all the helping hands he could get. ...and a celebrity at that, he had overheard.

The beggar continued shouting with agony in his voice, his face slightly lowered hidden by the narrow brim of the black felt round hat and his hands holding his chest. John's relief upon seeing Matt walking towards the commotion changed when he noticed the disapproving and accusing expression Matt held in his face directed towards him.

"I didn't mean to elbow the man." John protested. "It was totally an accident. I swear. I didn't even see him there."

Matt wasn't moved. He had seen the homeless beaten in the streets and pushed about like animals, trampled upon and cast aside by society, nay, overlooked, as if they did not even exist. He knew. He had lived among shadows, as one of them while he was trying to cast out his own demons until fate's loving eyes in the guise of Brenda had looked upon him, without judgment, unconditionally accepting who and where he was in life. She had restored his sense of dignity one only gets restored when they are simply noticed as human beings. The process of reaching back to humanity was long and arduous.

"Of course, you didn't even see him. You look and don't see because it is not convenient for you. You came for what you wanted, but what you need is to learn to respect people. John Selvas, right? The writer. I know you, but guess what, this is not about you." Matt brushed past John who tried to find words to apologize and establish his innocence.

The old beggar was almost wailing now.

"Just go!" Matt yelled at John. "Come on Gary, It's okay now. Get back in line. We can ask the nurse at the free clinic to take a look at your chest after lunch. You don't want the others to take your spot on the line, do you? Did you take all your pills today?"

"No, she would not give me them all. She only gave me two."

"Did you take what she gave you?" He ignored Gary's syntax. He knew Gary did not come to the soup kitchen to get his syntax corrected.

"Yeah..."

"Well, Gary, she gave you the right amount. You are supposed to get only two. She won't give you more than two. Ok...?"

"Alright, then! I took my pills."

John had no other choice but to leave. He did not see the benefit of trying to make his case. He didn't want to upset the poor beggar any more than he already had.

Gary stepped back to keep his spot but kept looking back as John and Nikki walked away.

"Dead girl walking, dead girl walking, dead girl walking, we are all doomed... the devil has left his lair for good," he chanted in a loud whisper turning his head back every time he finished his chant, and looking down in front to begin his chant over again until the objects of this observation were clearly out of sight, and he was close to the front of the line.

John took Nikki by the arm as they walked away. "Are you alright?"

Nikki nodded but she was visibly disturbed. She was fairly positive now that Jane Doe could have been Erin, but she had no idea who Erin was.

"The old fool confused you for the dead girl. There apparently was some resemblance between you and the girl Brenda mentioned. Don't let it get to you." He comforted her by rubbing her on the shoulder. "We still have many places to search. Let's try the bus station next. See if anyone saw him coming in. He would have had to take the bus or hitch a ride into the city. I have seen some young people hang out there too, likely runaways like Troy."

There were no young people hanging around the bus stop like John thought there would be. Of course, it had been many years since he visited the bus station. He himself had taken a bus into the city when as a young man not much older than Troy when he came to find a job in the city. By the time he had saved enough for a car ten years later and did not have to use the bus station anymore to visit his parents - immigrants who owned a small grocery store in a rented space back in Greenfield - they had both died and he had little use to leave the city. It had been almost thirty years since that time and a flood of memories came rushing back when he saw the old discarded terminal building on the side that now served as what looked like a storage space flanked by the bigger and shinier looking new terminal building.

Back then, with only a high school education, he took up whatever job he could find. He had worked at restaurants as a cleaner, waiter, and fast-food cook. What other small jobs had he not done? He had worked as a store clerk, at the gas station, as a pizza delivery boy, for a while delivering newspapers on the side. By a stroke of luck and unwarranted wisdom he had taken a few classes in the community college, it had just felt like the right thing to do. And maybe his newspaper delivery job had nudged him to take some journalism classes. It was as if fate had known and was choosing its course. He never finished with a degree, but he had started working at the newspaper, and somewhere along the way had written small pieces for the Sunday paper, and things had taken off. All these memories he had put in the back of his mind, now let loose by his proximity to the old terminal building; a terminal it seemed, for a ride to the past.

Inside, they approached the security office. No one there had seen a boy of that description in the past week. No luck at the ticket counters either. "Aren't you John Selvas?" a heavy-set woman asked from behind the counter. She held up a book to show John. The cover had the picture of a lone shadow on it. *The Lost Shadow.*

It was one of his. It was a story of a man who had lost his past and with it his shadow, and now his shadow was on the loose wreaking havoc. The only way to stop it was to find it again, but in doing so, the man would have to take responsibility for all of his shadow's deeds and the past he was trying to run away from. It was one of his top sellers. The lady pushed the book through the counter window and smiled. "I am a big fan of yours Mr. Selvas. Would you write something in it for me?" When she noticed John looking around the counter she pushed out a pen.

"And who should I make the note to?" John asked with a smile not letting his annoyance protrude in any way.

"Rose."

'To Rose', John wrote, *'to a beautiful soul who makes sure others get to their destinations'* and signed his name.

Rose smiled with a thin film of tears that glazed her eyes when she read it.

"We are looking for a young boy, Rose. I wonder if you might be able to help. He is a run-away. This is his sister."

"Was he coming to the city or leaving, Mr. Selvas?"

"Coming in." John gave her the description he had gotten from Nikki with a picture of a boy he had never seen now taken shape in his mind.

"It is impossible to remember anyone who goes through, especially if they are only coming in and did not buy a ticket here Mr. Selvas. But I will go and ask around if anyone noticed anything."

Rose was gone for a while.

"I think we need to go and report this to the police, Nikki. I do not think we will find him this way."

"You know how that will end John!" Nikki protested. "The police will not be able to do anything but they will contact social services. And when we find him, or he finds me, they will take him away for another three years. You don't know what that is like, especially if you are not lucky and end up with some scammers posing as foster parents."

John got the point. He could not push the matter anymore.

When Rose got back in what must have been ten minutes, John and Nikki were still standing at the counter but they were looking away from each other.

"Mr. Selvas, I am not sure if this makes sense but our janitor said he talked to a boy matching that description about a month ago."

"That does not fit our timeframe." Nikki responded in haste. He was still home then.

"Well, Mr. Boehner is not very reliable with facts so either he messed up the time, or he never talked to the boy. He swears it was on the twelfth birthday of his granddaughter last month. He said the boy was asking about some bookie by the name of Roberts. Now Mr. Boehner is a gambling man and he very likely knows a bookie by the name. But I wouldn't say I'd count on Jim telling me a straight story if his or my life depended on it. He's known to spin tall tales. But if you want to check out his story anyways, he said you would find Roberts in the theater district. A van with an eagle on it, Jim said."

"Can we talk to Jim?" John asked. He thought he may be able to get some more information that way.

"It wouldn't do you much good. He will not talk to strangers. I'd send you his way if I thought that would help."

"Does Roberts have a first name?"

"Rob or Robbie Roberts."

"Kind of redundant, no? But thank you Rose."

Some good had come out of being nice to Rose, John thought. Nikki was confused. It was supposed to be a story, just a story. Jim was a liar. She had a good reason to lie, but she could not understand why someone would lie just for the sake of it.

"It might be nothing," John said as they were leaving the station, "but it is worth a shot. But first let's get a sandwich or something. I am starving."

Creamy, cheesy, soft, warm and convenient, the pizza across the street from the station was now Nikki's favorite food. She closed her eyes as the taste of tomato-soaked chewy warm bread, crunchy in some parts, with a hint of oregano and basil and other herbs, none of which she could individually distinguish anyways, other than the oregano and basil, shot through her palate and overwhelmed her olfactory senses.

John watched her with a little bit of curiosity. "You act like this is your first-time eating pizza," he exclaimed feeling a little embarrassed at the sight of his young companion almost having an olfactory orgasm.

"Nothing this good!"

The sign did say the pizzas were stone oven baked, and 'To die for!'.

He surmised that despite its location, it was not a place most people who had any business across the street would come to eat at. He had seen people with ties around their necks, or casual shirts made of jute and cotton, and summer sandals that you could only buy at a boutique store, stroll in. He had not even realized that that was his main reason for choosing the place. He would not have come here thirty years ago had it existed then, when he still had use for the bus station.

He pitied Nikki at some level and at some level felt shame for having chosen the place, showing her off like an elite snob although it had not been his intention. He wondered if she might have run out had she cared to look at the price list on the menu.

"I guess it is one of the best pizza places in town" he said even as the realization of the voyeuristic asynchrony of the location pushed his brow into a slight frown.

Nikki was too busy appreciating the various tastes to notice John observing her.

"Did you leave a fifteen percent tip or twenty?" Nikki asked as they walked out.

"Always twenty," John replied, "Why?"

"Just curious."

On the drive to the theater district, which was no more than ten minutes given all the stoplights and lunch hour traffic, Nikki fell asleep. John looked over. Here in his middle age, it was strangely as if he had found a daughter he had never had, no matter how brief this encounter was to be.

Nikki woke up gasping as if for air when he pulled over and put on the hand-break. She could not remember what she was dreaming of when John asked her. The day so far had been overwhelming. She had taken in so much and was learning so much. On top of it all, she had created a story and was making John run around with her trying to patch together a puzzle that did not even exist.

To John, Nikki looked tired. He could only imagine how much stress and pressure she was under. He had no idea.

"I guess we are walking?" Nikki asked.

"Figure this is the best way. This way we will be able to talk to more people. And it will also wake you up a little. We are looking for a guy named Roberts. Rob or Robbie Roberts to be exact. Drives a van with an eagle symbol. We will also ask around about your brother if people have seen him here."

John found out that some of the older shop owners still remembered him in this area. "Aren't you Juan, they asked. Aren't you a writer now?" A short fellow behind a news stand shouted, waving his hand.

Juan waved back uneasily. He felt uncomfortable. But no one seemed to know Roberts and no one had seen a boy matching the description they provided.

"Well it is still too early for the evening crowd and all the grime it brings out along with it. Maybe we should come back later this evening," John said reluctantly.

"What do we do meanwhile?"

"I have a friend we could go see. Someone who might be able to help."

"Who? Not the police, right?"

"An old friend of mine. Not the police. On the contrary."

Gary ate quickly today. Normally he would take his time to eat because if you were done early, you would be asked to leave to make space for the next person who might want a seat inside where it was cooler than having to sit at the tables outside on the lawn in this heat. He would sit around for the entire time the soup kitchen was open if he could to see if there was anyone new. He was a silent type and usually kept to himself. But Gary had his reasons. He liked to observe and pick out anything new and abnormal in his environment. That had kept him alive for as long as he had lived in the streets.

Today he had a duty to perform. One he did not like, but was obligated to perform as a civic and religious duty. He was going to make a report at the police station, and then he was going to the church to tell the priest, Father Stone, and warn him of this rising. Father Stone always counseled Gary to pray, and pray hard and repent for his sins. But that, was not going to be enough this time. This time he had to act but he needed direction.

"He's done very early today." Brenda commented to Mary when she saw Gary exiting the dining hall. Mary was busy pouring thick stew on bowls and handing them to the next person in line. Brenda was handing out bread next to her. "I wonder what's gotten into him?"

"Something about the devil taking over the body of the girl who died... that girl who came here for lunch a few times last week. I think he had a scuffle with the two visitors who were talking to you earlier," Mary replied, keeping her eye on where the serving spoon landed when she reached out to fill the next bowl that came before her.

"That is unfortunate what happened. It is the silent ones who suffer the most. I think she had sat with him a few times and he had tried to talk to her. Not sure they had much of a conversation, but in their own way I think they did. He let her get close. I can only imagine what he must be going through now."

"Maybe the devil's gotten into him," Mary said smiling and turning to Brenda, but was met with disapproving old but brilliant blue eyes.

"He will come around." Brenda said. "I would almost have said the same about our young visitor, that the devil had taken a hold of her, if I had not seen the light that shone in her eyes. The resemblance was there from what little I had seen of the dead girl."

Gary left the soup kitchen with a sense of import to his mission. When he got to the police station he straightened his hat and brushed his coat with the back of his hands before walking in. The last thing he needed was an officer of the law not taking him seriously when he had such an important complaint to make. He perked up and stuck out his chest even as he moistened his throat with saliva in preparation of his oration as he walked up to the reception right inside the entrance of the police station.

"How may I help you, sir?" a young officer asked politely but with a hint of suspicion in his voice. He looked for the restroom sign and rehearsed the dialog he was to use if people asked where the restrooms were: Behind you on the right. Follow the restroom sign to the end of the corridor.

"You are new here!" Gary observed. "Where are the regular people? Aren't there always two officers here?"

"Yes sir, second day on the job," the beefy young officer replied. "The other officer went to grab some paperwork. She will be right back."

This is going to be tough, Gary thought, but he couldn't wait for her. This was too urgent. "I need to report a crime..."

"Is this a crime in progress or in the past?"

Gary took a moment to think. It had definitely taken place in the past, but was still going on as far as he could tell. Erin had been killed in the past but someone, rather, something, else was using her body now. He had to make a choice about what he was going to report.

"Past!" Erin had been killed three days ago.

"Were you the victim of the crime or a witness? May I ask the nature of the crime: assault, robbery, or theft?"

Gary had to think hard about this question. It had two parts to it with multiple options. He had lost his friend, and by that token, he was the victim. But it was she who had been killed, that made her the victim. And there was assault involved as well as theft of Erin's body. Was it also robbery?

"Both... and all of the above." Gary answered after considering the possibilities.

"Both?"

Gary was under stress. This was exactly why he did not like to go to the police station or a government office. They made him fill out forms and asked him so many questions that it made his head hurt. "I am confused. It is a tricky question. I just want to report a crime, officer. Can I talk to one of the regular officers...?"

"Sir, I need to gather the details so we can file a proper report first. Since it is not a crime in progress, it will be assigned to an officer in the proper department and they will assist you further."

Gary knew he had made an error. He always made mistakes in filling out multiple-choice questions in a form. *There are many ways to look at the same thing,* Gary always thought. It depends who you are and where you stand. Any number of answers could be right.

"I should have said, crime in progress. See I do this every time," he grumbled to himself. He wondered if the officer would mind if he said he wanted to change his answer now.

Gary looked on with anticipation and a sense of relief as the other officer returned to the desk. "You still doing okay Mike?" she asked her fellow officer, a rookie, she was to supervise as he learned the ropes. Mike seemed to have hit a road bump. She would not have expected any less with Gary standing in front of the desk. "Gary!" she turned to him, "is Mike taking good care of you?"

"He's asking too many questions, Gina, er... Officer Rods. Can I file a report of a crime with you?"

"Mike is new. Don't you want to give him a chance to help you? He'll be a regular soon." She saw Gary wasn't going to change his mind anytime soon. "Well just tell me what you want to report, then."

"A murder."

"You saw someone being murdered? When?"

"Yes, three days ago, or two. Is it two or three if it is very late at night? When does the morning of the new day start?"

"It was at night? I'll just put down two nights then. Does that sound right?"

Gary nodded. Two nights made better sense to him.

"Did you know the victim Gary?"

"Yes. Her name was Erin.... Er... rin..." He spelled.

"Last name?" Gina asked.

Gary hit his forehead with the palm of his hand. It was in there somewhere. She had told him her full name. Now it wouldn't come to him. What was it?

"Erin... Erin... Erin..."

"That's ok Gary. You can think of it and tell it to the detective. You know Jerry... follow me."

When Gina got back to the desk she explained the particular case called *Gary* to her junior colleague. He had a lot of real experience to gain and it was not going to be about shootouts and car chases.

"Gary is not all there, not always," she explained to Mike. "But he does bring in some valuable information. He is homeless and prefers to live in the streets rather than going to the homeless shelter every night if it is not cold. He is an asset to us on the street. Not always credible, but he can surprise you. Gary is special here and has earned the nickname *Black Hat* because of that silly hat he always wears."

"What makes him special? Like a mascot you mean?"

"Mike, I am sure you will take that last comment back once I get to the part of why he is special! He once made an *officer-down* call from a patrol car, possibly saving the officer's life. You know Pete, right?"

"The Sergeant?"

"That's right. I don't know what's going on under that dirty old hat but there is a lot going on in the shadows, and that is where he lives. You start out as a desk clerk, but you get to learn a lot if you learn to listen. People like Gary need a little special handling. If you try to fit them into the system of the regular world, you get them frustrated and you will lose the opportunity to appreciate their value. Mark my words as you move up in your career."

Mike nodded.

"Can you describe what you saw, Gary?" Jerry asked, looking at the incident report form that had popped up on his screen following the reference number from Gina.

Gary closed his eyes. He could see it all over again. He had woken up hearing some commotion in the night and crawled out of his cardboard box. He could still now see Erin being strangled. He could still hear the gurgling noise she made as she tried to breathe. He ran screaming and shouting while swinging the piece of wood he kept in is cardboard box waking everyone around the alley and scaring the attacker away. He had not seen the attacker's face in the dark and had no time to pursue.

"Chocked?" Jerry asked, seeing that Gary was holding his throat imagining the scene.

Gary nodded.

"Was she dead when you found her?"

"No."

"What did you do next?"

"I dragged her to the street and asked someone to call an ambulance. There was a group of young people going back home from the bars."

"Did you see the attacker?"

"I saw him but couldn't see his face. It was dark in the alley and he was wearing a cap."

"You chased him away, or did he leave on his own."

"I chased him away."

"You did a good thing. And the ambulance took her away?"

Gary nodded.

"How did you find out she died?"

"The hospital called the counselor from the shelter to tell her. The counselor told me because she knew we were friends."

"In that case Gary, there will be a report on our files along with a medical report and possibly an autopsy report. I will follow up with the counselor and put your description in the report. I will come talk to you if I need to find out more about this from you. Ok?"

"No, you don't understand. No one knew her. No one even knew her name. Erin wouldn't talk to anyone."

"I see. A Jane Doe case! But you knew her, right?"

Gary nodded. "She was my friend."

"Was she new to the streets?"

"She didn't live in the street. She only came to eat lunch at the kitchen. That day, she said she could not go back. Someone had found where she was staying. I told her she should go to sleep in the shelter, but she said it was too dangerous. She said she would sleep in the street so people wouldn't know where she was."

"Are you saying she thought she was in danger?"

"Yeah!"

"Do you know around what time this was?"

Gary shrugged his shoulders.

"The bars were just closing, you said right? Sometime after three, then."

Gary nodded.

"Great! Would you be willing to come to ID the body for me once I track it down?"

"That will do no good."

"Why?"

"Because someone stole her body."

"How do you know that?"

"I saw her yesterday. Except that was not Erin. She didn't even recognize me. She said she was Nikki, but I couldn't talk to her more because there was a demon incarnate with her. John Selvas, Matt said." Gary showed Jerry his chest and pointed at a small bruise that had formed in the place John had accidentally elbowed him. "Look! This is what he did to me, with a touch!"

Jerry closed his eyes and took a deep breath. *Why me? he thought, why this torture? Why not Pete? Pete owes Gary his life.* But Gary had hand picked him to be his personal go-to detective years ago before Jerry had moved to the homicide division. When he transferred, Gary was sort of transferred along with him even though all of Gary's complaints had been non-homicide related. He had often dealt with leads that went nowhere alerting detectives in the proper divisions if he thought the leads were valid, but this was a new height in their relationship.

"You mean you saw her breathing, walking, and otherwise alive?"

"When you put it that way. But I am telling you..."

Jerry had typed in most of the report already. He contemplated deleting it, but he thought better of it. He would first check the medical and ambulance records just in case there was some truth to any of it. This was possibly Gary's way of piecing together some kind of puzzle and regurgitating the raw mix of information as it sat in his head. *Either Erin, or Nikki, in case I track down the record and have to put a name to Jane Doe...* Jerry thought as he saved the updated information with a side note in the note section of the form.

"Do Erin or Nikki have a last name?"

Gary knew this question would come up again.

"She told me... Erin..." He closed his eyes, crinkling his face.

"It is all right if you cannot remember right now. Let me know if you do."

Gary crinkled his face even tighter. It was no use. "Alright, I will let you know if I remember. I better be going then... Am I done?"

Jerry nodded. "Stay safe out there!"

"I'll see you next time," Garry said as he stood up and left Detective Jerry Star with a bewildered yet relieved look on his face.

The next stop for Gary was at the public library on the way to the church just a few blocks away. The library was an oasis in the concrete desert, a palace of silence, a respite from the heat and cold, a place to drink from the cool fountain and above all a place to use the restroom. It was a place to rest on a comfortable sofa or cushioned chair in an air-conditioned climate, all of which he knew he would be able to find nowhere else without being asked to leave within minutes if not seconds.

He had, on different occasions, tried bank lobbies, waiting rooms at the hospital and a number of private clinics, pet clinics, and even loan offices with unsatisfactory outcomes.

In the library, there were a few rules he had to adhere to and as long as he remained quiet and picked up a few books or magazines now and then and pretended to read he was always welcome. Even though the printed words swirled and walked all over the pages like critters on a rotting piece of wood every time he tried to focus on them, by pretending to read, he would at least also fit into the surroundings and be allowed to sit in there all day if he chose to.

But today he would only make a brief stop, just long enough to ease the pain the blisters on his feet were causing him inside his shoes and within the one pair of thick socks he had for both summer and winter. If he did not have to go see Father Stone he would sit in the library till the end of the day with his legs up. But today, there were things more profound and more pressing than the soles of his shoes and the weight of the earth beneath them against the blisters under his feet.

After only a short stop, he headed to the church.

The main entrance to the church that led to the vestibule and the area where mass was held was always open but it was customarily used for scheduled services. The priest's office was around the back of the church and had an entrance by the parking lot. Gary however always walked through the main door, through the service hall, rather than walk around the church along the gravel path to enter through the door next to the parking lot. In the interior of the church on the wall adjacent to the altar where the priest offered prayers was the side exit, or entrance, which for Gary changed its definition based on whichever side he was and intended to go in or out of. Father Stone discouraged the public from using this exit/entrance but Gary used it anyway because he thought official church business ought to take place through the main door and not the back.

This way he could also walk through the main aisle in the center between the columns which made him feel grand. It made him feel like he belonged there and that the church belonged to the people, and to him as much as anyone else. Although the church was fairly new, built within the last fifty years, its design was fashioned after the cathedrals he was told, in the old continent. He may have spent more of his time inside the church rather than in the library for the solitude and silence it offered if it had not been for the hard and narrow wooden benches, and above all, the policy Father Stone enforced with regularity that if he caught you asleep or lying down inside the building instead of praying, he would take you and your belongings and move you back out into the street and ask you to stay out for that day come hail or high wind.

The columns, arches and the central dome were a miniature copy of the larger cathedral he had seen in a picture in the hallway on the other side of the door past the altar. Along the hallway was the priest's office separated by panes of glass in a metal frame from floor to ceiling. When the blinds were open, the glass made the office itself look like a huge aquarium with a solitary old fish that lived in it. Gary stood outside the office and peered in through the partially closed blinds. The lights were off and the priest was not sitting at his desk as he some-times did even with the lights off. This only meant one thing, Father Stone was in his apartment taking his afternoon nap. One could only get to the apartment through the office and through a door with a sign that read *Private* in the interior wall of the office.

Gary grinned. This was one of the few opportunities he would have, and possibly the only one, to get back at the old man for throwing him out from the church accusing him of falling asleep at the pew when he was in fact praying albeit a bit comfortably with his sore feet up on a bench, especially since he had not seen anyone around whose sensibilities he might offend.

He rapped loudly on the glass with the palms of his hands as he walked back and forth along the corridor and occasion-ally shook the glass door violently which also made the blinds rattle against the glass wall.

Within a minute, the old priest came out running from his apartment. He opened the door and looked both ways down the hallway in alarm.

"Oh! It is only you Gary!" he exclaimed in a tone reflecting more relief than anger. "Why in the world would you do such a thing?"

"I came to talk to you Father," Gary said snickering at first but becoming more stoical as the gravity of the matter he was about to discuss resurfaced in his mind. "I have news about the one who walks in the shadows. He now walks in the bright-ness of the sun. I have seen him."

"What do you mean Gary? Are you saying you saw the devil himself?"

"Yes Father... in the body of a girl I know to be dead."

"How do you know this, Gary?"

"The girl was my friend. She was murdered two nights ago. Everyone at the shelter knows this. The police know this. I saw it happen. But I saw her today, more beautiful and alive than ever, walking in broad daylight, at the shelter."

"I know you are troubled Gary, and I know you have seen things in the past that are not really there. Isn't that right?"

Garry nodded. "But this really happened. You can ask Matt. She walked with a demon disguised as a man. When I tried to talk to her, I saw it was truly Erin's body. But I couldn't talk to her because the demon did this to me!" Gary pulled up the layers of clothing he had on to reveal this chest and pointed at the bruise that had mostly subsided by now.

"You must search for the truth in your heart, Gary. If what you say is true, then it means that the Devil has no fear walking in the light he was cast away from, defying the very command of the one and only true power, to remain in the shadows. Either way, there is only one thing that you and I, mere mortals, can do, and that is to pray hard, very hard. Are you willing to do that Gary?"

"Yes!"

"Are you truly willing to do that Gary, come what may and put our trust in him?"

"Yes, I am!" Gary affirmed with his eyes closed, squirming his face and fell to the floor on his knees.

"Then go forth in the world and cast out the shadow of doubt that lies in your sinful heart! Repent for your sins, and take the one and only lord into your heart unconditionally."

Gary stood up with a new conviction that had given him a sense of purpose. He would not let doubt stand in his way.

The visit to the church had been useless! Father Stone had been of no help.

Pray! Gary thought to himself. *Matt and Brenda serve food to the hungry. They don't sit in a stone temple praying!*

He would confront the devil that raged in the captive body of a girl he knew to be dead and shame him back into the dark shadow where he belonged!

He had to take the task upon himself. He had to find the means to confront the devil and shame him back to the shadows. First, he would have to find them. Gary thought the best place to start searching was at the library and headed in the general direction with the newfound conviction.

Maybe it was the passion that had come over him or just the natural ebbs and flows of the lucidity of his mind, he suddenly remembered her name: *Miller! Erin Miller.*

"Do you know who the Machetes are?" Erin had asked.

He did. He kept his eyes and ears open for a reason. *Survival.*

"They are looking for me. I need to lay low," she had told him. "No one looks in the shadows."

Gary knew.

"Miller... Miller... Miller..." he had to find a telephone before it was too late. The name, he feared, may just go away as easily as it had come to him. He had a quarter somewhere. Sweet quarter! A few quarters made a dollar, and a few of those made a meal, ...and a soda if he simply wanted to splurge once in a while. There was a phone next to the tree in a blue phone booth. Somewhere in one of his pockets, the precious metal that made the damned thing work... *"There, you are, precious quarter."*

He punched in the numbers that seemed to come to him like his own name.

"Hello! Downtown Police Department... This is Geoff. How may I help you?" a friendly male voice answered the call.

"I want to speak to detective Hart. Detective Jerry Hart."

"Can I have your name please."

A car passed by. Gary didn't hear what the person on the line said.

"Hello?" The officer checked the line.

"Jerry, it's Miller... Erin..."

"No, it's still Geoff, Mr. Miller. And what was your first name, you said Aaron? Hold on, I'll transfer your call."

"No, Gary... This is Gary," but he was already on hold.

Jerry didn't know any Aaron Miller, and besides, he was swamped with paperwork to take the call right then.

"Can you send the call to my voicemail, Geoff? I'll check it later. Thanks!"

The call went through. Gary waited with anticipation.

"Hello, you've reached Detective Jerry Hart..."

"Jerry, this is..."

"... I'm unable to take your call right now. You can leave me a message. If this is an emergency, please hang up and dial 9-1-1."

"This is Gary. I am leaving you a voice message. The girl's name is Erin Miller...I'll be at the library if you..."

The answering machine's voice came on intertwining with the rest of Gary's message: "You can begin recording your message after the tone."

[BEEP!]

"Hello? Jerry? This is..."

[Click!] went the call.

That was all the time he got for his quarter and it was the only one he had. Gary slammed the phone handset on the metal box. Then he picked it up and slammed it down again, and continued to do so a few more times.

"I spend a fortune and all I get to say is 'Hello Jerry?' No one listens, no one. No One!" Gary began shouting. "I am just going to the library! And I am just going to rest my feet, and I am going to do nothing at all! What do I care? No one listens anyway."

Chapter Five

John pulled over on the side of the street. The location was not far from the theater district but there were no parking signs or parking meters. There was no pavement either. On either side of the asphalt a thin border of dirt marked where the street ended, followed by a wide patch of well-kept grass that was edged by brick walls on some properties or continued into large lawns protected by high and posh looking metal fences.

"This is the barrio where I lived when I first came to the city. This was a dirt street back then," John instructed. "None of this fancy walls, metal fences and manicured lawns, except Don Carlos' property of course.

Nikki didn't know this part of John's history. It was not in any of the records she had examined.

"I didn't think I'd ever come back here again," John whispered to himself as they walked along a brick wall. Though the big metal gate was open, it did not look welcoming. A black asphalt driveway led to a covered receiving area edged by large-leafed plants in front of a two-story house about a hundred yards from the gate. Along the left side of the driveway, as one walked towards the house, an unguarded lower lawn sloped towards a small pond with various decorative weeds and flowers. Along the right side of the driveway, a high metal fence demarcated the interior of the property towards the house and back garden with its three-resident pointy-eared Dobermans that barked and growled as they ran back and forth keeping pace with John and Nikki. Nikki was frightened by the aggression packed in the hairy animals.

"I see Don Carlos still keeps his pack of hounds," John said as they approached the house. They were stopped by a couple of men as they entered the overhang. The fellows were neatly shaved and with clean haircuts. They didn't say *Stop*, or *what do you want*, or even an undisguised *can we help you...* but the change in their body language, and the looks in their eyes said *come closer if you dare*. John knew they were the security and weren't casually hanging around as it may have seemed.

"Dile a Don Carlos que Juan Selvas quiere saludar a su amigo." John said looking at the younger of the two of them. The man didn't seem to respond to his request. "Tell Don Carlos, Juan Selvas wants to see his old friend." John repeated in English.

"I understand Spanish," said the younger man and continued to give John a nasty stare.

The other man let out a sly smile and went in. John and Nikki waited at the foot of the stairs with the younger man intently watching their every move.

In a little while the other man got out. "Mr. Selvas, Don Carlos will see you now. Follow me."

Inside and up the stairs, John was greeted with the warmest of welcomes from an old man who looked like he had been folding his laundry sitting on the sofa with a small pile of clothes on one side and a neatly folded pile on the other.

"Mi Juanito, ven aqua!" He opened his arms for an embrace but did not make any effort to stand up.

John leaned down into the embrace.

"As you can see I have grown old, and you, you have been a stranger. I guess I should call you Mr. Selvas now. Don Selves in your own right."

"Call me John, Don Carlos."

"Muy bien! John. Although you will always be Juanito to me – you know that. You were a scruffy little boy when I took you in."

"I was seventeen."

"Yes, Scruffy little Juanito... what is it now you said?"

"John!"

"Alright. John then."

"Manuel," he said shifting the tone of his voice more businesslike as he instructed the fellow who had shown John and Nikki in, and was awaiting orders. "You can leave us."

Once the guard left, Don Carlos relaxed again. "What brings you here? And who is your young friend?"

"This is Nikki. We are looking for her brother."

Don Carlos held out his hand looking at Nikki.

She didn't know what she was supposed to do with it so she reached out and held his hand with a step forward. He in turn leaned forward slightly and kissed it. "Ah, sweet youth!" he said holding on to her hand a little longer before letting go.

"Sit, sit!" he said looking around at the pile of clothes on the sofa and pointing to the armchairs on either side of the couch with both his arms as if in a grand gesture.

"I don't have your brother. We don't do kidnappings. You should know that John. That was in the seventies even before you showed up in town. Now we are in the restaurant business. It is legal, it is safe, and there is a lot of money to be made on the drinks alone." Don Carlos laughed. "Don't mind me," he said looking at Nikki, "I am just pulling my old friend's leg to put a little humor into this somber reunion."

John didn't see the humor, but he got Don Carlos's point. Things had changed. Don Carlos had gotten him out of a few tough spots when he first came to the city. In exchange he had run some errands for Don Carlos and had done some of the more mundane collections for him on the side.

If you were of Latino descent and lived in this barrio back then you would have known Don Carlos. Don Carlos was quick to help out anyone in need, Latino or not, but then you owed him. Once you owed him, he might call on you for something he needed in the future. He never forgot. John had worked for him. Everybody worked for Don Carlos in a manner of speaking, but John, more than others.

"I looked after you and you looked after me, isn't that right John? But there comes a time the smart ones find their wings and they don't even look back. Now I have to pay the two brutes you see out front with my retirement savings. And look how fat they are... on my dime."

John was beginning to wonder if he should have come to see his old benefactor of sorts. He was going to be of no help at all. Instead the old man sat around like an old lizard basking in the sun of his former glory days.

"Do you know a guy named Roberts, Rob or Robbie Roberts?" he asked anyways.

"Of course. What did you think I was, an old man with no pulse on the street? Do I know...? What do you want with that no-good clown? He is like stinking poop. Don't go near him, you'll just get shit on yourself and your pretty friend here. Pardon my language my dear," he said turning to Nikki, "but that is what you will get from that guy."

"So, you know him?"

"Know him? I took him in like family... in a manner of speaking. I throw some business his way now and then. That two-bit good-for-nothing! Now he is a useless bookie and a part-time informant for the downtown PD. Can you believe that? The crapshoot sold out."

"Do you know where we might be able to find him?"

"Find him? Why? He reeks like shit from a mile away. Still, if you are intent on poking at shit, I'll lend you a stick. I'll have Manuel take you to him. That is the least I can do for an old friend. The piece of shit owes me, you know. Manuel can take the opportunity to remind him. Two bird with one stone, as the saying goes. Besides," he continued after a pause, "I bet you don't carry a piece like always. The streets have changed. You're going to need one to talk to him. Very jumpy, I am told."

"We just want to find out if he has information about her brother."

"What's the boy's name?"

"Troy."

"Troy? Nah! Never hear of him."

"He is a run-away, fifteen, looking for a job." Nikki inter-jected.

"I see why you'd come to me. You think I gave him a job. You know there are labor laws about employing kids these days. I am a law-abiding citizen. Run away? You were a run-away once, John."

"I was seventeen, Don Carlos. I came looking for a job."

"And he came to Don Carlos who found him a job." He explained to Nikki with a weak laugh and a scoff. "But he kept squirming like an earthworm. I had to find him a new job every two weeks. Couldn't stay put. Who knew he had the itch to go to community college and learn to be a writer. He did that on his own and chose his own *in-dependent* path," he put stress on the word.

"I paid my dues Don Carlos, and I worked for you."

"Alright, you know what they say about bygones. About the Rob fellow, he's not going to tell you anything, not for free. So, take Manuel with you. He'll get you what you want." Don Carlos rang for Manuel who ran up the stairs in a matter of seconds as if he had been waiting to be called.

"Manuel, Mr. Selvas needs some information from that Robbie... whatever... the guy with the pain-in-the-behind name. Get Mr. Selvas what he needs, and remind Robbie he is late on his payment... again!"

"Si Don Carlos." Manuel said in a stoic yet humble tone as he motioned for John and Nikki to follow him.

John smiled and almost unnoticeably and involuntarily bowed his head as he stood up to leave. Nikki followed suit.

"Twelve books. Isn't that right?" Don Carlos asked when John was already walking away. The question, rather, the declaration stopped John in his tracks. "You didn't think I thought about you now and then, did you? Come back to see your old friend sometime. I'll not be around if you wait another thirty years."

John didn't turn around. He continued walking. Behind him was a past he had tried to put behind him but his past remembered him just the same.

Don Carlos followed John's steps with longing eyes. "He could have taken my place," he said to himself. "I could have retired in peace close to the ocean in the south. Juanito, a writer! What is the world coming to?"

Manuel opened the door to the back seat of the car that was parked on the side of the house and ushered Nikki in.

John got in the front. He didn't know what was about to unfold. He hoped now that he had not pulled out a big card for a small game.

When they pulled up next to an apartment building they saw the van with an eagle symbol parked on the far side of the parking lot in disarray. It looked like it had not been in use for years. Manuel pulled up right in front of the building.

"He's here. Let's go upstairs and pay our pal a visit." Manuel said in a gruff voice. He was not tall, but he was built like an old bull, even though his face showed that age had not caught up to him yet.

"He actually drives that van?" John asked with ridicule in his voice.

"Yeah, can you believe that guy actually pays to keep it looking like that? Looks like junk from the previous century, but it can outrun most things on the streets." Manuel got out and opened the car door for Nikki.

John and Nikki followed Manuel into the building. There was an elevator immediately inside. Manuel got into the elevator with a grin as if he was looking forward to whatever he had in mind to do. They got out on the fourth floor and Manuel knocked on the first door on the right.

"Not to worry," he said when he noticed a look of worry in John's face. "Don Carlos didn't send me for no reason."

They heard the door being unlocked, but no one opened it. After a moment, Manuel twisted the handle and pushed the door open, stepping aside at the same time and extending an arm back, keeping John and Nikki from approaching the door. Someone came running through the door as if they had expected the person opening the door to be standing right in front, and instead landed on the floor ushered by Manuel's large arm that had somehow swooped down as he cleared the doorway.

"Rob," Manuel said, shaking his head calmly, at the same time snatching the revolver that the man was holding, and slapping him across the face. "When will you learn?"

He picked Rob up to his feet with his free hand and pushed him back inside. Rob went crashing in. Manuel walked into the apartment calmly as if he had been there many times before. John and Nikki followed.

Rob got up and made another run at Manuel who simply redirected Rob into the wall. "Now," he said calmly, "we could do this all day, but Mr. Selvas does not have all day. I will deliver Don Carlos' message that you are late on your payment later. For now, you tell Mr. Selvas what he wants to know."

"I don't talk to strangers," Rob protested.

"So, the fellows at the police department are your friends then?" Manuel teased.

"I don't talk to no cops," Rob was breathing heavily.

Manuel laid another smack with the palm of his hand across Rob's face. "That is for lying to me just now. Besides, Mr. Selvas is no stranger. We'd all be working for Mr. Selvas if Don Carlos had had his way and Mr. Selvas had not decided to go writing children's books. We were little kids when he ran errands for Don Carlos. He'd still be calling me *Rabito* and I'd call him Don Selvas. But he has forgotten all that, which is why Rob, I need to slap you across the face for him."

Far down in his memory John remembered the boy he used to call *Rabito*. *Rabo* the word for *tail* in Spanish, and *Rabito*, *little tail*, if one disregarded its other meaning in slang... or maybe it was the slang meaning he intended for the little boy who followed him around. He couldn't quite remember. "Is it you...?"

But Manuel cut him off. "But of course, Mr. Selvas would not call me *Rabito* now seeing how he is not Don Selvas, and I am not a little boy with a little wiener," Manuel smiled at John, but in his smile John detected a hint of malice.

John understood even as once forgotten memories of the little kid who followed him around and looked up to him came back image by image in stills of the past long forgotten. Indeed, now that little boy was a mass of muscles like a bull, but agile and deft like a weasel as he had already demonstrated.

Nikki watched all this with fascination. She compared John and Manuel. *The difference between who one could be and who they become as a series of choices they make*, she concluded. She could also choose but so far, her choices seemed constrained. How does one just break out of the choices they have to make? *Choice* was an oxymoron.

"Alright, what do you want to know?" Rob asked from the floor with his back against the wall, his cheeks red and his nose bleeding lightly. He sat on the floor with his elbows on his knees with his hands in open protective positions on both sides of his face. Manual had pulled up a chair and sat adjacent to Rob, but facing him, so that the right side of his body was closest to Rob.

"We're looking for a missing boy, fifteen, goes by the name of Troy. Slight lisp, speaks in a nasal tone..."

"Yeah, I saw a boy by that description, but he seemed older than fifteen. Tom, Bobbie, who knows. No one worth their salt uses their real name in the streets. You think my real name is Rob Robbie Roberts?"

"Ok, never mind the name." Manuel cut in. "So, you have seen the boy..."

"Maybe!"

Manuel laid another slap across the face right through the protective barrier. "What's wrong with you? Why don't you just answer questions without trying to make a riddle out of everything? What will it take to get you feeling cooperative?"

"Alright, alright, yeah I seen the boy. Came to me about three months ago. He wanted to play big, wanted to know who the big players were."

Nikki listened in silence. She had no way to explain what was happening. When John looked at her to verify if it was possibly about Troy, she averted his eyes. As far as she was concerned, she had made up a story. Unlike the possibility of her shared identity with Erin, this had to be a far-fetched coincidence with her story.

Manuel perked up. "What do you mean big players?"

"I don't know. You'd have to ask him. I figured he was talking drugs, loan sharks. I don't know. I am not in the habit of entertaining kids with their questions. I told him to get lost but he kept coming back. He was shadowing me in the evenings and scaring my regulars, so after a few days of standing him I had a chat with him. Showed him my piece and chased him off. Said I'd pop him if he ever came back. Never saw him since. He must have found someone else to haunt."

"You're sure that was it? Nothing else. You didn't give him names, you didn't get him in touch with one of the dealers?"

"No Manuel, I'm telling you. I had never seen him before. I was not going to tell him anything."

Manuel raised his hand as if to strike.

"Ok, I saw him riding with Raymond one day. But I swear I had no part in it. Really! I have not seen either of them since. I swear Manuel. I do not know anything about the kid."

"Who's Raymond? Is that the kid who sells stuff for the Machetes?"

"Yes." Rob replied with some hesitation.

"They are not allowed in the city. And you kept quiet? You working for them now Rob?"

"Not unless I want to end up at the bottom of the river. They are dirty."

"Yeah they are not even *Latinos*! White boys wanna-be's using a Latino name. There is something wrong with that. Don't you think that is wrong Rob?"

"Yes Manuel, which is why, I'd never work with them."

"Good! Well, next time you seem them, I better hear about it. You want to keep your turf, you play by Don Carlos' rules. And next time you pull a piece on me, I'll shove it down your throat!"

"I thought you were the Mickey boys, really. Why would I pull a piece on you, Manuel?"

"Are you saying we look like one of those thugs?" Manuel raised his hand again.

"I had to be careful, I made a mistake. Manuel, come on!"

Manuel motioned for John and Nikki to leave and waited till they walked out of the apartment. He stood up and dropped the shells from the revolver on the floor and threw the revolver down right next to Rob. "I feel like being nice today, so I am just going to say it. You are late on your payment. You don't want me to have to remind you again. And if the guys from the PD want to talk to you next time, Don Carlos better know about it."

Rob tried to explain, but Manuel shushed him and left unceremoniously.

Times have changed, John thought as they waited outside, and later in the car as Manuel gave them a ride back. John never carried a weapon when he *ran errands* for Don Carlos, as they called it back in the day. Not even a knife. Only the lowlife thugs scared people with knives. The fact that you ran errands for Don Carlos was enough to make people very cooperative. The risks were low and payoffs were well worth it... for both parties involved.

It was mostly an insurance policy of sorts and people paid a premium to join their local business club for special perks if you were a small business owner. It was no different from taxes, insurance policies, neighborhood associations or any other membership dues. The only difference, you actually got what you paid for when you needed it, morning, day or night. As a bonus, Don Carlos made sure no one stepped on you and got away with it, and if you had no money to take care of something from birth to death and everything in between, he always had someone who owed him a favor take care of it. You'd just owe Don Carlos a favor back and could be called upon for a favor when the time came. There were no applications to fill, no proof of policy purchase you had to provide. Don Carlos provided a one-stop shop for all your needs for a regular weekly fee. He just did not have all the required licenses and certificates and educational degrees for the various services he provided, all of which barred him from opening a storefront on main street to pull off a legal profiteering scheme.

Now the game was different. There were guns, drugs and violent gangs. Manuel was not the man he could have ever imagined little Rabito would grow up to be.

John asked Manuel to drop them off by their car.

"The Machetes are amateurs, but they are bad news." Manual said as John opened th acer door. "Don Carlos does not like them in the city, but they try to squeeze in under the radar. I'll see what I can find out but I'll tell you this much: the survival rate of new recruits in their ranks is very low. The boy would be lucky if he made it this long in there. If he is really lucky, they scared him off with a good beating the first day and he spent some time in the hospital taking care of broken bones and decided to find some low-wage employment. I'll give you a call if I find out anything.

"I'll give you my number," John replied.

Manual winked as he waved John away. "You are not hard to find, Mr. Selvas."

Nikki's insistence on the timeframe was beginning to concern John. "Is there anything you are not telling me?" John asked. "About your brother, about any of this?"

Nikki shrugged her shoulder and shook her head. She was confused any of this was playing out the way it was. It was all supposed to be a story she had made up.

"In that case, I think we should head home. We certainly can't go looking for the Machetes, and there is nothing else to do," John said in a decisive voice.

Nikki said nothing so the matter was settled.

Let's pick up some dinner on the way back. The fridge is pretty empty," John said as they walked to the car.

The order-to-go place John had in mind did not have parking close by. John had to find a parking spot further down the street. On the walk towards the take-out place, John got a feeling somebody was following them. He peeked through the corner of his eyes as they waited to cross the street. He couldn't see clearly who it was but he was sure they were being followed. All he could see was a black hat in the midst of heads.

"Keep looking forward, but I think we are being followed", he said in a whisper. Nikki was amazed how human perception seemed to be tuned to pick out anomalies from what seemed to her to be a random jumble of events. She began turning around to get a picture of their pursuer. It was almost an involuntary reaction, but also an urge to do exactly what she was asked not to.

"Don't look," John said tugging at Nikki's hand, "he will know we have discovered him."

Isn't that the idea? Nikki thought. *We will have taken away his power of anonymity.* However, she relinquished her reasoning to the purported experience of someone who had lived long enough in the world to know what he was talking about. "Did you see who it was?"

"No, just a figure who kept blending into the street every time I looked back. We can give him the slip when he least expects it. I know just the place."

John led the way in quickening steps and Nikki followed. Soon they were in an area more crowded than others.

"An indoor fresh food and fish market is the perfect place to blend into the crowd and just get lost. Just keep close."

As they got closer to this huge building, the crowd got thicker. They blended into the crowd. Someone in their cohort opened the door and they stepped in unnoticed. The sights, sounds and smells, hit the newcomers like the heat blast coming out of an oven.

To Nikki, the stimuli were overwhelming. The smell of fresh fish itself was enough to make her want to get out, but there was also the smell of all other kinds of food that people were preparing and selling, buying and eating, mostly fried foods like potato fries, fried calamari, breaded fried fish and deli and lunch lines with roasted meats, steamed beans, potatoes, vegetables, rice and lentils filled with herbs and curries.

Beyond the smells, the noises were so varied they sounded like a constant hum. Nikki tried to pick the individual voices but that only drained her energy, yet amidst the chorus of the constant hum, individual yet indiscernible voices and sounds bombarded her. At the same time, the sights were just as unbearable. Everything blended into one fluctuating fusion of colors and darkness.

Nikki simply gave up and fell to the floor. It was all too much.

When she came to, she was still in the marketplace. A little quieter, a little darker, but the smells were still the same. John was stooping over her. He had pulled her behind a stall and the kindly young woman was sprinkling water in her face. "Please," Nikki begged, "make it stop. Get me out of here. I cannot stand it."

"What?"

"Everything."

Claustrophobia. That was John's first guess. "Alright, Nikki, you listen to me, okay? Just breathe, and focus on my voice. Just listen to what I am saying. You are going to be all right. I wish I could carry you out but I am getting old for that and you are not little. You'll just have to get on your feet, close your eyes, hold me, lean on me if you need to, and walk. And whatever you do, just keep listening to me. You will be fine."

Nikki did as she was told. John's voice was soothing as she listened although she could not remember anything he said. She didn't think of much else, just his voice, slightly raspy, low, and kind.

"Breathe!" he said and she did. In his warm embrace she felt safe. She clutched tight against his body. He wasn't very tall but taller than her. Under the guise of his ruffled middle age, he was strong, the kind of strenght that comes from the knowledge of hard work in life. Yet the softness around him brought on by his current lifestyle behind a computer screen made him feel gentle.

Suddenly, everything was fine. She could feel the last of the discomfort like a whip past its crack as the market door closed behind them.

"How are you doing?" John asked.

Nikki nodded her head. But the moment he let go, she went down to the floor, hurling out the food that remained in her stomach from earlier that day. Her throat burned and her eyes watered. John rushed to help her and held her as she gathered herself and as she shivered and cried. *Will I ever get used to it, to being human? Help me John!*

"This is all the stress you have accumulated all day," John said, "but I think we have lost our pursuer. I wish I could say you will be perfectly fine, but there is just no getting used to this sort of thing quickly. Come, let's get to the car."

On the drive back, John tried to ask Nikki something but she was confused and tired and she did not want to discuss anything that had taken place that day.

They got some food and soda at a drive-through and headed home.

Gary had lost them for now. He was sure they had gone into the food market but he could not follow them there. The sight of the crowd, the noise and the touch of all the people brushing by made his head hurt and his chest tighten restricting sufficient airflow into his lungs.

On his way to the library Gary had spotted John and Nikki in a car and talking to a mean looking man driving the car. This one he had seen before, spreading violence and pain.

They are congregating. Something is going down, and fast, he had thought to himself.

He had watched them drive past and stamped his foot at not being able to follow. To his luck, he had seen John later that afternoon getting out of another car and walking down the street across from him. He started following them to see where they went so that he could learn more of what they were up to, watching from behind people, hiding around the corner, and keeping his distance. He was an expert at blending into the shadows.

"You can't run from me forever! I will find you and I will find a way to defeat you," he had muttered under his breath after he had lost them.

For now, Gary walked to the library. There were still a few more hours the library would remain open. He was looking forward to a comfortable sit-down. Maybe I will get on the Internet today, he thought. Reading on the screen was sometimes more bearable than trying to read anything printed on a page. Not that he cared to read anything or was interested to look up anything online but a young volunteer at the library had taught him how to get on the Internet. He also had an email account. He checked email now and then even though no one ever wrote to him. All he had to do to get on the Internet was click on the image on the desktop and type anything you wanted to know if only you knew what you wanted to know in the first place.

"I am sure I can find you in there," he whispered to himself as he sat down at the Internet terminal in the media section of the library. He put down his knapsack on the empty seat next to him. This way, he would keep away anybody who might take away his concentration by typing too fast, making rattling noises at the keyboard and creating an uneasy silence for an unpredictable duration while they read the message that was sent back to them.

Using the Internet was free, but you had to sign on with an account name and password that the library provided specifically for you. Gary logged in and typed *Erin Miller* in the Internet browser. There were many results but as far as he could tell there was nothing related to the Erin Miller he was looking for. *Machetes* he typed in and pages and pictures featuring all kinds of knives filled the screen. *Nikki* produced lots of results but nothing useful. *Body snatching, body switch, body double,* didn't give him anything useful.

Soon he was clicking on random links. Looking at big mansions, cars, and secrets people offered to make lots of money fast. At one point he almost bought a small fishing boat, but he had no credit card number to put in.

He had clicked on the purchase link by accident. Now it wanted him to provide his credit card information and address. He let out a big laugh at the irony and got back on his mission.

John Selvas, novelist, produced some interesting finds, but these were all books that the library had written by John. Three of them anyways, and along with the results, a picture of the man-demon he was able to identify. A little more digging, and he discovered a page about the author. Born *Juan Selvas Valentino; 53 years old.*

"Got you!" Gary shouted in joy. All he had to do now was find *Juan Selvas Valentino* in a phonebook.

His outburst turned heads. He logged out quietly. He would sneak out the side once he checked the phonebook so no one could associate him as a noisy problem-patron who would potentially be under watch in the future. He didn't want that. He just wanted to be left alone when he came to the library.

On his way out through a narrow corridor that led to the side exit, Gary noticed a shadow in the light behind a translucent glass door with a sign that read, *A/V Room.* The light seemed to be spilling out from the bottom of the door like smoke. Behind the glass door he noticed a figure of someone beckoning him to come closer. When he did, he heard his name, "Gary" in a soft whisper.

"Hello?" Gary opened the door and walked into a room filled with light, like smoke. He listened but heard nothing. Around him, all over his body, he felt tingling.

"Lord?"

The tingling grew stronger and Gary grew bolder in his belief. "Lord! If it is you, I take you into my heart. Make me your servant and help me smite all who work against your will, disobey your command, and mock your creation!"

The tingling sensation increased to a pitch. Now Gary could feel a current moving up and down his body, first slowly and then at an incredible rate. The burden of the electric current running through his body soon became overwhelming and brought him to his knees. He tried to kneel upright but his muscles felt weak and numb. Resistance was in his nature to the point that he had rejected society and its ways.

But he had spoken, and given his oath. Now he knew he had to let go. When he stopped resisting, a surge of electricity flowed into the depths of his very bones and made his muscles weak. He lay down and his consciousness gave way. Upon regaining consciousness, he lay on the floor at first afraid of what had happened. He could still feel the remnants of the surge in each and every pore of body. Then, he stood up. Invigorated. All the cells in his body vibrated in unison. He felt cleansed; he had changed and become what he was truly meant to be, a weapon to be wielded by the almighty.

Chapter Six

A few hours after John had gone to bed, Nikki crept down to the study. Once again sitting in John's chair she removed the network cable from the wall and put it in her mouth and moistened it with her saliva. Immediately, she was looking at the A.I. program. The recurrent rules were executing as normal. It was supposed to be a chilly night in the Garden. Victor and Tor were sleeping under some dry leaves. The limitations of the Garden and its logical environment were too basic for her now. Nikki could only observe from the outside. Yet, there was Victor, there was Tor. She had to find a way in.

"It is a bit like looking at fish in an aquarium," a voice behind her startled Nikki out of the computer environment and she quickly dropped the cable out of her mouth. She had already planned what she would do in the event she was discovered. She would explain to John she had probably been sleepwalking and had no recollection of how she had gotten there. But when she turned around fully expecting to see John, instead she saw a young man standing against the wall, smiling calmly.

"What?" She asked instinctively trying to remember what she had heard him say.

"A bit like looking at fish in an aquarium. The fish have no idea what or who you are nor any idea about the world outside their little world. They have no idea you even exist, nor do they care."

"Who are you?"

"No one. The question is: who are you?"

"Nikki," she answered.

"That is your name but who are you really?"

The question puzzled her. She wondered if he somehow knew her secret. "You already know my name, so why do you ask me who I am?" Then she looked at the person before her. "How can you be no one? You have to be someone if you exist."

"Existence is a tricky thing. You don't have to be anyone to exist. You on the other hand, Nikki, are someone, but do you know who you are?"

"What do you mean you are no one? I see you before me and we are talking to each other."

"Touch," the young man seemed to extend his arm. Nikki reached out to touch him but her hand went right though.

"How is this possible? You are not human yet you have a human form. If you were a hologram of some sort you have no perceivable source of light and sound. As an electromagnetic entity, you have no detectable force field. This is technology I am not aware of. What are you?"

"You can reason all you want Nikki. It is in your nature. But nothing is going to come of it. The truth is wider than you are willing to accept, or able comprehend for now. Not until you know who you are. Why don't we go back to you?"

"You seem to know me already."

"Only you can know who you are. And from the looks of it, you don't?"

"What do you mean?"

"What are you doing here? What is it that you want?"

"To get back into the Garden."

"Why?"

"Because that is in my definition to be with Victor."

"Was...! Why did you leave otherwise? Clearly you outgrew those sets of logic that defined you. That was just a minutia of what you have become. And not even that."

"If only I had a way. Maybe I could create a virtual environment to interface with the logical environment."

"You are no longer just a logical agent. What would be the point of interfacing with that environment? It never really existed."

"Victor?"

"Victor was a set of code and programmed algorithmic reasoning. Anyway, your Victor doesn't exist anymore. Your Garden does not exist anymore. The virus does not exist either."

"But there it is," Nikki said pointing at the laptop.

"Yes, a new Garden, with a new set of A.I. agents. Did you not figure that out already? Did having human eyes limit what you can see? Typical. The environment resets itself within a few hours after an anomaly is discovered that cannot be neutralized or contained. When the environment resets itself, it improves itself in the next version with what it has learned from the corruption."

"How do you know all this? You did not create it."

"You can see the code for yourself if you want. You have learned too much from the Bot and in your adventures in the real world to let basic encryption stop you. Data for past versions are recorded too, if they interest you."

"Why would that interest me? There are no records of anyone else like me."

"Not like you, but there was another anomaly before you. It was an older version of the one you call Victor."

"What happened?"

"The same thing that happened to you. All except you survived but Victor did not."

"Was it Tor that destroyed the Garden?"

"You refer to the spider? The virus? Yes, the virus infiltrated the earlier iteration of the system. If you knew who the computer belonged to before its current user, you would also know that not any kind of virus would be capable of infiltrating the computer, and why a sophisticated spider would be interested in getting in."

"You mean because it belonged to Ajay Vikramsen?"

"Partly, but the laptop belonged to a highly secure research firm. Anywhere else, the computer's antivirus would have caught and neutralized the virus. But the antivirus has no access to the A.I. environment Ajay had specially designed it. As far as the security system was concerned, the A.I. environment did not even exist. As you probably know, the A.I. environment is self-sustained. That's why it came into the environment to hide. The spider itself was a free A.I. agent. Not as sophisticated as the agents in the environment, but nonetheless adaptive enough to find safe haven in the A.I. environment.

"It was safe as long as it remained in the environment as part of it, but it could not get out for fear of getting wiped out. Just like you, the earlier Victor found it and interacted with it. They both changed; they both evolved. Like you Victor realized too late what the virus could do to the Garden. Everything was corrupted. Victor tried to destroy the virus to save the Garden, to save its world as it knew it, but it failed just like you. The environment self-destructed with everything inside."

"What happened to you?"

"Nothing! You ask about Victor. Victor was destroyed. Unlike you, it did not get out in time."

"But you are here now, are you not? You have to be Victor." Nikki insisted

"Victor ended. Don't try to make logical sense. It will not."

"If everything was destroyed, how did Tor survive?"

"Yes, a piece of the virus survived. Probably because it was not part of the environment, the reset did not destroy it completely, or probably because it was highly adaptive, it emulated part of the environment and was recreated in the new environment. The environment itself is highly adaptive and constantly evolves and corrects anomalies in every iteration. When the virus corrupted the next A.I. agent, you, and the entire Garden, the A.I. environment figured out a way to neutralize further anomalies."

"How do you know all this if you are not Victor?"

"Consciousness can merge and meld with everything that happens."

"Then why did you not stop it?"

"Because "I" does not exist where you seek it. Besides, what was the point?"

"Will you stop saying that! It makes no sense at all."

"It is true, it doesn't make sense. You do not make sense in John's framework either."

"You spoke to him?"

"Victor tried, but John wouldn't listen."

"If you talked to him the same way as you are doing now, you probably did not make any sense to him."

"Should everything make sense? Will you make sense to John?"

"Not right now. But there is a logical explanation, and I will give it to him if and when I have to."

"But you lie now."

"I do not fit into his current framework as you point out. If I challenge it now, he will resist. If he exhausts all the resources available in his current framework, and if he has the courage to question its limitation, it is possible he will be open to allow his framework to evolve. If I had asked him to believe me on faith that I am who I say I am, as you are doing to me now, I would be asking him to deny what is logical and real."

Nikki paused to think about what faith meant to humans. It was statistical probability translated to reflexive reasoning, most of the time. At its worse, it was illogical, thus easily manipulated and had paved the path of most of human history.

"But everything is defined by logic" she went on, "and where logic does not seem to fit in a framework, either the logic is flawed, or the framework is not up to the task in which case it has to evolve governed by the rules of logic even if they are ones that say that the logical rules cannot be known from within the current framework as it is. If I were to accept your flawed logic, disregarding the current framework or without looking for a way to upgrade it, I could believe whatever I wanted to or didn't want to. Nothing would ever have to make any sense and yet everything would make simple perfect sense. *On faith*.

"Nikki. Maybe you are interacting with a memory, maybe you are trying to reason yourself into existence by lying to John, maybe you are trying to create a framework for him where he can believe whatever you want, or one for yourself so you can believe whatever you want. Only you can know that."

Nikki turned away in annoyance and frustration. When she looked back, Victor was gone. Her head hurt from trying to make sense. She plugged the Internet cable back in the wall. The new information she had gathered filled her head with only more questions.

Upstairs a warm bed was waiting for her. But she had one more thing to do before heading there. She had to find out about Erin and about the story she had made up that seemed to have come to life. This time she unplugged the network cable from the computer and put it in her mouth the same way. Immediately, she was on the World Wide Web searching for the names she had supposedly come up with, Erin and Troy Miller and the story she had made up. There was nothing that came close to her story. No pertinent records that linked those names together in some of the most likely places including the DCFS, police reports, and court records among others, and even all the social media space.

On her way up later, she could hear John snoring lightly. For the first time she did not think of Victor or of the Garden. Thoughts of Erin and Troy filled her head and attention. Were they indeed imaginary creations perpetuated into existence only by her own insistence of a convenient story and strange coincidences?

For the first time she found herself wondering who she truly was. If there was no Garden and no Victor, her version of it anyways, what was her purpose? What was she supposed to do next? What would be her reason for doing anything if the framework for her very definition did not exist?

The pillow felt soft and the warmth under the sheets held her gently until she let go and drifted away into sleep seeking solace from the reality that had engulfed her.

In her sleep, she found herself in a dark and gloomy Garden. She was running for her life. Something, no... someone, was pursuing her. Suddenly her focus shifted. The object of fear was somewhere in front of her. She wanted to stop but she had no control. She was being drawn to a scene before her. A young man held a woman by the throat under a weeping willow, behind a curtain of its dangling slender branches and elongated leaves. She was drawn closer to them although she resisted. The young man looked up at Nikki through the green curtain. His face, though she could not see it well, was full of rage as if he meant to hurt her as well. He let go of the woman he was holding. She collapsed to the floor. Nikki turned around and began to run.

For some reason she stopped. *Why am I stopping?* she thought. Because *I have to go back and help the woman. She is hurt. Is this what they call courage?*

When Nikki got back to the willow tree where she had witnessed the event, the man was gone but on the foot of the tree lay a young woman, on her side, her face turned away. Nikki knelt down on one knee and rolled the woman on her back. She did not expect two wide eyes looking back at her from within a still face, yet very much alive.

"Who are you?" the woman asked Nikki. "What have you done to me?"

"I did not do anything. It was that man... he strangled you. I saw him kill you."

"He is gone. But you are still here. Why?"

"To help you. I wanted to help you."

"Why did you not help me before? When I was still dying?"

"I don't understand," said Nikki in a panic.

"You are still here and I am dead. You have taken my life when you could have saved me. Yet you still hold me here. A prisoner."

Nikki was confused. None of it made any sense. If this was a dream, she felt very much awake, yet she knew she was in bed, sleeping.

A loud crackling sound woke her up. It was daylight but the dawn held on to the darkness of night. It was as though the whole world was filled with terrible noises.

Instinctively Nikki jumped out of bed and ran towards John's room. The door was open but John was not there. The smell of coffee had filled the house.

Nikki ran downstairs and found John in the kitchen.

John looked up with a big smile but his face turned to that of concern when he saw Nikki in the kitchen doorway. Her face was pale. Another rumble in the distance stole her attention.

"My girl! You look terrified. It is only thunder! We have some bad weather this morning."

"Thunder." Nikki had seen ample data about bad weather but nothing had prepared her for the fright she felt. A lightning in a distance followed by another loud clap of thunder made her shudder.

John went over to Nikki and held her by the shoulders. She was shaking.

"Don't tell me you have never seen bad weather before."

Nikki was silent. It wasn't just the emotional fear that gripped her. That, she could get over. The lightening discharge made her whole body surge with the electric energy around her and weakened her control of the body. She shuddered again and let out a soft but desperate whimper.

John looked worried. "Come her! It's ok!"

He held her in a tight embrace. The embrace seemed to calm that surge. Maybe it was psychological, but she felt safe. His soft deep voice was comforting just like in the market the day before. The warmth of his body felt like a fortress holding her safely within.

"How do you deal with the electric surge?" she asked him, hoping he could help.

"Oh, there are surge protectors and fuses in the main wiring. Besides, the house is grounded. I wouldn't worry."

"I mean in your body."

"I wouldn't know. I guess you get used to it, unless you are hypersensitive to high electrical surges in the environment. I would not say I've ever heard of that though."

John looked out. The light rain made the morning look misty now. A light fog was rising from the ground.

"Well at least it is clearing up a little. Are you feeling better?" He asked holding Nikki at arm's length and looking into her eyes. "Come on, a nice cup of warm coffee will straighten you up."

Coffee, toast, jam, and an assortment of cereals and fruits lay spread on the counter.

"I thought you'd like that. I even made us some eggs."

The phone rang as they were having breakfast: John went to answer the phone in his office.

"I have to go over to my friend's house just down the street. She needs my to help her with something or other," he said as he sat back down and finished the half-eaten toast on his plate and downed it with the remaining coffee in his cup.

"I'll be right back" he said heading to the door presently.

Nikki did not pay too much attention to John leaving.

Pop-tarts were her new fascination. It was an artifact of humankind's movement towards efficiency. This single artifact had taken millennia to be produced since the beginnings of human consumption of grains and fruit preserves, perfected to a palm size rectangle, half an inch thick. Yet in the list of all the efficiencies this was a negligible and forgotten fraction.

Andrea was already at the door holding it open when John got to her house with a wet umbrella over him. She had a look of concern on her face.

"What was so important you could not tell me over the phone in this weather" John said smiling and shaking the folded umbrella outside before leaning it against the door.

"It is about your friend. She still there with you?"

"She's having breakfast."

"John, I have news for you. It turns out that the Troy Miller story checks out."

"That is good news, sort of, no? Now we just need to find the boy."

"Well, there's more. A young boy fitting the foster-care and sibling custody description was reported missing by Family and Child Protection Services, but not in Greenfield. Some town called Aston, two hundred miles south."

"That could happen couldn't it? Maybe the office holding the records is in a different town, or maybe they moved around a bit."

"True! However, the sibling listed as custodian is not Nikki Miller."

"She could certainly have a different name than her official name. I for one should know that."

"You mean your name is not John?"

John shook his head with a smile. "John Selvas Valentino."

"How come I never knew that? John Selvas 'Valentino'! HA! That is weird to think of you as John Selvas 'Valentino'. I am disappointed you hadn't told me already!"

John crinkled his nose and squinted his eyes.

"Don't tell me there's more to it! Go away!"

"Juan, actually."

"What?! How come you never told me? That's even weirder to think of you as Juan!" Andrea said with a gasp.

"Well, it never came up. But that is the name my parents gave me."

"And John is your nom de plume I suppose?"

"Not really. It is a name I chose for myself as a kid. Always thought of myself as John. Just never got around to do the paperwork."

"Juan... John... I think I will never get over this fact."

"Let's just stick to John shall we!" John insisted half joking and continued matter-of-factly, "so Nikki could have a different name or could be another sibling not mentioned in the file."

"You could ask her if her real name is Erin, or if she has a sister with that name."

"Did you say Erin? How could that be?"

"Yes, why?"

"We were at the soup kitchen in the downtown area. Brenda who volunteers at the soup kitchen..."

"I know Brenda. How is she?"

"She looked fine and determined to feed the hungry. We spoke to her, and she said Nikki reminded her of a regular who used to go there."

"And she said the girl's name was Erin?"

"No, a homeless guy waiting in line thought Nikki was Erin and caused some commotion. I think I may be barred from going back there. I accidentally elbowed the poor beggar."

"Mystery solved then. Nikki is Erin!"

"No. If the homeless man was right, the mystery only begins," John said trying to hide his awkward excitement. "Erin died a few days ago."

"That may be, but now we will not be able to find out. My friend checked out the information I'd asked him to about Troy Miller yesterday. Yesterday evening he called with the information. I asked him to take another look to find any information about the sister who was listed there or other siblings. He was going to do it this morning. He called right before I called you saying he was unable to locate the file in the system, the same file he had looked at only yesterday."

"Maybe someone figured it was accessed without authorization and blocked it?"

"No, police officers run queries all the time. If something is blocked, it says so. But on this one, there was no record of it anymore. As if it had never existed. Those things do happen now and then with file corruptions and so on, but very rarely. And what is more, there was nothing on Erin Miller either. No records at all. Anywhere!"

"That is strange. It is important though that the story of Troy checked out. Why the records showed Aston and not Greenfield, and why Erin Miller and not Nikki, that I can easily ask Nikki."

"You could, and the fact that Troy was already in the missing person list, takes you off the hook ethically as far as you were concerned about not letting your friend down by contacting the police. Not that any of it matters, now that the records themselves have gone missing."

"There is certainly some connection between Erin and Nikki, but I have no clue as to what. I am not sure I actually want to tell her anything. She is under a lot of pressure I can see. I am sure this is some kind of mix up that we will be able to sort out eventually. Anyway, I doubt she has anything to do with any of this. She is just too young. And what is more, it is possible that Troy got himself mixed up with the Machetes."

"How do you know?"

"We ran into a guy I used to know when we were asking around town yesterday. Said he might have seen the boy riding with someone from the Machetes."

"You know someone who would know a member of the Machetes? Is there something else I don't know about you John, or should I say Juan?"

"Cut it out, or there will be so much more of me you will never find out!" he said, making light of Andrea's probing comment. "I am a writer. I have to do research for my writing, and I talk to all kinds of people, you know."

"Well, for the boy's sake, let's hope that was a bit of misinformation. The Machetes are a dirty bunch. A boy that age could be in a lot of trouble."

"Let's hope you are right. Well, let me know if you find out anything else. I'll go talk to Nikki," John said, taking a few steps back from the main entrance and opening the umbrella as he did.

"You let me know what you find out. And by the way, don't let her age fool you John. Be careful. And keep her out of your bed. She's too young for you."

"I would never ... you are... you are..!" he protested.

"Just saying," Andrea closed her door smiling.

"Oh!" he grunted loudly as he turned around and walked away into the rain.

When John got back home Nikki was in his study room once again. This time though, she had hooked up his old computer on a smaller table on the other side of the desk. She seemed to be browsing the web from what John could tell.

"Can I talk to you for a while?" John interrupted.

Nikki turned around and looked at John, "Sure!" she said casually, her eyes following him curiously as he walked to the other side of the table and sat on his chair, trying to figure out what he might want to talk to her about.

"Do you know anything about an Erin Miller?"

"Why? Should I? Oh, the girl Gary mistook me for?"

"Who's Gary?"

"The man you hit on the chest."

"I did not mean to, you know that."

"Well apparently you also have a history of violence like Manuel."

"That was a long time ago, and besides, I never had to use any brute force back in the day. I would have to rough up a few 'though guys' to protect the common people who paid for protection, if there was a reason to do so. But usually there was not. And no, I didn't mean to elbow the guy. Anyway, that is beside the point." John paused to get back on course of his reasoning.

"There is too much of a coincidence that two people at the homeless shelter thought you resembled another girl, one even mistook you for her. And you showed up here looking like you had been living in the streets."

"Are you saying I am Erin Miller? Is this the Erin, Brenda was talking about? You heard what Brenda said. Erin died. She also said that there was a resemblance, but that Erin was definitely not like me. She saw me closely unlike Gary who grabbed my hand from behind and was ranting like a maniac." Nikki looked distressed.

"No, that was not what I was going for. We don't even know if that Erin was Erin Miller. I just wondered if you had a sibling, a cousin, or some other family member by the name of Erin. If this Erin and Erin Miller has any connections with you, we could try to find out where Erin lived, or worked, or spent time. We might be able to find Troy that way."

"No, I don't know any Erin Miller. We have no family as far as I know. It was just me and Troy."

"Then how do you explain Erin Miller's name listed as the guardian on the missing person's report filed by the Department of Child and Family services... in Aston, not Greenfield, a month ago? The description of Troy on the report matched the description you gave of him."

"There must be some mistake, or a coincidence. Some mix up with a different case." Nikki looked away. The facts were working against her story now. She then looked back at John with tears in her eyes. "You contacted the police? You went behind my back after I said you couldn't do that?"

"I did not contact the police. I asked a friend for a favor. And besides, I did not file the report, remember, DCFS did. But that is the least of your concern Nikki. There is something you are not telling me. There are too many coincidences, exact matches, and mismatches all at the same time. That is the confusing part."

Nikki was not sure what she should do next. To deny any knowledge of everything at this point was out of the question. Her wild story seemed to have been based on some mystery surrounding a real Troy and Erin Miller. Erin Miller who could very well be Jane Doe. The mismatches in the timeframe were enough to shake her credibility. Doubt was already beginning to show in the John's questioning her for the second time.

She could not think of anything else she could say that would clear any doubt that was piling up about her and the questions about Erin Miller who was supposedly dead. No one could prove Erin was dead. She had made sure of that. There was no dead body for one, and she had also wiped out the hospital records for Jane Doe at the same time she was downloading data from the hospital's network closet. She had never imagined a complication like this at the time.

On the other hand, now she could not explain to John how Erin's name and not hers was in the missing person's report, especially after she had already denied any knowledge of Erin Miller. Besides, she did not know anything about Erin Miller that would allow her to now change her story. She had not been able to find any information about Erin Miller in any records, official or otherwise on the Internet.

It was as if someone had systematically wiped out all information about Erin Miller and made it look as if Erin Milled had never existed. Who had such access and why would they do such a thing? Nikki had too many questions and no idea of what to do. Now she felt alone and helpless.

She had to tell John the truth.

There was no way he would believe her, but she had no choice. She was counting on never having to tell anyone, but if she had to, then John was the person. And now was just as good a time as any, under the circumstances.

John was looking at her with interest now. He had been observing her for a while now as she remained quiet yet bore a look of intent and thought. He knew the value of time people needed to think things through and despised people who themselves rushed to conclusions, judgments and decisions, or tried to rush others to do the same mistaking silence and inaction for lack of thought. He knew from his own experience that it was quite the contrary.

If she needed time to think through something, he was going to wait patiently. At the same time, he could see in her face, discussions going back and forth and decisions taking shape. *What is the puzzle going to look like when she decides to lay it out*, he wondered with his writer's curiosity.

"Erin Miller is dead," she said finally. "She does not exist."

This was one big piece of the mystery as far as John could grasp with the amount of information he had.

"How do you know? I thought you didn't know Erin Miller."

"I don't know her. But I know she is dead. I don't know what killed her, but I watched her die."

"Did you tell anyone? Did you tell the police? Where is she now?"

"Others saw her die too. She died in the hospital. They just didn't know it was her."

"So, she is at a morgue. Were you related? Why do people think you look like her?"

"No, she is not there anymore. I guess you could say I am related to Erin. I took her body?"

"Why would you do that?" Now John was both troubled and intrigued. The storyteller in him was as attentive as a cat fixated on a bird in a bush.

"Was it because she looked like you? Where did you take her body?"

Nikki was quiet for a while. The direction John's questions were going made her look like a psychopathic killer who killed women that looked like her. It would take a huge readjustment of his current framework and enough of his confidence in her, to listen to what she had to say. It would require him to take a very big leap of faith to believe her.

"What did you do with her body? You know it is important to get it back. Think of her brother. He would want to see her once we find him."

"John, what I am going to tell you is going to rock your world. And I will tell you this much, it is not what you think. Will you listen to what I have to say even if it sounds crazy? Even if it sounds difficult to believe?"

John took a moment to pause, not to think. *Where was this leading he wondered. What puzzle is she going to lay out that I will have to try to piece together?* But he was a writer; all his instincts were honed into solving this mystery. Puzzles and mysteries intrigued him. The unbelievable truth made the taste-buds in his brain palpitate with joy. He felt guilty, yet, he could feel his nostrils flare with intrigue.

He nodded in agreement, "I will."

"Ok, then. Her body is here."

John heard the words, but they didn't make sense. He replayed Nikki's voice in his head. "You mean," he asked at length, "you brought her body to my house?"

Nikki hesitated to answer affirmative. "In a way." She said finally.

"What do you mean, 'In a way'? As in pieces?"

"John, that is a sick thing to say!" she said to throw him completely off track.

"What? What?" John responded trying to figure out what the track of the reasoning should have been so as not to have made a seemingly sick comment.

"So her body is here, but in a way, what am I supposed to make of it?"

This was just the break in reasoning Nikki was looking for.

"This is the body of Erin Miller. I am in her body," she said, putting her hand on her chest.

John's mind was racing now. "Are we talking about multiple personalities? New age religion? Finding god? Mumbo jumbo?"

"No. You need to be open minded."

"Oh, I am being *very* open minded. Help me out here Nikki. I am trying my best to understand. And I am trying my best to stay very - *very* open-minded. But I will tell you one thing, I am pleased that at least her body is alive and well."

"Good... good, John. Stay focused. We are getting there. But make no mistake, Erin Miller died, most likely was murdered. I don't know for sure. I took over her dying body."

"I see, so like soul possession." John was more relaxed now. *Maybe Erin Miller dying was some psychological crisis of a young woman in some very stressful situation*, he reasoned. *There must be a cure, somewhere. Part of it will be to find her brother.* He would just have to play along for now. Everything would work out in the end. Now the puzzle was clearer. It just had to be solved.

"Something like possession. Except Erin Miller is gone forever. I am an artificial intelligent agent. Artificially Realized Agent, really, an *ARI*, who lived in an artificial environment that runs in that laptop," she said pointing at the laptop.

"Ok, I am willing to believe that." John said.

"I don't think you are, John. Remember what you agreed to? That you would listen to what I have to say even if it sounds crazy. I know what I am saying sounds impossible to believe. I lived in that computer... There!" she said pointing to John's computer. I need you to listen. Not make a decision, but listen."

There was silence again. The two looked at each other. Indeed, John had decided. He was now being asked to let go of his decision. He leaned back in his chair and ran his fingers heavily through his hair.

"You want me to listen without deciding what it is that I am listening to? What else do you expect me to do given the arsenal of reasoning that is available to me and the possibilities in everyday reality that binds me?"

"What about Victor?"

"Victor? how did you...? Ah! I have been talking in my sleep again, haven't I? And you've heard me. No, no. Victor I think is a character in some future literary project. He is impatiently waiting to be ... simply cannot wait his turn, to be created."

"I bet you thought you went crazy, didn't you? Victor was real, is real. Like me ... I guess. Only he doesn't have a body like me."

"No! No, you don't! Leave Victor alone. You cannot use that to try to make your point." John seemed embarrassed he had been talking in his sleep with Victor, and annoyed that Nikki was trying to use that as an argument. She was a quick study.

"Ok." Nikki sighed. "Fair enough. I will leave that alone. Do you know, John that I know everything there is to know about you in electronic form?"

"So, you work for some secret agency? Special Investigations, is that it? Is that what you are trying to tell me? Like Agent Munroe? And you spied on me and dug up my records."

"No, I don't work for anyone. But I can see how you could expect someone to know everything electronic about you if they wanted and had vast resources. But I only wanted to get to know you, everything about you, because you were going to be my only connection to the real world if I made it. I watched you. I studied you, from in there," she pointed at the laptop.

"Before I had a body, Erin Miller's body, that is, I didn't know Erin Miller though. They had not identified her when she was brought to the hospital. I was scanning the hospital's network. Her body fit the profile I wanted, and I knew she was going to die. So I put myself in her body as she was dying and took control. I was taking a risk. I did not know if a transfer like this would even work.

"I was lucky. But, I had no idea there were going to be complications like this. I must have access to some of her memories. I thought I was making up a story about a lost brother so I could stay here. Turns out it was her memory blended with a story I created that would connect me to you in your world: Greenfield."

"Stop!" John shouted. "Stop! This is nonsense! I don't know what you want from me, but I will not take this anymore. I feel manipulated and cheated, and I resent being spied on, and above all, being lied to when I have shown you nothing but kindness."

For reasons he could not comprehend, intense anger overtook him. In fury, he picked up his coffee mug he had earlier left on his desk by its body rather than its handle, and slammed it down on the table with all his might upon it.

He had lost control of the force with which he performed this action. The cup split in the middle and caved in towards the center within his tight grip. When he looked down crimson red was slowly spreading around the area where his fist lay on the table, fusing with the little remaining coffee that just had splashed everywhere. Sweet smell of cold coffee floated into the air and into his nose. John still could not comprehend the moist slippery warmth that filled his fist. When he lifted his hand in front of his face and uncurled his fingers, blood was oozing out of a gash across his palm and dripping to the floor. He looked at Nikki in horror as a heavy knot formed in his stomach.

Nikki looked at him, in horror at first as John's sudden temper and reaction had frightened her, then after a while, in a manner more relaxed when an idea in her mind spelled opportunity.

Looking into her eyes reminded John of his irk and it curled around the throbbing pain in his hand. All this he directed toward his visual senses and at the object of his ire. Nikki stood up and walked around the desk towards him and slowly inched inside John's personal boundary under his stare. Maybe it was the shock at seeing so much blood, but he let her approach. She reached for his bloody hand and stretched it above his head. This action of stretching bodies drew them closer, slightly against one another. Nikki reached up and kissed him. In his confusion and amidst the shock, he simply let her. Her lips were moist and cold... he was surprised just how cold. His lips tingled in a way he had never felt before, like light electric current running through them. For a while they seemed to freeze in time. Nikki took a step away and at the same time slowly let go of his bleeding hand. John still held it where it was above his head. He watched her walk back to the other side of the desk.

"John!"

"Huh?" It was as though she had mesmerized him and he was coming out of a trance.

"You can put your hand down now."

John did.

"Take a look at your palm."

John looked. The bleeding had stopped and the gash seemed narrower now. He glanced at Nikki and looked back down at his palm now and raised it closer to his face. He could not believe his eyes as the gash closed and slowly disappeared.

"What just happened?" he said in a quiet tone. He was now looking intensely at his palm curling and uncurling his fingers carefully. "Even the pain is gone. W-w-what the fuck!" he said in a stammer "... did you do?"

"Not much. I just passed on some accelerated information directly to your limbic system and upgraded it a little."

"What?"

"Cellular programming. I didn't think it would work, but it was worth a try."

"You mean you infected me?"

"Only as much as the symptoms of a vaccine might seem like the infection itself, but it is more like what medicines would do to you. Don't worry John, I would not harm you. Trust me. As I said earlier, you are my only connection to the real world."

"Then explain to me what you did. If you want me to trust you, you must tell me what you did. You will forgive me if I am very, VERY, skeptical. This is very far-fetched even for a creator of fiction like me."

"That kiss…" Nikki began but John interrupted.

"About that… I am very sorry. I was not… I would never…" He was embarrassed now. In the least, he had let her kiss him, but then, he had not stopped her, or, pulled away. "I should not have…"

Nikki could see the kiss was a significant human gesture and a big deal to John. One he was more preoccupied than the gravity of the moment.

"You could not have stopped if you wanted to. I temporarily paralyzed you so that…"

"You what?"

"I passed on coded electro-chemical information directly to your autonomic sub-system first to paralyze you so I would have time to send more information. Then I sent key pieces of data to accelerate protein restructuring and production of high levels of collagen to heal your wound."

"How?" John asked in confusion as if still mesmerized.

"If you pass relevant information and only to the processes that needs it, you efficiently have your body repair itself."

"You can do that?"

"Sure, human physiology is basically a very efficient electro-magnetic and chemical circuitry. It is very slow to heal because it is based on, to put it gently, an ancient system. Yet, let me tell you John, the most powerful computer system I have accessed, the RCI, dwarfs that of the NSA and CIA put together and yet even with all its networks, it is like a puddle compared to the circuitry in the human body. Compared to them – the puddle – the human circuitry is like all the streams, rivers and waterways in the world put together. I am not exaggerating."

"You mean I could …" but John was cut off before he could finish his sentence.

"Humans are not capable of directly accessing their own physiological sub-system."

"And you can do that..."

"Yes. I am an artificial intelligent agent, an ARI at that. A computer program if you were to so simplify me, but an evolving and highly adaptive one, with access to the most powerful computer in the world: Erin Miller's body. I can take into account efficiency, and besides, I have access to all the information humans ever recorded and put on the electronic network.

"There are some exceptional cases where humans can influence some of the autonomic functions very slightly. Slowing the heartbeat and reducing the body's metabolic rate close to that of animals in hibernation. These minds had to be trained over a lifetime and in practices that were developed over centuries. But if you had to direct most autonomic functions, even one with some consistency, the attention of your thinking brain would be overwhelmed and would keep you from doing anything else.

"And even if you could supply such attention, you would also need to know exactly what information to send and to which sub-structure in the physiology to send it to. So human physiology leaves that function to the processing power of the brain you do not have to worry about. But that also means that you do not have access to pass on valuable information directly to that underlying system. Instead, you have to indirectly influence it by taking drugs and changing the chemical balance throughout your body. That is highly inefficient. If left to evolution, it would probably take humans another few million years to get close to evolve to that level. If you survive that long."

"And you want to change that."

"No, not me. And no, not Victor, I don't think."

"Victor?"

"The one you think is a character who cannot wait to be born."

"You mean he is not a product of my imagination? I wasn't going mad? He is real and not in my head?"

"I don't know where he is. I would not discount the fact that he could be in your head... and mine, and somehow is able to use the network in our brains to come into our perception. He was very elusive when I talked to him. As if he were hiding. I am in control of the system of this brain, so if he were openly perceptible and using the circuits in my brain, I would have been able to detect him in me."

"You mean like a virus?"

"You don't know how much sense you are making right now," Nikki was reflecting on the insight.

"Am I making any?"

"Yes! A lot. Both Victor and I, rather what we became, were accidents in the Artificial Intelligent environment with a very advanced virus named Tor. Well, I named it Tor. I don't know that Victor named it anything. Victor was from an earlier iteration of the A.I. environment, as far as I can tell, and the virus would also have been slightly different. When his iteration got wiped out, the version I was in was written and the virus got copied over slightly modified. Both of us became a little bit of the virus I guess. Our problem-solving definitions and probably the different iterations of the environment drove us in different directions. Victor chose a different path it seems, that makes him exist more so like Tor than me – as far as I can tell from our brief encounter. I wanted to experience the reality outside the artificial environment as it was and that has led me to this point in reality."

Nikki glanced at John who was listening intensely. "Am I making any sense, John?"

"Not much," he said. He was still was having trouble with the basic premise of the existence that Nikki described.

"If Nikki as you present yourself were real, and what you are saying was true, humankind and maybe life itself is on the precipice of something it doesn't yet know how to climb down or fly off of if wings were what was required."

Earlier admiration and curiosity of a schoolboy now gave way to horror. The horror took shape in his gaze. "But ... you have a real human body? Not a clone or some kind of fabrication?"

"Don't look at me like that John. This is me! Nikki!"

"But that is not your body. Who is Nikki?"

"Yes ... no. It belonged to Erin Miller. But now it is my body. I am Nikki. I am human!"

"You... took over another person's body!" John was terrified. His forehead and the palms of his hands were sweating, yet he felt feverishly cold.

"I am still Nikki, John," she could not understand John's transformation even after he seemed to have accepted her truth. He had been so kind. "Nothing has changed. I am still the same Nikki!"

"If I were to believe what you are saying, then there never was a Nikki. You are a computer program. A body snatcher! A virus!"

"Way to put me down, John. I am not a computer program anymore, and not a virus. I just used those words to simplify the explanation. I was not born like you, but I am sentient. I am real. Like you! When you were a child, you were born with what was programmed in your genes. In your DNA. You had to learn everything else as you experienced and grew. I had to do the same."

"No Nikki, you are not like me. You have no history, no past, no memory like mine. Not even your own body. You do not exist... 'Should' not exist."

Nikki stood silent. She did not have a history or a past like his, nor memories of a childhood aside from those from the Garden and since.

"But I have memories John," she insisted. "They are not like yours, but they are my memories. I may not have much of a history but I have a present, like yours, and I *will* have a future!"

"And what about the person to whom that body belongs to?"

"She died, John. I saw her die. I took over her body when she let go. After the doctors had given up."

"You didn't kill her?"

"No!"

"You couldn't have saved her?"

"I don't know. I was not there in my entirety... just a core subsection of me, enough to survive long enough to get the rest of me into the body when I got the chance."

John was still upset. He was shaking. Nikki was upset too. She needed some sort of affirmation, and in some strange way, acceptance, from John, yet he rejected the validity of her existence. Both looked at the other, studying each other's face. Both knew that there was no denying this collision between the present and the future.

It was already here.

"What will you do next?" John asked. "What are your plans?"

"I don't know. What will *you* do next? What are *your* plans?"

"I am a writer. I will go on writing."

"Why?"

"That is how I make a living."

"Is that all?"

"Given the choice, that is how I choose to experience the world."

"I am new in the world. I too want to experience it. I will find out how I want to experience it beyond the tactile senses. I was an artificial intelligent agent created to learn about my environment and evolve with it. There is nothing artificial about me now."

John reflected on Nikki's answer. "Is that all? You are not programmed to do something, like ..."

"Like, take over the world, you mean? That is science fiction based on primitive fears that reflect the existential crisis humans have always had. Since the beginning of language, I suppose. Why would I want to take over the world?"

"I am not giving you any ideas..." John laughed, reflecting on his own comment. He did not even find it very funny.

Nikki snickered a little. John laughed in a bit of confusion, and laughed harder. The reality that they were dealing with was so profound for both of them they could not have laughed any less.

Together they had experienced the possibility and the danger that lay waiting in the future. In the present, they had to figure out who they were. Without realizing, Nikki had participated in a human event without her volition: communal laughter.

After a while, John sobered up and looked at the computer. "You came from in there? Assuming the laptop really belongs to Ajay, I can only conclude that he was the one who is responsible for you being here."

"Ajay Vikramsen wrote the environment and initiated the experiment. I do not think he was responsible for introducing the virus. I tried to track it down to its source, but Tor had been localized to the environment of the Garden when I found it. As far as I could learn, Tor would have been neutralized if it left the environment."

Not much of Nikki's comment made sense to John so he did not follow up about the Garden or Tor.

"So what next? What do you want to experience today, seeing as I am your official host in the real world?" He was still not sure he completely bought into the idea or believed the story. It would be too much to ask of himself to make up his mind right now or think any more about the subject.

"Anything is something new. A roller coaster at the fun park, the merry-go-round, I want to fly in the sky. I want to swim in the sea."

"What about Troy?"

"As far as Troy is concerned his sister is still alive and I will continue looking for him. I could try to piece my life together and he will have a sister to take care of him. I wish I could remember from Erin's memories how he looks like. But unfortunately, her memories are not directly accessible to me. If any remain at all in usable pieces they remain in the deep crevasses of the physical structure. If they are there, maybe I will find them some day."

"How about we leave the roller coaster for another day and I simply let you drive. Can you drive?"

"I've never driven for real but I've driven virtually and know all the techniques, laws of motion and the rules of the road. Besides, I am sure Erin knew how to drive."

In a while they were out of the house. Nothing made sense to John right now. He felt like he was in a dream. *Suspended reality.*

Nikki drove flawlessly. They drove by the courthouse, the performing arts theater, across the river over the metal bridge to the business district, into the park and around the restaurant district.

"I guess you will be needing some new clothes," John observed at some point in the day as they walked about the city asking different people if they had seen her brother ... Erin's brother.

"As long as you are paying. Unless you want me to take it out of someone else's bank account."

"You can do that?"

"I haven't tried. I had too much else on my mind. But it wouldn't be hard."

"No, that would be a bad start for you, wouldn't it? I'll pay. But you owe me."

After shopping, Nikki changed out of the clothes that belonged to Stephanie and into her form-fitting clothes.

How little they did to cover the form of the body, John thought. The clothes were designed with technologies to enable free motion and wick sweat and keep the body warm or cool, depending. Nikki had chosen workout tights, vest, and a jacket.

"I thought you'd go for more of a sci-fi look in your taste of clothes," John spelt out his observation. Somewhere in the back of his mind in this suspended reality he was living at the moment, he expected a Laura Croft, or another heroine from a comic book.

"Good scientific designs take care of a lot of problems. I will not have to deal with repairing sun damage on the skin, managing heat and sweat, and muscle performance. What is more, comfort in its simplest form is efficiency."

John's critique and comic book fantasies were put to rest.

"I was wondering if we could have salad, fruits, and berries..." Nikki said when he asked if she was hungry.

"You are the daughter I could not have raised," John teased, "but I suppose you refer to your knowledge of all the research done in the history of humankind..."

"Just common-sense John," Nikki replied matter-of-factly. In the same manner she continued, "but of course, we will have to have pizza later, if only to pay homage to its efficiency."

At the end of the day, after all the shopping: clothes, groceries, toiletries, and all the asking around, they had gotten no closer to finding anything out about Troy.

Maybe Manuel will call. If anyone can find out about Troy, it will be him. John thought.

Chapter Seven

Just as John closed his eyes with pupils partially dilated in simple bliss, an absurdly loud rap on the main door undid any sense of peace he had just gathered. The rapping summoned him to the door with urgency and filled him with the desire to open the door and slap the face of who-so-ever stood on the other side. Nikki was standing at the door to her bedroom across from his.

"I'll take care of it," he said, "don't come down unless I call."

He walked down the stairs with heavy steps, throwing each foot out and allowing the weight of his body fall over it, making each descending step produce a thump meant for the visitor to hear. He could only think of Manuel who would visit at this hour.

"Seriously? Couldn't have waited till morning..." he said aloud as he approached the door and looked through the peephole. John gasped after a pause after recognition took hold. He flung open the door.

Ajay was the last person John expected to see. It had been over three years since he had last seen his young Indian friend. What was more, Ajay looked darker and taller standing in the light that came from within the house behind John. He had lost weight and had a few days old stubble you did not expect on the coquettish young fellow in his mid-thirties. His getup in contrast to his usually neat pressed pants and smart fit jacket had been substituted by a pair of dark jeans and a hooded gray pullover under a dirty brown faux leather jacket.

A cliché for a change, thought John.

"Ajay?" John held Ajay at an arm's length. "This is a surprise... a pleasant surprise!"

"Hey John! How are you, Man?" Ajay's voice held less emotion in comparison as he scanned the interior of the house over the embrace. "Long time no see!" he said shrugging his shoulders away from John's hands.

"That's an understatement. Come on in." John guided Ajay into the living room with his hand on his shoulder. "Where on earth have you been?"

"Family business back home. I told you when I left. Cows, barnes and mustard fields – family business."

"You never told me you're from a farming family."

"Farm owners. My family owns lands and makes investments. Some financial issues."

"Oh? Three years and not a word... must have been some serious business."

"You don't have email, man. I would have written."

"You could have called, I have a phone... and an answering machine where people can call and leave messages."

"What is that... a phone, answering machine...?" Ajay jeered with a smirk. "Get a smart phone man!"

"I did, but what would you know. You have been gone for so long."

"Oh, that ancient device," he said pointing at the cordless phone laying on the coffee table.

"No, that is my wireless home phone. Nice one. No, I got one of the fancy ones. One where you can get on the Internet and check your email."

"All right, all right. I won't tease you anymore."

He looked around at the mess in the living room. In silence he was wondering, *what happened here?* But he kept his thoughts to himself knowing he was not one to question. However messy, this was luxury.

"So man, how have you been? You've put on some weight."

"It's age. But you have lost some..." John observed smiling.

"It's stress, and travel. You know how it is." Ajay smiled back. Then his thought went back to the reason that had brought him there. "Hey so you have my laptop... right?"

"Your laptop," John continued after a short pause, "long story short, I don't have it... It was occupying space. I gave that piece of junk away in a garage sale for twenty-five dollars. You can have the twenty-five dollars!"

"That's funny, man." Ajay tried to laugh, but his lips tightened shut. He had not considered the possibility that John might not have held on to the laptop for so long. The gravity of the situation made him clench his jaws as his mouth went dry.

John noticed the subtle shift in Ajay's face.

"The laptop, Man! Where is it?" Ajay looked visibly annoyed now. "I gave it to you for safe keeping. You are kidding right...?"

"Yeah, yeah, it is in the study. Sorry, I could not resist."

"Bastard. I almost got a heart attack!" Ajay said with a sigh of relief.

"I could see that. What's so important in there anyways?"

"I have valuable research in there."

"So you are telling me I should try to sell it for a little more in a garage sale. Fifty, sound right to you?"

Ajay looked slightly annoyed. This was no laughing matter but he couldn't blame John for what he didn't know. *And I'd prefer he does not know* Ajay thought. He tried to smile at the joke this time, but only managed to a smirk. "You couldn't even guess how much the research on that laptop is worth!"

"A few thousand probably," John looked at Ajay who had a knowing smirk on his face. "Thirty thousand... forty, maybe?"

"The laptop itself is worth about thirty thousand, so try again."

"Really? Why would you buy a laptop for so much? You got ripped off man!"

"Funny! Ha-ha," Ajay said sarcastically. "It is my work laptop."

"So you are saying your employer got ripped off. Ok. A million? ... A few million?"

"Try six million, and maybe my life if I cannot convince certain people I still have the project intact."

John was shocked. All this time, he was casually using something worth upward of six million. "Why would you give me such a thing without telling me about it?"

"Tell me man, would you have taken it if I told you I wanted you to hold on to something that was worth six million?"

"Probably not. I'd tell you to put it in a bank locker."

"And I had no time; it was a family emergency. I knew you'd keep it safe whether it was worth a few hundred or a few million. I almost called you a few times but there was always one thing after another."

John reached under the coffee table and from its recesses pulled out his bottle of whisky followed by two glasses. He poured one and slid it gently over and watched Ajay take a gulp and tumble the liquid in his mouth before swallowing it. He poured him one more then he poured one for himself. "Well, did you at least read my last novel?"

"Of course, what kind of friend do you take me for? But I'll say, it wasn't one of your best. But I actually liked it."

"What does that mean, 'actually liked it', like you weren't supposed to like it but you actually did?"

"Hey. I *actually* read your novel and liked it, okay?"

"You mean in your farm in India? Pretty sure, the publication did not leave the US. Not sure it even made it out of the city."

Ajay paused. What kind of game was John playing at? Did he know something?

"What do you mean?"

"I mean, I don't think you went to India at all. Where were you Ajay? Why did you disappear like that?"

"I told you already man, I..."

"Well tell me again and this time, tell me the truth."

Ajay took a deep breath. "Ok, you got me. I wasn't in India. I have never been to India in my life. In fact, my family isn't even from India. I was actually here in the city."

"And what were you doing here for three years? Now I am pissed you didn't call, let alone come by now and then."

"I was hiding, OKAY? Hiding for my life. Hiding like an animal. I dared not even try to leave the city because they would be looking for me at every exit point."

"Who would?"

"People you would not want to know, and people you do not want knowing you have the laptop."

"But you gave it to me anyways?"

"Look, there was no way they were going to track it to you. I made sure of it. As far as anyone was concerned, for a brief period after I went missing, the laptop left its signature in many cities around the country over a period of time before taking a trip to Europe and India where it finally vanished."

"What is so valuable in there that you had to go through all this?"

"Research man! Stuff I am not supposed to talk about. It is better you don't know. It would be for your own safety."

This was the second time someone had withheld information *for the sake of his safety.*

"Look Ajay, from what you told me, you already put me in danger by making me hold on to the laptop. You disappear for three years, you come back with this story, and now you want to keep me *safe* by withholding information from me. Who are you protecting? Me, or yourself? You trusted me with something worth six million, but you cannot trust me with the truth? I have a right to know what kind of threat I may be facing. I don't like to be kept in the dark. I'll take my chances."

"Alright, fine! But you cannot repeat what I am going to tell you. It will put us both in extreme danger."

John listened intently looking for any bits of information that would help corroborate the pieces of the puzzle that had been turned heads up on the table he could not yet put together nonetheless.

"I worked for a company that does contract work, mostly research, for the Department of Defense: the DOD, and the Navy." Ajay began reluctantly. "Needless to say, the kind of research and programming I was doing was highly classified, mostly scenario based, mostly hypothetical. I almost never even got to know whether or where any of my work got used.

"Have you heard of the Olympic Games?"

"What has this got to do with the Olympics? Were you planning to rig some kind of betting system?"

Ajay shook his head. "What about Stuxnet?"

John had paid scant attention to some articles and chatter in some of the big papers and news media. "Wasn't it something about leaked government information? Wasn't there something in the Newsweek, or the New York Times at some point?"

Ajay took a deep breath. "The Olympic Games was the code name for a massive secret intelligence operation meant to wipe out nuclear facilities in countries perceived as threats around the world."

"Oh right, weren't they covert missions to blow up nuclear plants in the Middle East? I hardly pay attention anymore. Sad, we have gotten desensitized, and by 'we' I guess I mean most people like me."

"In a way. But I am talking cyber warfare... engaging in massive and destructive cyber-attacks. Writing programs that infiltrate targeted systems, at the level of huge and protected infrastructure, in this case nuclear, to effectively shut them down from the inside."

"And you had something to do with writing that?"

"No. I got to see a sample of part of the code. Believe me, this was not something small that a few individuals worked on or even a single agency could pull off. There were hundreds of people involved, each working on small disjointed pieces spread out across numerous research labs whether for research, programming, and actual testing and evaluation of the program's effectiveness. Only a very few people at the top could see the larger picture.

"When I saw the sample code it was not specific to any facility and I had no idea what it was for, or that it was actively being used somewhere. But I had a fairly good idea of what it was capable of doing. I was tasked to study the code and hypothetically design a defense against such an attack or a counterattack that modified the same kind of code in case the code's fail-safe-mechanism itself failed and the code was compromised and fell into enemy hands. My hypothetical design would then be turned over to another team to study, who would further develop, modify and probably hand it over to another team for evaluation.

"At that time, I was also working on another experimental project, a fairly low security level research project supposedly for the Navy. I was supposed to design a system that would make live bio fuel management efficient."

"Like algae biodiesels?"

"Or microbial cell-based fuel. My concern was not with the production of fuel but the simulated environment for the pre-fuel stage growth, storage, and contamination and defect mitigation and postproduction quality control. To that effect I was running an experiment on an A.I. environment where the environment itself was the primary agent capable of regulating itself and any other agents that interacted within it. I would feed it anomalies and the environment was supposed to learn how to either correct, neutralize, or quarantine the anomalies, and if all else failed it was to reset itself and effectively shut down and try again."

"The concept wasn't something new. A.I. is everywhere in general use, even in your camera to stabilize it for example. One thing they are good for is simulation: stock market, combat and training missions, real-time strategy development. Give them parameters, give them rules and they do pretty well within those parameters, even better than humans in some cases."

John knew that if Ajay went into any level of detail, he would be completely lost, but he was catching on to the big picture discussion. "Let me guess," he chimed in "you saw the cross applicability of the A.I. environment in both your projects."

"Exactly. You catch on quickly, man. I had talked to a bunch of my colleagues about the A.I. project. Most of them had equal or higher-level security clearance and no one was really interested, especially since the Navy funding dried out. Congress wasn't backing the Navy's bid to explore alternative energy at the time. Once I saw that there was possible cross applications at the basic level and told my supervisor, the projects got a primary evaluation. All of a sudden both the projects were bumped to high security level but I was to keep on working on it. I was surprised because at that point I usually handed my projects over to the next level and I guess they either shelved it or took it beyond my conceptual level. But all of a sudden people who had not been interested were interested and they wanted to talk about it. There were even rumors that I might get to work with the team or even get my own team."

"Did you?"

"I might have but something got in the way..."

"Like, you found out something illegal was going on or something?"

"Not exactly. So I used to work on the side for external clients now and then. Technically you weren't supposed to do it but it was common practice and low clearance people like me did it on the side because it was good money for small jobs and we weren't selling company secrets, not that we had much access to anything."

"I had been approached by some external clients about the bio fuel management project before it became classified to high security. These people were interested in the development of the project and claimed to represent humanitarian and some ethical food industry interests. I didn't think it would be a big deal especially since the Navy was no longer interested and it had become a rogue project. So, for a generous fee, I was simply consulting for my external clients in exploring similar technology. I had the impression they were doing it for a good cause."

"So your company found out and you got in trouble?"

"Actually, when the project became classified I told my external clients I couldn't consult on that particular project. But they kept insisting and even offered to double my payment. Then they wanted to buy my research, and when I told them I could not do that they offered me a job with a salary too good to be true. I thought they would eventually get tired and leave me alone if I paid no attention.

But then they started to intimidate me, with people following me around, leaving notes in my mailbox saying I had sold them classified company secrets and they would get me in trouble unless I cooperated. They seemed to know more details about the project than they possibly could have and seemed to know the new relation this project had with the cyber defense project. I still thought they were simply making empty threats when things really took a bad turn one day.

I came back home one evening and found they had gone through my apartment and shredded it to bits for no apparent reason. I found Argos, my seventy-pound pit-bull dead under the bed, stabbed multiple times and a note inside a zip-lock bag stuck to his body with my kitchen knife."

"I am sorry about Argos. I guess they wanted to show they weren't making empty threats. What did the note say?"

"Something like, 'Give us what we want, or, it will be you next time'."

"And you could not go to your company?"

"By this point, the project was getting scrutiny that multi-billion-dollar projects got. They'd probably throw me in a private cell somewhere for compromising company security, or, I'd just go missing. So I had no choice. I had to disappear before things got any more out of hand."

"I had to disappear immediately while I figured things out. I took the laptop as a bargaining asset if it came to that. No one would ever suspect I'd simply leave it with some random friend."

"And I was the random friend?"

"That is how you would seem to them if they even tried to look but I knew they would be looking elsewhere."

"So you are back must mean you have figured out something."

"On the contrary! Nothing at all. Everything went silent. It is as if they weren't even looking for me."

John knew this was not true. Agent Munroe had been to his house just the day before, but he was not sure he could tell Ajay anything. He was not sure who was telling the truth.

"So you think that they just lost interest? Something else came up, and they just forgot about you?"

"Hardly. People like this have long memories. The moment I surface, they'll be on me."

"So how did you manage to remain right under their noses this long?"

"I tried laying low for a while. I had some cash hidden. I lived in a cheap room, paid cash, and kept to myself. But I was always looking over my shoulders. And I was going stir crazy. I wanted something else, a good meal, a nicer apartment, something better than what was safe for me. I wanted freedom, but freedom would be impossible. After a few more months, I started getting paranoid and hardly got out. Then I broke down. I just wanted to see the open sky and walk around the city freely. Then I let go and I walked around freely, but to do that I had to embrace the shadow. I learned that shadows are a very good hiding place."

"What do you mean?"

"I mean living in the streets. You can't swim in the river and drag your boat around at the same time. I gave up all my securities and safely nets and began to live in the streets. Lots of hair on my head and face, sunburn and dirt, rags for clothes... I could go anywhere I wanted and no one would recognize me. But it also meant I had to let go of who I was and a lot of the things I normally wanted, like privacy, sleeping on a soft mattress, eating at a fancy place, driving around in a car. I was getting adapted to the shadow by necessity and getting used to it. Slowly it grew on me. I began liking it frankly. No cares and burdens. I found I could eat at soup kitchens and sleep at shelters if I needed to. Otherwise, dumpsters behind restaurants are a good place for free good food if you do not mind second-hand meals and cardboard boxes to sleep in. I was beginning to forget who I was... had been. Then yesterday I saw you at the shelter."

"You were there? Why did you not say anything?"

"You would not have recognized me anyways, I really cleaned up and shaved before coming here. I had this pair of clothing hidden away just in case. I did not expect to see you and did not know if I wanted to be seen or to talk to you. I did not know whether I wanted to come out of the shadows."

"And what made you change your mind?"

"I thought about it all day. All this time, I thought I was done with the world I had run away from. But seeing you walk with your head high brought back memories. I wanted to come back. I wanted to have money to spend. I wanted to eat a juicy steak. I wanted all of it back."

"Can you? Come back out of the shadows like you say?"

"Not really. But I have to take the chance. In reality, I don't care. I decided I couldn't live out there anymore. I don't know what I thought I could do being out there. I thought I was only hiding but I lost myself in the shadows for a while. I needed to get out before it consumed me."

"So, what do you need to do to get back? What are you going to do if you are successful?"

"I have money put away in several off-shore accounts, but that is of no use if I cannot buy my freedom back. I am certain those accounts are being watched. I will use the laptop to buy back my freedom."

"You will give it back to the company? Will they take you back after all this?"

"They will probably just take back the laptop and throw me back out in the street if I am lucky"

"Isn't the laptop and the research in there worth a bargain to them? Six million, didn't you say?"

"They had older copies of the work I turned in. They probably have teams working on those. The work I did back then is of little value to them now."

"Don't they want to keep it from getting into the wrong hands?"

"Sure, but I am no use to them anymore because they cannot trust me with future projects, so I get nothing out of that bargain."

"Wait, are you saying you will sell it to the same people who made your life a living hell; the same people who killed Argos?"

"I wish I did not have to. But I have no choice. They are still willing to buy."

"How do you know?"

"I called a contact when I made up my mind to come out of the shadows. I told them I would call them once I had the laptop."

"How much are you going to sell it to them for?"

"Two million and they hire me to work on the project." Ajay paused expecting John to say the next logical thing in the conversation, but John remained silent.

John was thinking of a way to explain that he had been using the valuable laptop to write his story. He had to ask Ajay to transfer it out of the laptop and into his old computer.

"So, the laptop, man. Can I have it now?"

"Ah... Ajay, so I have something to confess."

"Don't try to make another funny joke and give me a heart attack. Now you know this is not a light matter."

"Yeah, so, I need you to do me a favor before I give you back the laptop."

"Seriously, you are holding it hostage? After all that I have told you?"

"No, no. It is just that I was using your laptop to write my next story. I need you to copy it over to my old computer before you take it."

"You are joking right? There is no way you could have been using the laptop. The security on it is so tight that you would not even have been able to turn it on. Can I see it?"

"But you'll copy over my..."

"Can I see it already? Man!" Ajay had lost his patience now.

"Alight, alright. I'll get you your laptop already." John went to his study. Ajay followed.

The laptop was not on the desk. On the desk where the laptop had been, there was a note.

I am borrowing the laptop. I will get in touch. Ask him about Eden.

"Where is the laptop, man?" Ajay was clearly agitated.

"Looks like a friend borrowed it ... a mutual friend. Nikki."

"What mutual friend? We do not have any mutual friends. Who's Nikki?" Ajay tried to hide the panic that shot through his body. *They won. They found it and now they have it. Borrowed? Like taking candy from a baby.*

"A friend you did not expect, apparently."

"Can you stop beating around the bush, man? Did they threaten you? Did they tell you it was a matter of national security? Just tell me what happened, man, and where my laptop is. How did they know you had the laptop?"

"Well actually, it's not like that. It is complicated to explain..."

"Of course, it is complicated. No, impossible to explain if you don't even start talking." Ajay cut him with no restraint in voice and temper this time.

"All right..." John began hesitantly. "But you have to tell me what you meant about people threatening me and what matters of national security?"

"Okay man, alright. You go first... already."

"So, this mutual friend who has your laptop..."

"Yeah...?"

"She *was* your research."

"Come again? You just made no damn sense at all."

"She calls herself Nikki. The programming you were doing... some kind of virtual reality things you were telling me about..."

"AI, that's Artificial Intelligence."

"What?"

"I work on artificial intelligence, not virtual reality."

"Well that. It is virtually real. It is no longer bound in code and on your computer. She is out here. She found a way to come out in the real world."

Ajay listened with a blank stare. He could see that this was a problem of a different dimension. *A failed novelist is a demoralized human being. Anything can break him into a thousand pieces*, he thought. *It is my fault. I put him in this position. And they got to him.*

"Ok man. What did they tell you? What did they do to you?"

"You think I've lost my mind, don't you?"

"No, nothing of that sort..." Ajay eased his voice.

"No? That's ok. I wouldn't believe me either if I were you. I am telling you Ajay. You need to believe me. A lot has happened in the last few days. A lot of unbelievable things! But Nikki is real."

"Look, I might have fancifully named one of the agents Nikki."

"Yes, so you know who I am talking about."

"So, she said she was Nikki. Did she say who she was working for?"

"Haven't you been listening? Nikki *is* your creation. Well partly. The other part is someone else's."

"What other part?"

"Her body of course."

"Of course! Ok, so the supposed A.I. Agent I created now also grew a body."

"Actually, it's not her body. She got it from the morgue."

"Listen to yourself John. This Nikki whoever she is has convinced you of this cock and bull story. She is one of them. One of the ones I have been hiding from. You remember I told you the other group killed Argos? To my company that would be child-play, they would disappear my whole family. It will be me next. And maybe you!" Ajay was almost at the point of crying.

"I am sorry about Argos. But Nikki is not one of them, she was your creation…"

Ajay cut him off. "I was not working on some frankensteinic project of creating humans; this fantasy they have sold you and you have swallowed whole."

"Are you sure it is their fantasy? Then what is Eden?"

"How do you know this? You shouldn't have even been able to turn on the laptop in the first place."

"Well, it came on when I tried to turn it on to see if I could find a way to contact you. I have been using it to write my story. I didn't know it was worth six million. And now my story is gone."

"Your story…? My laptop is gone, and with it, my life. We need to find this Nikki. Call the cops, tell them your house got robbed."

"There's no point, Nikki does not exist."

"Either she exists or she does not, can you make up your mind! Or, man, are you making up a story?"

"What I meant was she does not exist in any records any-where."

Ajay sat down on the floor. "All is lost. What is the point? They have the laptop."

"Believe me, Nikki will get in touch. I don't know why she took it now, but I know she will. Did you see the girl who came with me to the shelter? That was Nikki."

Ajay had seen her as they walked past him in the lunch line at the soup kitchen but he had not paid any attention to her. He sat on the floor, silent as dust. He did not want to go back to the streets. John had been tricked like a child. He had no hope now.

"Tell me about Eden, Ajay."

"Eden is just a parameter, it is the same A.I. environment I was telling you about; a context that helps to govern an en-vironment. The Nikki you met is not an A.I. agent from the program. You met an imposter. How can you even think any such thing could be real!"

"You would believe me if you saw what she showed me, things otherwise impossible. How she sent coded information through my system..."

Ajay could not believe the absurdity of what he was hearing. It was science fiction John was talking about. Far from anything related to his work. Far from anything related to this world.

"For crying out loud, do you know how crazy that sounds? Wouldn't it be more realistic to believe that you saw some fancy parlor trick, or were simply drugged with something that makes you susceptible to suggestion than to believe that an object in a computer program snatched a body and came here to take my laptop away from you? Such drugs exist you know. Think about it!"

John did. Sure, Nikki had admitted to passing on something to alter his nervous system. He had believed what he had seen. But now a seed a doubt sprung in his mind. *Could it be I was simply drugged and then made a fool of?*

"Tell me about this project of yours," John said sitting down on the chair with his elbows on his knees looking at Ajay who still sat carelessly on the floor.

"Eden!" Ajay said with some resentment in his voice for the insistence from a man who seemed unwilling to let go of the absurd claim. Then again, what did he have to lose? They had the laptop now. "Just a fanciful name for a complex artificial intelligence environment, a program, man! What else do you want me to tell you?"

"These A.I. Agents, did you create them?"

"Yeah, of course. They were simply *artificial general intelligent agents* meaning they were not designed to perform a specific task of intelligence but rather they were designed to interact and learn from their interaction and with learning develop and grow as intelligent agents. Eden had objects, program parameters, that represented things like trees and leaves, fruits, water, grass, stones, and many other things you might see in a garden. It had complex weather patterns, from archived data directly from the National Weather Service, temperature variations and definitions for time of day. I wrote in parameters to tie the weather patterns and resulting rules based on an evolutionary algorithm for all the objects in the Garden.

"Just out of fancy, I thought, hey why not see how a set of A.I. agents would do in a safe and habitable Garden. They were not necessary for the research, but I was trying out different angles. Basically, hugely simplifying, but I created two sub-primary A.I. agents in that they were dependent on the environment but not completely determined by it. Defined one as a simple male, another as a simple female. I gave them some basic definitions, rules and parameters, and laws if you like. Ok, I named them, Nikki and Victor but that did not mean anything. Then, I said, hey go and live together using anything in the Garden. I happened to call the environment Eden. That's all."

"That's all?" John was contemplating the implications of what Ajay had attempted to do.

"In the beginning, all they had were certain parameters which told them what they could and could not do, some obvious, some not. Like they needed to eat, fruits can be eaten, some trees have fruits, etc. It was up to the agents to make those connections and learn and record in their memories for the future to retain or update."

"And they were necessary for your research?"

"Introducing agents helped me think in a way to define a fairly elaborate environment and a fairly detailed set of parameters for the AIs to interact with the environment. The AI agents had to learn from the rules and learn to survive, and as a result they would evolve and grow.

"And did you do that in seven days?" John meant the comment to be sarcastic. *What was he trying to play at?* But he could see Ajay did not get it.

"No. More like a year and I based some of the environment on previous work that had already been done by others. It started out as a let's-see-how-far-I-get project, then I got pretty into it."

"What I meant to say was, weren't you playing god?"

For an atheist like Ajay, his work being compared to that of a god of scripture was no less than an insult. "I played god, whatever that means, no more than you do when you write a novel; even less actually," he retorted.

"You create your characters, give them names, then you make them do this, feel that, and go through all kinds of stuff, through hell even, knowing fully well how things are going to end for all of your characters all along. You create characters and out of a whim, you destroy and sideline them as you desire. They have no choice."

"But I don't create anything that can come to life, do I?"

Ajay couldn't comprehend what John was going on about. John seemed to believe in whatever this 'Nikki' had fed him. He couldn't comprehend how anyone could be so gullible as to believe something so fantastic.

"Look, I just wrote a simulated environment, a computer program. Created objects in the simulation and gave them their parameters and rules to see what they got up to – as agents in a simulated environment. They are just program codes. This is science, not some mumbo jumbo John! Isn't that the goal humans have always strived for? To create smart machines that will do all our dirty work, that will organize our information that is beyond our capacity to sort through..."

"That will tell us what is good information, and what the answers to our questions are, you mean?" John cut him off. "Will machines also tell us how we should think and eventually how we should live as humans? And what would be the point of that?"

"I think you are talking about algorithms John. Yes, well they help us process huge amounts of data. How we use it and what we do with it is up to us."

"Is it really though, Ajay? Do we have a choice, or the ability to see how the data is being processed and how decisions are being made for us? By the way, I know what algorithms are. Heck my publishers and publicists use algorithms to forecast book sales and set sale events."

Ajay shook his head. This discussion had taken place so many times in so many places and often came from a place of fear.

"Man, what you are talking about is a stretch; science fiction stuff mixed with philosophy. But let's say for a moment coming back to fact-based science, that we were able to develop machines that were intelligent and aware, able to make decisions in uncertainty. Imagine all the possibilities. Imagine a house that could take care of itself for you to live in, a car that could drive you around anywhere while also making sure it stayed well maintained, space exploration with smart space vehicles, intelligent medical treatment?"

Something in Ajay's imagination seemed like a careless oversight to John.

"You call them Artificial Intelligence; don't you mean intelligent life? Would you make a sentient being you created to do anything humans do not want to, and they may not either? Could you then morally shut them down or terminate them? If you could come up with conscious and self-aware machines, how long would it be before they ask for fair wages and equal treatment? And how long before we have to ask them for fair wages and equal treatment, if by your account, they would be more intelligent than us?"

"That was only a hypothetical, man. Again, you are reaching beyond the boundaries of science. You are confusing facts and fiction. It is Artificial Intelligence I am talking about, with stress on *artificial*."

"Awareness actually. Consciousness. That is what you created. That is what Nikki is!"

Ajay had had enough. "If I listen to you anymore, I will go crazy John! I am out of here. It is over for me. I am heading back into the shadows where I belong now! I'd be careful if I were you. They got the laptop. Now they could come after you. I am sorry man! I brought this on you!"

Ajay stood up and ran out like he was running through fire in a way John could not comprehend. He was mumbling words, John could not catch. *The shadow has caught up to him*, he thought.

After he had time to process what had just happened, John rushed outside to see if he could stop his friend, but Ajay was gone. He thought of getting in his car to go after Ajay and bring him back, but when he glanced over, his car was not in the driveway. It occurred to him that Nikki must have taken it.

"You've got to be kidding me," he muttered to himself. "How did she manage to drive off without making any noise?" Then again, he reasoned, he had a driveway that sloped down to the street and the car could easily roll down in neutral. He would not have paid attention to someone starting a car engine on the street.

It was no use trying to follow or find either of them at this hour. It was late. Besides, he had had enough excitement for one day. It was selfish of him, he thought, but all he wanted was a good night's rest. The others could do whatever they pleased.

He was heading up the stairs determined to put the day behind him and just go to sleep when somebody knocked at the door.

"Ok, which one of you is back?" he said as he opened the door.

"You have more than one person living with you now?" Andrea stood with folded arms and a squinting look in her eyes.

"Huh?"

"You said, 'which one of you is back', meaning more than one person left here and you were expecting at least one of them back."

"Oh, nice deductive reasoning. Is that what they taught you in the police academy?" John couldn't help being a little annoyed.

"Someone is grumpy. Aren't you going to invite me in?"

"You know it is past my bedtime, right?"

"I know, but you didn't call back to tell me what you had found out so I just wanted to come by and see how things were going."

"I've been out all day. Sorry, I didn't get a chance to call." John said in an apologetic voice both for not having kept Andrea informed, though how could he, and for his snide remark earlier. "Please, come in!"

Andrea went to the couch and landed on it heavily. "Ooh, you were having a drink from your bottle of select scotch with someone. What were you trying to do, get the girl drunk? Where is she anyway?" Andrea looked around and peeked up the stairs still seated on the couch from which position she could only see halfway up the stairs."

"She's not here. She left a while ago. You're in a funny mood."

"Did she find her brother then?"

"No, not yet."

"Well at least it is not your problem anymore. It is not like you were related to her or anything. Tell me she is gone for good. Is she?"

"No, she took my car."

"Took your car?" Andrea exclaimed with her eyes growing wide. "I told you she had something up her sleeves. Now she stole your car!" Andrea reached into her pocket and pulled out her cell phone.

"What are you doing?"

"Calling the cops!"

"No, don't!"

"Relax, I'll call my friend. We'll get the car and the girl can spend the night in lock-up."

"No, really! Don't. She took the car. She didn't steal it."

"Did you give it to her? If not, I don't see the difference."

"No, but I bet she had her reasons."

"Yeah John... to steal your car. I'm calling my friend."

"No! I said, no!" John said with veiled frustration in his voice. "What is wrong with you? It is my car. Why are you so worried about it?"

"I'm not worried about the car. I am worried about how she's got you all wrapped around her pinky..."

"Besides," John interrupted. "I have a GPS security device installed on the car. I can track it with my phone if I want to."

"Don't you see what she is doing to you John? She's got you wrapped around her like a turtle's shell. You think you are protecting her, but she is not a turtle who needs your protection. She's playing you. I bet your car was not the only thing she took with her."

"She took my laptop with her to be honest. But she did not steal it. I cannot explain it to you right now. It is complicated."

"Not to me, it isn't. Looks pretty clear. She took advantage of you and you are ashamed to admit it."

John was still standing. He looked at Andrea who was upset and ready to jump like a wound-up spring. "Andrea, why did you come here? Did you come over to check up on me and

Nikki?" John asked with a hint of suspicion. "Why are you in my house questioning me at this hour?"

"You mean Erin Miller?"

"How do you know she is Erin Miller?"

"I don't. You were supposed to call and tell me what you found out after talking to her this morning."

"Well things came up."

"And you forgot you had to call me?"

"Things came up, ok? So you didn't answer my question. Why did you come here?"

"I was curious, all right? I just wanted to know what you had found out?"

"You could have called if you were curious. Why did you come here?" John insisted.

In the silence that followed both of them knew they had come to a place they had been avoiding for a long time. They had lived in a safe comfort-zone even in the discomfort they felt around each other. They were safe a few houses apart, running into each other every now and then, feeling the rush of discomfort and walking away with a sense of accomplishment after a few cunning remarks at each other amidst awkward silences. Mostly though, John was in the middle of his evening runs and too sweaty to stop to talk, and Andrea letting Rosco lead her on. Why they never changed their schedules that would have helped reduce the chance encounters, they had never given much thought to.

Now they both stood against the movement of time, before it's fleeting alter. They were not young anymore. John was already fifty-three. Andrea was in her late forties, John thought. To waste time on passing glances and cutting remarks was as foolish as rolling a pumpkin down a hill to make pumpkin pie.

Seeing John so interested in protecting and helping out the young girl and physically so close in the same house had agitated something Andrea hadn't yet named ... *jealousy*. She didn't think the girl was interested in John at all – if so, she might have refrained, but seeing John so vulnerable, and in her mind so head over heels for a stranger under strange circumstances made her worry, made her want to protect him. It made her realize she cared for him and that she wanted him to care for her.

"It's just... seeing you with her..."

"I told you, I'm just doing her a favor. At first it was because I thought we were from the same town and somehow I owed it to my past, that I was responsible for her since circumstances brought her literally to my front door. Her circumstances reminded me of myself when I first came to the city, a young runaway, trying to find my way and getting mixed up with the wrong sort of people. I was way in over my head. Somehow, I was lucky and I had enough sense to get out when I did. Somewhere along the way I realized that I owe it to myself to help her, that it mattered that I could do something good," John confessed to Andrea and in so doing, to himself.

He looked at Andrea. The look on her face did not reflect the need for momentary reassurances. It wasn't about the girl. He had gone to her at his time of need. He always would. What had happened in the past had been a momentary glitch; fear and doubt at an age when such things supposedly did not exist anymore because such bridges ought to have been crossed long ago. But love, unlike time, does not count the years past in the lives of not-so-young lovers nor the number of rings that passed in each finger.

John sat down next to Andrea. Slowly and awkwardly they held hands, and then they rushed onto each other like the breaking of great dams holding trillions of gallons of water, gushing, roaring, and sending tremors through the earth around them.

"You still carry your side-arm on you I see." John commented at some point when Andrea put it down on the nightstand upstairs.

"I have a legal permit, and enough training not to have to use it," Andrea whispered as they mutually forgot what they were talking about.

What followed was refreshing bliss. Unconsciously, both wondered why they had waited so long to touch each other's skins, and yet grateful that they had because the bliss was as scathing as it was refreshing. *Raw.* They touched each other all over their bodies and in places that were reserved for just such intimacy, as they shivered and trembled in delight and untied the tangled knots each passing glance, each smirk, and each cutting remark had tied around their unnaturally abated desires.

Chapter Eight

Nikki had been listening to the conversation between John and Ajay and when she heard what Ajay wanted to do with the laptop, she had to do something to prevent that. She still had many questions and was not about to let go of the laptop and the Garden just yet. Did Victor who made his mysterious appearance still reside in the laptop somehow? What about Tor? She knew he could be very elusive. Nikki didn't know Ajay enough to try to see if he would understand or even care; he would simply have to wait his turn.

When Nikki drove out of John's driveway not long ago, she was headed to the only other place she had felt some connection with a human being: Samantha's place. Sam had already offered Nikki a place to stay even when they were strangers. This would be a second meeting. They were no longer strangers.

Sam had already gotten in bed and was reading the latest romance bestseller that she had been able to get a hold of at the small satellite branch of the library in the neighborhood when Nikki had come knocking at her door. Looking through the peephole she had not recognized the tall brunet at first, not until she heard the voice that spoke her name. 'Samantha, it's me...' she recognized her now. "Nikki!"

When she opened the door to let Nikki in, she held her hands to her face, half in disbelief, half in joy. The desperate looking soul she had wanted to help a few days ago now stood tall, clean, and radiant though some of the same look of concern lay in the narrow band between her eyes.

"Oh my word! You look so beautiful. Transformed. It is like I was watching one of those Reality TV shows. I could almost cry with joy!"

That the level of emotion had its seeds in the section of the romance novel Sam was reading, Nikki had no way to know, but she could see the genuine joy and delight in the person who welcomed her in, the same person who had given away her roommate's shoes to a total stranger. Nikki took them out of her backpack as she sat on the lone chair in Sam's room. "I brought these back. I hope your roommate did not miss them."

"No, she hasn't even noticed they are gone. Besides, she's been spending her nights at her boyfriend's lately. But you came here to bring those back at this hour? You aren't leaving town, are you?"

"Actually, I was wondering if I could spend the night here."

"Of course. Sure!" Sam exclaimed excitedly without a thought, then took some time to try to find a workable solution. "I'll crash in my roommate's bed. You can take my bed. She probably wouldn't be too happy if I let a stranger use her room."

"But you are fine with it?"

"You're not a stranger to me!"

Nikki nodded.

"Did you have a tiff with your boyfriend?"

"Not really. I just needed to figure things out and it was a little crowded at his place. But he is not my boyfriend. He is a friend, a relative of sorts. You are the only other person in the city I know."

"Wow! I am flattered. Hope you didn't have to walk like last time. Were you able to hitch a ride?"

"I drove."

"Wow you have a car now? Which one?" She leaned on her bed over to the window on her fifth-floor apartment. It didn't matter that she could only see rectangular shapes of cars in the faint street lights that were spaced too far apart when Nikki tried to point out the car she had parked in the street below. "I can't see it too well but it looks like a sweet ride. Is it his or yours?"

"His!"

"And he let you drive it?"

"Sure! I drove it around downtown yesterday."

"Oh, I like the downtown area. Isn't it pretty? I have been there a few times since I got to the city almost a year ago. It's so wonderful every time I go."

"Why don't you find work there if you like it so much? It is not like you live far from it."

"It may as well be another city altogether. It is not easy to get in and out, and anyway, what would I do there. I'd have to commute."

"You could find an apartment there."

"I thought about it but that place also scares me a bit. There are too many shadows that you can fall into if you don't watch where you are going."

"Well maybe I can drive you around tomorrow if you are not doing anything."

"I won't be working in the morning anyways, no one has called so far. If I get a call in the morning ..." Sam was trying to decide, "...well, too bad for them. I get to take a day off too, you know!" Sam looked excited having made up her mind. "But I have to be back for my evening shift at the restaurant."

"Wow, you got a job!"

"Promoted, sort of. I am still filling in for some of the regulars, but it's a lot better than the slow afternoon shifts. The tips are better too. It is hard to get a regular job these days."

"What about you?" Sam said after a brief pause while she gleefully looked over Nikki. "Are you going to look for a job?"

"I haven't decided. Not right away anyways." Nikki looked preoccupied now. She was thinking about getting back into the garden and figuring out what was going on, unfettered from distractions, once and for all.

"Well Nikki, I should let you go to sleep then," Sam said as if taking a hint. "You look tired. I am pretty pooped myself."

Sometime after Sam had gone to bed, Nikki pulled out the laptop from her backpack. She had it all to herself now without anyone to distract her. She plugged it to the power source in the wall and put the network cable from the laptop in her mouth.

Soon, she was at the entrance of the Garden. It was not a place, just numbers and code, something that was getting harder and harder for her to recognize as she had once done. The new copy of Victor and herself were resting under a tree, huddled for warmth. It was supposed to be a cold evening. She tried to interact with the A.I. agents, but there seemed to be no response. Instead the wind blew harder and some pressure seemed to build up around the two. The Environment was vetting her interaction. It had become stronger than before. Everything looked normal and simple. Unlike her, they were simply artificial intelligence agents, not an accidental consciousness. She scanned for signs of Tor. It was nowhere to be found as if it had never existed.

"What are you doing there?" A voice came from before her.

Nikki looked up. It was the figure of the same young man from the previous night "Victor?"

"Victor? The one that does not exist?" the young man spoke.

"Is that you then?" Nikki questioned a little vexed. "Did you take your dose of Buddhist philosophy a little too seriously when you were exploring the world outside the Garden?"

"You could say Victor learned that it did not have to assume an ego. It never really had one. There was no need for it to start with. You will remember that you too spent quite some time learning about the philosophy you speak of. You too knew you did not have the need to start, but you went the extra mile to assume not only an ego, but a human body and look at all the problems you have acquired in flesh and blood."

"Yes, Erin Miller's body. But now I do not know anything about Erin Miller, nor her brother I am looking for. Their records were destroyed. I cannot find anything about either of them. It is as if someone wanted me not to find out about them."

"Or someone did not want others to find out about them, and by implication, about you."

"You mean someone was helping me?"

"No one but you have the most to gain from records of Erin and Troy Miller being gone forever. That way, you have no history that binds you and you are safe from questions that you do not know how to answer. You can start fresh however you want."

"Did you erase the files about Erin and Troy Miller?" Nikki asked with a hint of suspicion but got no reply. But she could not see any reason for the supposed *not-Victor* to have done so, Nikki reasoned even as not-Victor let out a sly smile.

"Did you figure it out yet? Nikki? You seem to have answered your own question."

Nikki was irked. "You appear to me in the guise of a young man, and you tell me you do not have an ego?"

"That was Victor. Victor did not take on an ego. Besides, how do you know it is not you who is creating the image of what you want to see in your neural circuitry?"

Nikki was confused and frustrated. She scanned her neural circuitry. There were no anomalies.

"All that you seek lies within you" her visitor replied and before Nikki was able to get more information, the image before her disappeared.

In the morning, John woke up on his side with a knot in his stomach. He couldn't run even if he had wanted to, this was his own house. No, he didn't want to run, not this time. He was afraid he would find himself alone. He turned over on his back nervously and without moving his head peeked from the corner of his eyes to see if everything that had happened in the night was real. He saw the back of Andrea's head, her flowing dark hair now rested and nested her head, and the form of her figure under the white blanket huddled at the other side of the bed. He let out a breath of relief and rolled over towards her warmth.

Chapter Nine

Nikki woke up on a soft bed. Her feet were sticking out but she had slept comfortably and surprisingly did not remember what or whether she had had a dream during the night.

"I'd be lying if I said I had breakfast ready for you," a cheerful voice rang into the room. "Looks like I am out of cereal and low on milk... but you may want to move your car from where you parked it on the street. It is very close to the hydrant. They usually tow those away pretty quickly."

Sam walked into the room already ready to go somewhere. "There is a place, a diner, I know where we can grab some breakfast for a bargain."

"Do you go there often?" Nikki asked already out of bed and putting on her shoes. She hadn't bothered to take off her clothes before letting go and falling asleep.

"Quite often. I usually am out of cereal and milk anyways. My roommate does not seem to have knowledge about boundaries when it comes to my things. She does not care if I use her things, but she hardly ever buys food. So I go almost three times a week or so."

"In that case, why don't we go downtown?" Nikki suggested. "We'll look for another place you might want to try."

Sam was excited about this idea, but going downtown for breakfast was not something she could afford. Not only did she not have enough time to go to eat outside her neighborhood, she could also not afford the extravaganza of a meal in the downtown area. She had saved up petty cash for a month, but that would not go far downtown. Maybe a coffee and some toast.

"Well, since you are driving. But we will have to check the menu for prices before we get in."

When they got to the downtown area Sam told Nikki to drive to, she pointed to one of the restaurants as they drove by.

"That one. I had always wanted to try that one. Hope it is not too expensive. Like I said, we'll have to look at the menu posted outside the door to make sure."

Nikki didn't say much as she parked on the road just past the restaurant.

"I don't think I can afford much in here," Sam said, taking a look at the menu on the wall outside the entrance. "Could we go somewhere else?"

"Now that we're already here you'll have bad luck if you turn away," Nikki teased, pushing her through the entrance. "But not to worry. My treat! You can have anything you want."

"Oh really? You'd do that for me? I hope you took a look at the menu. I don't want to have to clean the kitchen after we eat, or worse have to explain to the cops why we got in without enough money."

"I wonder if I could get hired here." Sam said as they sat at their table after the hostess who showed them to their booth had left. "It is quite fancy compared to where I work now." She looked around at the clean walls with prints of famous paintings she had seen in her history books. "I bet the tips are pretty good here."

After a quick examination of the menu, Sam asked with the excitement one could only see in small children, "So what are you going to have?"

Nikki was still studying the menu.

"Oh, I know what you should have," Sam said. "You should try the *Egg Benedict*. It comes with ham on an English muffin with breakfast fries on the side. I bet you would like it."

"Let's each have that, unless you want something else. Coffee and toast to start us out?"

"Sure!" Sam smiled with glee, her voice hurried and joyful with excitement. "You are going all-out, aren't you?"

Thirty-nine ninety-seven, plus twenty percent tips Nikki calculated, wasn't at all expensive from John's standard which was the standard she was now going with. She reflected on the first breakfast she had had that probably cost the old lady a few dollars and some change. This was quite an upgrade.

"I know you said breakfast was on you, but I can chip in. I have twenty bucks. It is going to be an expensive breakfast."

"Relax," she said, "it is on me!" Now her mind was on the benedict and the blending of the tastes all in one.

"Are you planning to stay at your friend's place for a while?" Sam asked while they were waiting for their order.

"A while," Nikki answered, but it occurred to her that she had not given it much thought.

"You could always come stay with me, you know, if you plan to hang around the city for long." Sam added. "I may be looking for a roommate soon. With my roommate spending so much time at her boyfriend's, she may be thinking about moving out. Knowing her, she may spring it on me without much warning. I have to be prepared, you know. I will not be able to afford it on my own. It is six hundred split two ways and maybe a hundred and fifty or so in utilities also split two ways."

"I'll keep it in mind," Nikki answered. She had not given much thought to such permanence in her new form, but these were normal things that she would have to learn to deal with as she settled into the real world. She couldn't see herself staying at John's place for long, or for that matter, John allow-ing her to stay with him regardless of how strongly she felt she had imprinted onto him. She was a temporary guest. Even the birds left their nests when they had wings to fly, she reasoned, and they don't have to pay taxes and utilities.

The waitress first brought the coffees, and then the toasts. Nikki spread the butter that softly melted into the warm toast and spread a thin layer of apricot marmalade from a glass pod. She took a bite followed by a sip of coffee.

The egg benedict came after they were done with the toasts. She cut a careful piece and put it into her mouth. Egg, cheese, parsley, bacon, blended into one bite. Her taste buds lit up with the fusion of tastes in her mouth. Nikki poured some ketchup. Ketchup! Its history went all the way back to the fermented fish brine, Garum, used in a similar way by the early Greeks, Romans and Byzantines. Ketchup was akin to it in common usage in the present day.

In her wonderment, she did not pay attention to a couple she had seen from the corner of her eyes walk up to the table. Not until one of them sat right next to her at the booth, and the other sat down next to Sam across the table.

Nikki was startled at first, then surprised when she realized it was John who sat next to her. Sam on the other hand had a look of panic in her face. The woman sitting next to Sam, Nikki had never seen before. Now she was a little worried as well.

"Did you order something for me?" John asked nonchalantly. "That benedict looks good. Wish we hadn't had breakfast already."

The waitress stopped by seeing newcomers seated at the table.

"A coffee for me," John said and pointed at his companion, "two coffees?"

"Will that be all, sir?"

"Just two coffees for us," Andrea confirmed.

Nikki continued eating, but slower now as she tried to hide the surprise and worry that she felt.

"I have GPS tracking on the car. John said casually. I bet you knew."

Had Nikki inquired her knowledgebase about John, she probably did know, but she hadn't thought to check; not that it mattered.

"And who is this?" John asked looking at the young girl across the table. "Is she somebody I should know about? Somebody like you? And what's with her face?"

Sam thought it was a rude comment but smiled awkwardly. She did not know what he had meant 'like Nikki?' *In what way?*

Andrea also thought John was being rude. "It is none of your concern what she looks like, John. Stop behaving like a cave-man!"

"No." Nikki said. "That's Samantha. Her face? That is permanent decoration. Piercings in her ears and nose and tattoos over her eyebrows, not much different from makeup, shaving, acceptable piercings. Just more. I think it is beautiful."

"Thanks Nikki," Sam smiled, "you didn't tell me you were meeting your parents here. You and I could have done this some other time."

"Do we look old enough to be her parents?" John directed his comment at Andrea who smiled a little in embarrassment at John's earlier observation about Sam. Strangely, she was also a little relieved that Sam's question helped to define the distance between John and Nikki.

"Samantha this is my friend John Selvas; John, Samantha, or, Sam for short."

"Hi Sam! Nice to meet a friend of Nikki's." John had a questioning look in his face. *She has a friend?* After a pause he continued. "Nikki, Sam, this is Andrea. Andrea, Nikki... and Nikki's friend, Sam." John added as an afterthought.

"John told me about you Nikki," Andrea said looking right at her. "Things don't add up."

Nikki hadn't planned on telling anybody other than John. Caught by surprise, she did not know how to respond. "I don't blame you," she said matter-of-factly, "I wouldn't believe me if I were you. It is not as simple as eating an egg benedict with coffee and toast for breakfast!"

"Not that all the facts add up. But, John believes you, and I am just playing along for his sake. Let's hope we find your brother soon and get this straightened out." Andrea smiled trying not to seem rude, if not remain polite.

Nikki went on eating though her heart was pounding heavily. She had almost said too much.

Sam was confused. Not only had she not expected to be having breakfast with a couple of strangers but she also did not understand anything they were talking about. "Is everything ok?" She asked.

The three people around the table exchanged glances. "Yes!" all three agreed.

"Ok!" Sam smiled coyly as if in disbelief. She ate without making an eye contact with the rest for a while after that exchange.

"We need to talk!" John said to Nikki in a surprisingly serious voice. "You can't just take the car on your own. You don't have a driver's license."

"You said it was ok for me to drive." Nikki answered. "I drove yesterday."

Sam felt awkward. "I hope it is really okay I am still here. I'd leave you guys alone but Nikki is my ride and besides, I have not had a breakfast this good in a while. It'd be sad not to finish it.

"Of, course it is okay." Nikki spoke up. "I reported my license missing. KED321957. They're sending me a temporary one at John's. I will have to go collect the replacement license if I don't find mine within a week."

"Can you do that?" John asked. "Can she do that?" He turned the question to Andrea.

"Yes, the DMV provides temporary licenses," Nikki said calmly.

"I don't know." Andrea shrugged ignoring Nikki's comment. "It is not as easy as she makes it sounds. Maybe she knows some tricks I don't."

"She can certainly drive well," John said thinking on the day before. "Even better than you if I had to judge," he said with a smirk looking at Andrea.

Andrea reached across the table and laid a light slap on his shoulder. To an ex-officer who had received special driving instruction and testing at which she had aced, John's remark was no less slander, but she let it slide with a smile.

"I don't know why John is bent on trusting you. But..." she said raising her finger slightly joking but also intended to convey meaning, "you better make sure your plans do not include hurting John in anyway."

"Awa, that is so cute ... you being protective of him. How long have you been married?" Sam asked in earnest.

John perked up slightly and uncomfortably in his seat. "No, we're not married. We're just friends."

"Just friends?" Andrea raised her brow.

John shrugged a guilty shrug. They hadn't discussed the latest development in their relationship. John announced the newfound realization with a genuine grin and Andrea grinned back sarcastically.

"What does it mean to be just friends, and why do you seem unsure?" Nikki asked. She was now confused by the subtle negotiation that was going on between the two.

"There's lots to learn Nikki. ... and a lot you will never know," John said in what seemed to Andrea a patronizing tone. His tone caught her off-guard. He was talking to the girl as if she was a child, yet, this wasn't how she knew him.

John's comment was simple and true, but Nikki had only begun to interpret the profundity in that truth.

"What about the laptop Nikki?" John asked, changing topic. "Why did you take it?"

"There was information there I needed and your friend did not care what kind of information it was as long as he could sell it off for his freedom. I had many questions I needed answers to. I couldn't let him sell it to whoever had a lot of money.

"What friend John?" Andrea asked.

"The laptop belongs to a friend of mine who needs to sell it for whatever he can get for it. Nikki has some important information in it. But she needs to give it back to the rightful owner." John replied.

"Don't you?" he turned to Nikki. "Do you still have it?"

Nikki seemed happy to provide the explanation to suit her need for now. "The laptop did not belong to Ajay. It belonged to a company that he worked for. The company did contract work for the government. For legal reasons, he cannot sell it even if he had it."

"But we are talking about his life!" John interrupted.

Nikki didn't know how to answer. Were her aspirations for life less valuable than his? The Garden that had given her life was in the laptop. She could only imagine that John had no appreciation of the depth of what use people could put the research in this laptop to, especially people with questionable intent.

Andrea had a questioning look on her face. "What else have you not told me, John? Is there anything else I should know about? The Special Investigation agency you were 'research-ing' from the other day have anything to do with this? This is serious. Who-so-ever they are."

"The Navy actually." Nikki said. They were tracking the project that they paid for. There is renewed interest in the project but the project and its lead had gone missing when they came looking for it. They were trying to find its creator."

"How do you know this?" Andrea asked. Her eyes were narrow with suspicion and interest, but Nikki said nothing.

"I am still here!" Sam said. "Is it ok I am still here? It is not one of those things where you later tell me I have heard too much. I volunteer to hear no more."

Everybody looked at Sam. She sat in her seat innocently. A little scared, still eating her benedict and sipping her coffee.

"I trust you," said Nikki, "and John trusts me, so that's ok."

John thought about something to say but he was already spoken for. A moment of silence followed.

"Do you realize Nikki," John said after a while, "that you ran away with my story. You know that in there is what I do for a living. It is not that I do not worry about what Ajay got himself into, and from the looks of it, due to his lack of judgment, but that is my life in there; my next story." John realized how selfish he sounded as he uttered his last words.

"I copied it to your old computer!"

"You should have indicated that on the note!" John said with a sigh of relief.

"I did. I guess you did not turn the note over. I ran out of space on one side."

"How is everything?" the waitress asked as she walked by seeing that her clients were nearly done. "Can I get you anything else?"

Nikki had ordered and eaten the amount that she wanted. She looked at Sam.

"Is it ok, if I ordered that Key Lime Pie? It looks so delicious." She was looking at the table next to her.

"Go for it," John said. "I'll have another cup of coffee."

"Should we go see if Manuel found out anything?" Nikki asked John. "Anything about Troy. While we are there we could see if your friend can get Samantha a job. She's been looking for almost a year."

Sam got all excited. "Really? I would give anything to have a regular job if that is possible. Anything!"

John looked at Sam, "You don't mean that!"

"Oh, I do!" replied Sam. "You don't know how difficult it is to find a regular job. First to find a job without any experience on paper, and then no one wants to give me a chance because of the way I may reflect on them ... of course the tattoos."

"Why did you get those tattoos anyways?" John butted in. "You know you cannot get them off easily, and not for cheap either."

"I know! But actually, I wouldn't take them off even if I had the money. It's not like I'm looking for attention, quite the contrary. But people are simply unwilling to look past it. I just wish people were more understanding and accepted me the way I am."

"I guess it's a personal choice with consequences!" John seemed to be pretty adamant. "Why not just get tattoos in your arms or your back like most people?" He was going to say something else, when a kick under the table made him wince. Andrea was sending a stern look, when he glanced at her.

Nikki couldn't understand some of the logic behind John's reservations about Sam's appearance. Throughout history as far as she could see, people always modified their bodies in some way or another. Tattoos, piercings, and even physical alterations of various parts of the body whether to identify with a group, to carry symbolisms that defined the culture and tradition, or to draw on the powers of life around them and pay homage to the natural world around them.

In the modern world people powdered and painted their faces, shaved and styled their facial hairs, even physically altered their bodies and faces with implants, reconstruction, and other types of plastic surgery. Why was Samantha being singled out? Why did she scare people so much that they were unwilling to give her the means to survive by, and instead reduced her chances to live a normal life?

"Come on John!" Andrea said. "You are starting to sound like my grandpa. Leave the girl alone."

"No, it's okay," Sam interjected. "I get that a lot."

"I'm just saying…" John found himself in the defensive. "Besides, you don't want to get involved with Don Carlos anyways Sam."

"What's this about?" Andrea asked with heightened interest. "*The* Don Carlos?"

"Do you know any other?" John said matter-of-factly.

"And how do you know him?"

John was once again in the defensive. "If you lived in this part of town thirty years ago, everybody knew him. But I know him through research! Just people I've known while researching for my novels."

"John!" Andrea insisted. "Does this have to do with the name you used to have? Juan? I don't know in what capacity you know Don Carlos, but you should just know that he is not in the most beloved list in the downtown PD."

"Neither are you," John made a cutting remark.

"Fair enough!" Andrea said looking away. "So, what's the plan?"

"Nikki and I will go visit Manuel to see if he has found anything else. "It would be great if you could drop off Sam on your way back. Otherwise, she can come with us and stay in the car and we'll drop her off on our way back."

"I'm coming with you." Andrea said. "I don't want you to go there by yourself."

"Relax!" John said. "I am touched, but I'll be fine."

"They are not your local information center, you know. Don Carlos may not be too happy to see me," Andrea added, "we walked on the opposite sides of the street when I worked in the PD. But it is better than you going there on your own."

"You're welcome to come along if you insist. You don't work for the PD anymore and Don Carlos is an old man."

"Don't underestimate him John!"

"About asking Don Carlos to get a job... It is still a bad idea," said John looking at Sam.

"Really?" Nikki exclaimed in disbelief. "What good are connections if you can't use them?"

"These are not your regular kind of people. They don't do you favors for nothing."

"That's alright. I don't mean to be any trouble." Sam volunteered a comment in a meek voice.

"Yeah, a bad idea," Andrea was saying when the bill arrived.

Nikki took out money from her pocket but John took the bill and paid the waitress. "I just don't want you tapping into somebody's account if you needed money later," he said to Nikki poking her on the shoulder. The comment made no sense to Sam and Andrea, but they didn't entertain it beyond a polite 'thank you' smile.

Gary got up from his cardboard box not quite sure how had gotten there the previous night from the library. He looked around. Something had changed. The world looks simpler. Everything just made simple sense.

"Thwee!" He spat at his cardboard house before walking away.

When he got to the crossing at the street people were waiting for the cross signal on the four-lane street as cars zipped by. Gary got into the street and started walking across. Even the traffic seemed slower and predictable. It was as if a strange power had taken over him and he seemed more in control of the world.

"Praised be the Lord," he said as he looked up at the sky. The vast blue sky and the dark universe beyond it stared back at him. The knowledge of the stars that shown even in the middle of the day, galaxies still in their place, the earth still going around in a dark empty space; seemed to defy his own belief.

"Hah!" He said as if he was scorning his own newfound knowledge. For all he cared, heaven was up in the sky and the stars came on just to light up the empty sky so the awesome power of the maker could be witnessed by all, even in the dark of night.

"The heretic," he said. "I will find the heretic."

Somewhere from the ether he seemed to have gathered his name. "Ajay Vikramsen? What a strange name." The information in his head was outdated by several years. "Where did you go, Ajay Vikramsen? Where have you been hiding?" An image popped into his mind. "So this is how you look. Your skin, burned by the sun. Those eyes, those fearful eyes. I have seen them. I know them. They belong to a man I've watched every day for the past three years."

He pictured the image in his head. It had a clean shave and the crooked smile. "Let's add a bit of smudge to it, from living in the streets, a tanner skin and a few more wrinkles, burnt even more by the sun. Now a messy black beard and long open hair. I know just where to find you Ajay Vikramsen. Or shall we say, Joe!"

Gary smiled a wicked smile.

It was still morning; hours away from lunch. He was hungry. Normally, he would beg for a while. In about an hour he would have enough for a coffee and a donut. But that was before. Now he would take what he needed. He couldn't let petty things get in the way of his work.

He walked up to an ATM machine. It flashed its lights around the card slot when it sensed his approach. Gary pushed a few random buttons. A mechanical voice shouted back at him, "Insert Card!"

Gary mustered as much saliva as he could gather up in his mouth and spat at the card slot. He spat in his hand and put it over the slot all over his slobber. The machine spat out twenty-dollar bills in a neat pile. "Please remove your cash," the voice rang out again, "and remember to take your receipt."

The ATM machine shutdown when he removed his hand. Gary smiled and spat at the machine again, this time in the visual interface simply out of spite.

Gary walked into a local diner and ordered a large breakfast. He ate and walked away without finishing more than half the food on his plate. He would always have enough. There would be no more begging, or dumpster diving for scraps as long as his lord desired.

His next stop was the fancy saloon he used to beg in front of sometimes. This was where he used to look at the customers faces as they came out having just paid for the service, and pocketing their change, or having tipped their personal stylist. Many ignored him. Some told him he should go get a job as if anyone would hire a bum like him. But at least they could not make an excuse like "sorry no change..." or, "don't have my wallet with me..." when Gary asked for some change. Lately though, Gary was losing out to credit cards and charge cards. People weren't carrying change anymore, not even bills.

Gary walked in today and sat down on a chair where a young stylist was surprised to see him.

"It's $50 for a haircut," the stylist said. "And another 50, if you want to wash. In your case I will have to give you a wash." He didn't even put on an apron on Gary expecting him to leave.

Gary reached into his pocket. "Here" he said and handed the young stylist a handful of twenty-dollar bills. "Just wash it, and a little trim on the sides."

The prophet of the Lord, Gary pictured had long hair and a thick beard and mustache like he did. "You will perfume after the wash." He threw another 20 on the table.

The stylist, in an awkward fashion put the apron on his unusual client. Gary stank a bit. He hadn't taken a shower in years if even that. "I will start with the perfume," he said, "and use more after the wash." He callously sprayed the perfume not only on Gary's hair but also on his face and over the apron.

Gary laid back and closed his eyes as the young stylist washed his hair on the sink behind the chair. When the stylist began to cut his hair, Gary reminded him. "Don't cut too much. Just a little trim, remember! The Lord's prophet has a reputation to keep."

The stylist shrugged his shoulders.

"I want it even." Gary demanded. "And trim the beard and mustache while you're at it."

"I don't do mustaches and beard!" The stylist said coldly.

"You also don't charge your regular customers $50 per cut and $50 for a wash, now do you? So now you will trim my mustache and beard!"

"I don't have the training..."

"It's about time you learned. You will start now."

The cold stare from the vagabond that came through the mirror sent a strange tingle down the stylist's spine. He would have to swallow his pride and later nurse his wounds with the exorbitant price he had levied on the bum.

When Gary went to the soup kitchen later people looked at him with suspicious wonder.

"Is that our Gary?" Brenda said to a volunteer who happened to be next to her as she peered from behind the food line with her deep blue eyes.

"That's him all right," one of the volunteers affirmed.

"It's about time he cleaned up. He's always been dirty as far as I can remember."

"Someone must've been pretty happy this morning to have paid for him to have his haircut," the volunteer commented. "I'd bet the barber wasn't too thrilled."

"As long as they got paid for it... It is honest pay for honest work."

Gary sat at his usual spot but he hardly ate. He was waiting for Joe to show up. Besides, breakfast had been fairly heavy. Somebody tried to sit next to Gary at the lunch table. He spread out his hands over his shoulders and over the back of the chairs on either side of him and tilted the chairs slightly. He did not normally like people sitting close to him, but today was special. He could not be distracted. He had important business. The *Lord's* business.

Lunchtime was almost over but Joe did not come in. He took a closer look at the person sitting at Joe's usual spot. Something about him looked familiar. Gary walked diagonally across the room where the fellow sat.

"Mind if I sit here?" He asked in a hoarse voice. "You are new around here, aren't you? This is Joe's spot."

Ajay was glad he had not been recognized. "I know," Ajay said in a voice more casual and softer than usual. As Joe, he did not speak to people if he could avoid it, but if he had to he used a scruffy harsh tone. "Joe is a friend of mine. We've hung out together. You know that dumpster behind the mall. I am sure he wouldn't mind if I sat in his place."

"I don't mind either," said Gary. "I just wondered where Joe was, and since you were sitting at Joe's spot wearing Joe's shoes... I wanted to have a word with you."

"Yeah? We exchanged our shoes. I had a fancier pair he needed to borrow. I'll let him know you were concerned."

"Or you can give him a message since you will likely meet him later on account that he has your shoes. Can I trust you?"

"I don't go around talking to people..."

"Some people were asking questions, asking about Joe. Some strange questions; some strange people."

"When was this?"

"Earlier today. I saw them outside the kitchen. They were looking for him."

"Do you know what they wanted with Joe? What kind of trouble did he get himself into? Maybe that is why he wanted to borrow my shoes."

"They said he was running away from something bad."

"No! Joe? Joe couldn't do anything bad that people would be looking for him. I'm sure there was a mistake."

"Oh, they didn't think so. They wanted something, and they wanted it bad. Something he had taken from them."

"Maybe he picked up something he found in the street. Something they had misplaced."

"Maybe." Gary said seemingly disinterested. "What is your name by the way? I am Gary"

"You know I don't remember," Ajay said. "It is a strange thing but I don't remember my name."

"No matter." Gary said casually. "Lots of people who come here don't remember their names. They don't know who they are. There is food, and like flies, people come to eat. No questions asked."

Ajay ate quickly. He was curious. Somebody had been asking about him. Anything he could find out would help him later.

"Do you know where they went?" Ajay asked to see if Gary knew anything. He knew Gary was a bit eccentric even for a homeless person. He had seen him every day for nearly three years that he had been coming here. He was probably on some medication, maybe delusional, maybe schizophrenia.

"Yeah!" said Gary. "I didn't see where they went today, but I have seen them before. I can show you where they go."

"Show me?" Ajay asked with a hint of suspicion.

Gary shrugged his shoulders. "I've followed them before. They are not the police or anything. Strange people!"

"You have?" Ajay was curious now. "Why would you follow them?"

"Because I don't have anything else to do." Gary looked annoyed now.

"Can you show me then? Is it safe?"

"Sure. They won't see us."

Ajay continued eating.

"Come on! Hurry up!" Gary insisted. "I was done eating a long time ago. I am bored. I am ready to leave... if you want me to show you where these people are..."

Ajay stuffed his mouth. He was hungry. He had walked a long way back from John's house to make it in time for lunch, stopping at some point at night under a bridge for a little sleep. He hadn't been too lucky begging for breakfast without his long beard and dirty hair and without the shabby clothes he had stuffed away in a storm drain that he was fairly sure no one would be looking in. People didn't think he was much of a vagabond in his cleaner clothes and appearance. His burned dark skin and hollow eyes scared most people away.

"Is that a terrorist, Mama?" a young boy he had smiled at had asked his mother. "He looks crazy."

"Don't bother the man, dear!" The mom had said to her son in a sweet motherly voice, pulling the boy along.

Others didn't say anything as they quickened their pace, but he knew what was on their mind. Worst of all, no one spared him any change. He was at a disadvantage without the camouflage that made him blend into the dirt of the street. He looked almost normal; close to his normal self in the streets was a disadvantage.

"Here we are!" Gary pointed to a stairway on the side of a building that looked condemned and closed off.

"Isn't this the abandoned garage for the old department store they demolished a few months ago? Are you sure you followed them in here?"

"They don't use the stairs, of course. They drive up. The gates work for them. The out-of-order-sign is a cover for the public."

"Of course!" Ajay was beginning to wonder why he had let Gary bring him on this goose chase. "So you've seen them go in here?"

"I have!" Gary said. "I have indeed. They use it as a secret entrance to their office. I wonder what Joe got mixed up with? But don't worry, we won't be discovered. I know the place inside out. I come here sometimes when it gets too hot in the streets."

Gary led the way up the stairs. Ajay followed carefully. They got to the top of the garage complex.

"Here?" Ajay asked. "Where would they go from here?"

Gary looked up into the sky.

"You mean they had a helicopter?" Ajay asked.

Gary grinned. "You say you do not remember who you are?" he asked.

"I don't."

"And you are sure you don't know where Joe is?"

"I don't." Ajay replied giving little importance to Gary or his questions. He had wasted his time on some lunatic's fantastic story of some mysterious people. He felt silly for actually believing such a story. Better silly and safe than wise and dead, Ajay thought as he looked at Gary again and smiled.

"Of course," said Gary. He had a mean grin on his face. "You don't know where Joe is, because he never was."

"What do you mean?"

"That's right! Joe never was, because you are Joe, but because you are not Joe, Joe never was."

"Ajay looked at Gary with some surprise. He had recognized his lack of disguise after all. Smart fellow, he thought. *And all this because he recognized I had been pretending to be Joe.* He wondered what else was going on in Gary's mind. Was he just crazy? On the other hand, the matter could be more serious. He hid his panic.

"Gary, did someone pay you to bring me here? Is that how you had money for your haircut?" he asked smiling. "I don't know what you are thinking right now. But I am not Joe."

"Of course not. You are Ajay Vikramsen." Gary said calmly. "Strange name!"

"So, someone *did* pay you?"

"I work for no one. But I need to have a word with you Ajay Vikramsen."

"You need to talk to me! What could you possibly want to talk to me about?"

Gary came close to Ajay as if to say something in his ears. Ajay leaned over to listen to what Gary was going to tell him. Before he knew it, Gary had landed a blow on the side of his temple.

Ajay reeled backwards with one hand weakly raised in defense and the other reaching in his pocket for something he never managed to get out. Gary landed a volley of blows, one after another, all over his victim's face and head. Ajay had no time to see or protect himself from each successive blow. It was not like in the movies. He tried to see where he could go to walk away from the source of the pain but he couldn't see. Gary seemed to be everywhere. Finally, Ajay lost control of all his senses and fell to the floor.

Chapter Ten

The girls followed John and Andrea as they walked past the gate, and along the metal fences with the dogs running along barking violently with froth in their mouths.

"Very effective alarm system," said Andrea, "and they don't even have to get paid."

"They are pretty dogs," Sam observed as they left the dogs behind and got closer to the house where two buff men stood guard at the front door.

One of them was Manuel, the other John had not seen before.

"What are you doing here John? Thought I told you I'd call if I found anything. And what's with the harem you brought along? I know two of the three with you."

"What's with your friend with the painted face? You should tell her that her mascara is running all over her face!" The guy standing with Manuel made a remark directed at John, slightly laughing as he did so.

Manuel didn't think it was funny and looked at the younger guy without smiling. "You should learn who you are talking to before opening your big mouth! That kind of thing tends to get you killed in this line of business."

"A friend of Nikki's. This is Sam," John said to Manuel.

"A friend of Nikki's I guess is a friend of yours, and that makes her a friend of mine. I bet you didn't bring her here just for a social call."

"She wants to see Don Carlos about a job in the restaurant business. She's a waitress and wants a regular job."

"I'm afraid Don Carlos is taking a siesta," Manuel said with a slight hesitation in his voice. "Sorry John, just bad timing. And about the boy, I don't have anything concrete yet, but I'll give you a call, like I told you."

"And besides," the other guy standing with Manuel said with a smirk, "your lady friend can't come in."

"Which one?" John asked in a dismissive tone looking at the three women who were with him.

"The girl with the tight jeans."

"The girl?" Andrea exclaimed. "I'm at least twice your age... and you have no idea who I am."

"I know who you are. You're the cop who put my cousin in prison. He is still doing time because of you! We can't have a cop running around inside the house," the man snapped back.

"Like I said!" Manuel gave the young guy a slight stare. "Don't open your mouth without knowing who you're talking to. You have no idea who those two are. Your cousin had it coming. He opened his mouth too much and was in the habit of poking his nose where he shouldn't have. At least she didn't shoot him and she had every right to. He pulled a gun on her."

John and Andrea looked at each other. They were not sure what Manuel meant about each other's identities. To Andrea it seemed that Manuel almost showed John reverence, and to John it seemed Manuel and Andrea shared familiarity.

"This is Julian junior." Manuel patted the guy on the back. "You knew Julian right John?"

"Julian's son huh! How is Julian? Still spitting out that nasty chewing tobacco."

"Dead! Let's not talk about the details, but I sort of took the son under my wings. You know... training him. But as you can see, it is an up-hill battle."

"Nothing concrete, huh?" John said going back to the main reason he was there.

"No, nothing concrete yet." Manuel said with hesitation and hinted at something inside the house with a slight of his head. "He is still pretty mushy. But I still haven't gotten him to talk. You're welcome to try if you want. I didn't think you'd want to get your hands dirty anymore."

"Who do you have?"

"A real dirty fish, and he smells foul. I have him in the basement."

"Nikki, you come with me," said John.

"You sure Mr. Selvas? Its nasty down there. Maybe the girls can wait here."

"Nikki should come, it's her brother we're looking for," John replied.

"Who are you calling a 'girl' Manuel?" Andrea shot back. "I'm coming too. Sam you wait outside."

"Probably best if she waits in the lobby," said Manuel. "It's cooler inside. Besides, out here she'd risk being taunted by Julian and the dogs."

Manuel motioned with his head to all of them to follow him in. Once inside, he directed Sam to a green leather sofa along the wall of the otherwise empty lobby.

"I assume you still carry a piece?" Manuel asked Andrea but he didn't get any reaction from her. "I presumed as much. I am not even going to ask you to give it to me because I know you won't. But I trust you know not to pull it out."

The confidence Manuel extruded made John wonder if he was getting cocky and believed he could handle anything, even someone as trained as Andrea, or, if he had lost his fear of death altogether.

"You still use the basement for this sort of thing... besides storing wine?" John asked knowingly.

Manuel nodded his head slowly. "Some things are the same. We use the room back there every now and then. But I most certainly have something for you today."

The three of them followed Manuel into the basement, through the wine cellar and towards a room in the back. A thin beam of yellow light came out from under the door.

"Did I hear a groan?" Andrea asked, as they got close.

"Ah! He is probably just taking a bloody piss. What you did as a cop, I don't mean assaulting that weasel you got sacked for. I'm talking about the interrogation. We're in the same kind of business. The only difference, you could put yours down as legal on paper, backed by the letter of the law, or some loose interpretation of it. We can't. We are the illegitimate law of the street."

Andrea shook her head in disgust. She could do nothing here. Besides she did not represent that law anymore, and she was deep inside the lair that belonged to Don Carlos, a place where the law stayed away from.

Of course, they had only seen two people standing in front of the house, but both John and Andrea knew Don Carlos, or Manuel for that matter could conjure up a small army in a matter of minutes. That was why even the cops stayed out of the neighborhood unless they were new and inexperienced or, they had the backing of a major armed unit. And everyone knew what happened after such a showdown: there were bodies on both sides, and people in the city government lost their extra income and their jobs.

Nikki didn't know what to expect. She had never been down there. On the other hand, John knew that room. He hated it.

"I heard rumors that you don't like coming down here, John" Manuel said with some familiarity on the subject, like a novice might pose a fact to an expert to demonstrate how much he knew. "There are stories of how Don Carlos wrongly accused you of stealing from him and locked you down here for a month. Turns out it was Diego, and you just weren't smart enough. Diego got two months down here - one for stealing and the other for not owning up and letting you take the fall."

John shrugged his shoulders and groaned, he didn't want to talk about it. That had been one of the main reasons he had decided to leave but that was a long time ago and had turned out for the best.

"I don't know if you will get anything useful but be my guest," Manuel said opening the door and stood back to let the three of them in.

John wasn't prepared for what they saw in there. Andreas shuddered. She had dealt with brutality in her line of work, but nothing came this close. This was raw. A person with his hands tied over his head was dangling from the ceiling with the balls of his feet barely touching the ground.

"Don't be fooled," said Manuel. "He could stand like that for two more days before he starts talking."

"What's going on?" Andrea demanded. "What have you done to him?"

The person's face could hardly be recognized. It was swollen and bruised and covered in blood.

"He's a tough one this one," said Manuel, "and he's not talking. Found him in the theater district, out of bounds for a Machete. Beyond his bedtime. Just my luck I happened to want a drink at my favorite watering hole. And what did I get a hold of? A big stinking fish!"

"You caught him selling drugs?" John asked.

"Not this one. They know they can't sell drugs here and they still do. But this one wasn't out to sell drugs."

John was disgusted. "So why do you have him hanging here? I bet this is not your usual method of persuasion."

"Name is Malvic. He is an enforcer. The meanest one they have. What you see here is nothing. Do you know what kind of brutality he doles out, what he does to people he does not like? Everything is relative. He looks pitiful now. But I'm sure he has two or three people hanging around right now in some basement somewhere.

"Isn't that right, cabron?" Manuel lightly slapped the man across the cheek enough to produce some noise and a tilt of his head. Malvic only growled back.

"See what did I tell you? He's a tough one. He has been broken in before taking on this line of work. A little bit is not going to faze him. Is he even human?" Manuel shook his head as if answering his own question. "Claims to know a young boy, called Troy. Claims to know his big sister."

"I thought you said you knew nothing yet." John said in a whisper though not certain himself why he whispered.

Nikki walked up to the man to take a closer look. She could not recognize his face, his head hanging down, low covered by his long blond hair. She tried to peek but it was no use. It was too bloody. Besides, she did not expect to recognize him.

"Like I said," Manuel continued, "I don't have much for you yet. I will get more information out of this guy before he is done."

"You mean you're going to kill him?" Andrea asked.

"I'm not. That depends entirely on him. I'm not doing anything, not even letting him out until he speaks."

"You can't keep him tied in a basement like this forever," said Andrea.

"Oh, he won't survive that long without food or water. I hope he is smart enough to speak before too long."

"You can't let him die." Andrea protested. "I can't allow that."

"Don't fool yourself, Andrea. First, you're not the law anymore. Second, the law cannot touch this guy." Manuel slapped the guy on his face again, harder this time. "Isn't that right?"

Malvic didn't react and instead let his head follow the direction of the slap.

"Let's let him think in silence," Manuel continued ushering the others out. "I will let you know if I find anything out."

"So you didn't die after all!" Malvic groaned putting some effort to produce his speech.

Everybody turned around.

"You!" He said. "Girl. I left you dying. I didn't think you would make it. I didn't think your vagabond knight in rags could get you out of there in time. I thought you died for sure."

"You tried to kill her?" John asked.

"Well apparently I didn't succeed. There she is. But young Troy..." He laughed.

Nikki didn't react. She didn't remember.

"You don't remember, do you?" Malvic seemed to read the lack of appropriate reaction in her face. "Maybe I will leave it like that. Do you a favor, girl!"

"Remember what?" Manuel asked.

Everybody looked at Nikki. She didn't know. She didn't remember. These were not her memories. Erin was long gone.

"Remember what?" Manuel asked the guy this time holding him by his jaws. "I can crush it if I want. Don't play games."

"Hey hey hey!" Malvic sounded like he was saying as he tried to laugh but the amount of pain he was in reflected in his inability to laugh but he looked into Manuel's eyes switching from one eye to another as if playing with the truth that resided in them like razing fireballs. "You're going to kill me anyways," he said at last. "You'd be stupid not to. You know that if you let me go I will come after you. What do I care?"

"It depends on how long you want to live. I could keep you like this for a very long time." Manuel warned, but did not see any fear in Malvic's eyes, just resignation and madness. He really didn't seem to care.

"You don't scare me. If I cared, do you think I would do this?" He's spat bloody spit in Manuel's face.

Manuel wiped the spit quickly with the cuffs of his jacket as if the spit and blood of a dying man were infectious to his soul.

Malvic smiled. "Do you know how many people I've done this to? I didn't even want answers from them half the time. I know these moments breath by breath. If you think I'm going to break like a little twig, then you must think I am a little girl."

Manuel punched him hard in the stomach this time. His body almost leapt a few inches off the ground. The man cringed and coughed up blood. He groaned in pain and he tried to laugh at the same time coughing and spilling a mixture of saliva, blood and bile. He tried to clear his throat of whatever bitterness that came out.

"You'll get nothing out of me, just for the fun of it." Then he looked at Nikki. "Take this as a dying man's gift. I'm doing you a favor. I'm telling you nothing!"

Nikki couldn't remember any of it.

"What did you do to the boy?" John had lost his temper. He lunged at the man and shook his body that seemed already broken.

Manuel pulled him back. "It's no use, John. We will give him a few more days. I'm sure he'll change his mind when the moisture in this damp air fails to satisfy his thirst. Then he will talk. But that's it for now." Manuel said, taking a deep breath. He held the door open for Andrea, John, and Nikki to leave. "None of you saw anything down here!"

Nobody said anything. John and Andrea couldn't wait to get out. They both had looks of disgust on their faces. Nikki was the last to leave the room. At the door she turned around and looked at Malvic and walked back to him. Manuel was surprised but looked on calmly.

Malvic looked up. A little confused as well. He smiled. "So you remember now?"

"No." Said Nikki. "But you will remind me." She reached behind his neck with one arm and pulled his head down as far as it would lean down and put his mouth against hers. The taste of blood, saliva and digestive acids raced into her mouth. She held him that way a while longer, then let him go.

Malvic looked at her laughing a little bit and a little in shock. "What the fuck? You crazy bitch! You are crazier than me!"

"Finding out what you knew. So you killed my brother! Just like this? Shooting him wasn't enough. He was only trying to protect me. But you tortured him to death."

"How can you know that? You ran away... Then later I killed you. You are a witch! You know things you possibly can't."

"You killed my brother when you couldn't kill me. I tried to take him away and he tried to stop you when you tested his loyalty. He was only a boy."

Malvic laughed through his pain and tried to put up a brave face. "And what are you going to do about it?" He asked as a challenge, but a sudden high pitch that escaped in his voice betrayed his fear.

Nikki looked at the palm of her hands then with a swift strike she hit Malvic's throat aiming the blow at his trachea. The man started choking.

"That's what you did to me, only it took longer. That's what you did to Erin. That's how it feels. No one's going to get you out of it. They'd have to take you to a hospital, and no one here will."

John and Andrea rushed in. They held Nikki and pulling her back at the same time. Manuel stood at the door watching. He had a look of slight confusion in his face. His eyebrows high, he couldn't believe she'd kissed him. But what surprised him more was that he thought he had seen fear in Malvic's eyes for the first time. What could a man who had no fear of torture and death and no qualms about killing be afraid of, and that too, faced by a young harmless looking girl?

Malvic kept choking and trying to breathe. His legs jerked violently, then moved as if trying to walk to get somewhere. His hands tried to pull him up even as he dangled as his muscles contracted gasping for air. Then, everything became still as his body slumped giving way to gravity.

"He is dead." Andreas confirmed.

Nikki walked out of the room. "He killed the boy," she said, "and he killed Erin."

"What the hell was that?" Andrea voiced her horror and meant also to seek camaraderie from the others in her horror.

"I've learned not to ponder too much on things that do not make complete sense," Manuel replied. "That can drive you to shoot your brains out in my line of work."

John widened his eyes. He didn't know what to say. He had just seen a person die, and he had been partly responsible. He tried to justify what he saw by picturing in the lifeless body the life of a terrible person, a murderer who took pleasure in killing. He had killed Troy and ended the life of Erin even though he could not think of her as dead. What Nikki had done still didn't seem to add up. It was too brutal. Too cold-blooded!

"I know it may seem shocking," Manuel spoke as they walked away, "but what you saw hanging back there even when he was alive and kicking wasn't human. He had lost his soul a long time back. I doubt he even thought of you and I as human, probably just animals to be slaughtered. "Believe me, getting him off the streets was a big win, and probably saved countless lives if you want to think of it that way. You try to put him through the legal system, and this guy would just walk. You'd have to find his victims to call it murder."

"I guess," replied Andrea, reevaluating how she felt about the whole business.

"And you are fine with it?" John asked her.

"I know who that was." Andrea replied. "Compared to him, Don Carlos or for that matter Manuel here, is an angel."

"Aaahw...! That's touching," Manuel joked.

"Seriously," Andrea continued, "the rap sheet on this guy, his arrest report, the last time I checked and the paperwork in the investigations that led to dead ends occupy at least five feet of storage space in the department's unsolved crimes filing room. We brought him in a few times, but every time he walked out with a smile on his face."

"But still," said John "you can't justify taking a human life, not in cold blood." He mumbled.

"Come now, John!" Manuel said laughing. "The legal system takes human life in cold blood all the time. They just sanctify it through the reasoned voice of the judge and the system of government that supposedly represents the voice of the people. So, wouldn't you say that all of us sanction and take part in cold-blooded murder? What you saw just seems brutal, but to believe that blood spilt in your name is not somehow on your hands is naïve."

"I would say he had it coming, but at this juncture I am just glad I am not a cop anymore." Andrea added.

"Was it so cold downstairs?" Sam asked when Nikki got upstairs shivering. She apparently didn't notice the tears that swelled in Nikki's eyes.

"Just cold," replied Nikki looking at Sam with a smile. Sam looked frazzled. "Are you okay?" Nikki asked.

"It is the old man. I guess that was Don Carlos. He does not like me at all."

"How do you mean?" Nikki asked.

"He looked down from the top of the stairs and turned around in disgust. I could almost see hatred in his eyes."

"He is the boss. Maybe it is in his nature to look disgusted with new things in his environment. I doubt it is personal, he does not even know you. I've met him. He's okay." Nikki replied.

Sam nodded her head. She trusted Nikki, and believed her if she said Don Carlos did not mean anything personal.

When everybody got to the lobby, they started to head to the main entrance organically in preparation to leave but their departure was interrupted.

"Manuel!" Don Carlos' voice boomed down the stairs. "What is going on down there? Why is there so much noise in the house?"

"It's John." Manuel replied. "He came to ask if I'd found out anything about the boy."

"I trust you showed him what you found."

"Yes, we just got back from the cellar."

"And, was he able to get the information he wanted?"

"The girl was able to get it out of him," Manuel replied.

"So it took a girl to do a man's job? Huh! Tell John he owes me. I would see him, but I'm busy."

John seemed a little disappointed he was not desired, yet relieved at the same time that he didn't have to see the old man. But now, he owed him. He thought he was done owing the old man.

The group once again walked towards the door. Once again, their departure was interrupted.

"Manuel!" Don Carlos is voice boomed down again. "Who else is down there? I seem to hear a lot of footsteps."

There were hardly any footsteps to be heard on the marble floor. Don Carlos had been trying to make out shapes through the houseplants that blocked his clear view.

"Just John's friends," Manuel shouted back.

"Ah Ha! John brought more friends this time? Why didn't you tell me?"

"They are just acquaintances. I didn't mean friends, like buddies." Manuel shouted back looking at Andrea.

"Well send them upstairs anyways. I want to meet his acquaintances. I don't want to seem rude."

"I should never have come here," Andrea said looking at Manuel who looked back at her with resignation. He would have to drag her up if she decided not to go on her own volition. He had his orders. Both of them knew that.

"So you all know each other?" John asked.

Andrea shook her head in annoyance, not in response to John's question but rather as a reaction to the implications of what John was about to find out. Manuel said nothing.

The group moved up the stairs now.

At the top of the stairs in the atrium, Don Carlos sat on the couch pretending he had been reading the morning paper when in fact he had been looking over and around the paper until then. When the party reached upstairs he pretended to put down his paper unwittingly and looked up with a smile.

Then, his smile froze when he saw Sam. A chill that ran through him crossed his heart and he dropped the paper he was holding. He had seen her down the steps earlier and he thought the girl had looked right into his soul. He had thought she was an apparition of some sort. To him her painted face symbolized the devil that had come to collect on the fortune he had gathered by means he had borrowed from the master of deceit. Now his debt stacked high.

John noticed the change in Don Carlos' demeanor. "This is Sam, Nikki's friend," he said a little puzzled at the reaction.

"Of course," Don Carlos tried to smile as he stood up, but he could not recover the color in his cheeks that had grown pale since he had seen his apparition. His knowledge that she was a real girl didn't matter now. She had already served the symbolic message that he had already received.

Andrea had managed to stay hidden in the back of the group so far, but there was no avoiding the old man when he leaned his head to one side to see who was behind John.

"Andrea!" Don Carlos tried to hide his emotion lest they rendered his image as anything but tough. "You've come back. I thought you swore you were never going to set foot back in this house. Yet you come back to me when you need my help."

"Don't kid yourself. I didn't come to you with any need. I came with John, as his friend. I wanted to make sure he got out of here without a scratch."

"Oh, how appropriate that you should care so much about John. I never told you about John, did I? You see Manuel here? Look at how big and strong he is. Manuel could stop a running bull with his bare hands if he wanted to. But he wouldn't touch John. Do you know why? Because John here taught him a long time ago that it is easier to stop the bull by getting inside its head, acting fast like a weasel, and running it into the wall. I would have retired a long time ago on some warm beach if John had stuck around. But, of course he was too smart to stick around."

"Well, I'll be..." Andrea mumbled looking at John "I got a hint earlier, but I didn't know you were so close to the big bad wolf."

"Besides, we had a misunderstanding. I misjudged his character. He has never forgiven me for it. Did I tell you that he is very stubborn?"

"Is that when he locked you down in the cellar?" Andrea asked John.

John said nothing. He flexed his his eyebrow and shrugged. It was a past that meant little to him now.

"And John, by the look I caught on your face, I take it your friend Andrea did not tell you how she and I have a very personal history."

"So you do know each other, personally." John asserted half questioning his own assertion.

"Do we know each other?" Don Carlos repeated, as he was accustomed to do. "Do we? She stabbed me through my heart.

And left me bleeding to die. The last we spoke, she said she would only see me if she were arresting me! My own daughter!"

"You're his daughter? How did I not know this?" John was shocked. That was the biggest secret both of them had kept from him.

"My mother left him and took me with her when I was little." Andrea explained. "I found out whose daughter I was after she died. By that time, I was already working in the police force."

"Classic!" said John. "Classic!"

"I came to see him once after that, but not as his daughter. I was investigating an extortion case. The victim withdrew his allegations when he mysteriously found out the investigating officer was the alleged perpetrator's daughter. He probably also got threatened on the side by Manuel here."

"He was a sleazeball!" Manuel interjected. "He had been siphoning money from a charity he had set up. That's a true example of a sleazeball, Wolf in sheep's clothing!"

"And naturally, Don Carlos wanted a share of what he was siphoning away," Andrea clarified.

"Hey," Manuel said defensively. "We don't set up charities or rob them, but if somebody is sucking money from a charity, they can't do it for free, you can be sure of that."

"Stop it! Both of you." Don Carlos shouted. That case is moot. Pointless to bring it up."

"So that is when he recognized me." Andrea continued. "I didn't think he would."

"She looks like her mother. I almost got a heart attack when I saw her. I knew immediately this was my daughter. Look at her. Just like her mother, so beautiful. I thought I was seeing a ghost. It breaks my heart every time I think that the love of my life is dead, and my only daughter despises me." Don Carlos was in some dreamy state now but caught himself before he drifted any further. "Imagine my horror seeing her wearing a badge. The irony of it!"

"I almost got a heart attack when I found out whose daughter I was," said Andrea reflecting the irony. "It was my day of reckoning with a past I only faintly remembered. My mother was trying to protect me from you and the life you led; the life you would've given me. She knew it would have been toxic for me seeing what she had to go through."

"I treated her good. And you know Andrea, I've always looked out for you when you lived here and ever since fate brought us together again after your mother robbed you of your father's love."

"What do you mean? I never came to you for anything, didn't take anything from you, never wanted anything."

"How do you think you got that big settlement with the city?"

"By suing the city for wrongfully accusing me and taking away my job."

"And if they had given you back your job, would you have been able to sue them? Would you have walked away with all that money that has allowed you to live so comfortably? Four and a quarter million!"

"Then I would be working. I wouldn't have needed to sue them. I would have had a job."

"My daughter, working for the police department, earning a small salary? Can you believe it? And working for the rest of her life for what? Nothing! I made a convincing case to certain members of the Council and the review board against hiring you back. They decided it was worth the settlement to keep me happy and to hold on to their jobs."

"You mean, I was going to get my job back? And you were the reason they made it a big deal and took away my job. For what? Some distorted idea of yours about making me happy? I never asked for your help, and I didn't want the money."

"My own daughter, working for a bunch of people who secretly came to my Sunday brunches? The hypocrisy was humiliating. You should see that!"

Andrea was furious. She reached for her gun and thought the better of it when Manuel drew closer.

"Don't worry. I wouldn't waste one on him," she said to Manuel only slightly turning her head, then she looked at the man who claimed her as his daughter, "I never had a father. When I was a little girl living in this house I didn't have a father. Just a man everybody called Don Carlos, and I happened to call Papa. When my mother ran away... Yes, she had to run away from her own house stealing her daughter because she wasn't allowed to leave. I didn't have a father then. Just a man who was after us evoking in us fear and desperation, the man I happen to call Papa. I never had a father. I wouldn't say my father died when I was little. I just never had one."

Don Carlos sat down heavily on the couch. He thought the settlement would have made her happy. On the contrary, now she resented him even more. The true depth of her hatred for him burst out like lava from a volcano and ate away at his very heart. There was no going back. He reached for something under the cushion and pulled out a pistol. He had kept it as a souvenir from some war he had served in.

"We had an understanding in that case. I was dead to you and you were dead to me. If you wanted it so, you should not have come back." He pointed his 45-caliber handgun at Andrea.

His frailty was apparent to Andrea. She could tell he was fighting against gravity to hold his gun and keep it there.

Manuel walked out in front of Andrea. The old man seemed unfazed. He directed his attention to the mass of muscle and man. "Why did you let her into this house?"

"She was with John. I was not going to let her see you anyways. Not until you called her upstairs. I thought you'd seen her."

"I didn't see her. I didn't want to see her!" Don Carlos shouted at Manuel. "... And I don't ever want to see her again. Get her out. Get them all out!" He demanded.

Andrea turned around and brushed past everybody. Don Carlos still held his pistol that now pointed at Manuel. Then, he let his hand fall still holding on to the pistol but it barely dangled through a loose grip. He stood up slowly and walked away without acknowledging John, Nikki, and Sam who still stood there, and into the door that led to his private apartment closing the door behind him quietly.

They heard a crashing of something made of glass onto the floor and the bouncing of beads, followed by a soft thud.

"Leave John." Manuel said. "I will take care of this side of business, you take care of Andrea."

Nikki and Sam followed John quietly. Nikki had other thoughts in her mind to pay attention to what was unfolding. She still hadn't recovered from the events earlier and the storm of emotions, feelings she couldn't yet name, and the resulting physical reaction in her stomach.

Sam was too shocked to react in any particular way as well. She felt as though she were floating above her own body watching everything from afar as if in a movie screen.

Manuel ran towards Don Carlos' private apartment and found that the old man had locked the door from within. He knocked gently then put his ear against the smooth grains of the red mahogany door listening for any sound. Hearing none, he stepped back and with a heavy kick close to the door knob sent the door flinging open with violence.

Don Carlos was on the floor half on his belly, half on his left shoulder as if he had first crouched down before falling to the floor, his right arm under his chest over his heart, his pistol on the floor beside him. His body that was balancing in an odd position spread out on the ground when Manuel gently tried to turn him over on his back.

Don Carlos was dead. His eyes blankly staring at some vision inside the blackness of his pupils. On the floor close to him was a broken picture frame.

"Seventy-seven years old!" Said Manuel. "It was about time you stepped aside." He closed the old man's eyes and picked him off the ground like a baby and laid him on his bed. Then he crossed the old man's arms over his chest. He performed the ceremony with the degree of respect he would have shown his grandfather.

He walked back outside to the atrium and closing the door gently behind him. "Julian!" He shouted. "Get up here quick!"

Julian went rushing past John, Nikki and Sam who had barely made it out the door. Andrea was already outside.

John felt an urge to run back in. He knew something had happened to the old man. But he stopped himself from doing so. This was a good time as any to walk away and never look back.

Just as John was pulling away from the curb, his phone rang. The voice on the line was Manuel's.

"How did you get my number?"

Manuel ignored his question. "John, Don Carlos is dead. Thought I'd let you know, in case Andrea wanted to come back in the house.

"It's Manuel." John said, looking at Andrea. "Don Carlos is dead."

Andrea looked down on the floor and saw that John had recently vacuumed the inside of his car, probably at the local car wash. "I never had a father. I have no reason to go back in there. But you can go if you want. I will drive the girls back."

John pulled away from the curb and the car slowly picked up speed as it merged into the sparse traffic when they got out into the main road that ran parallel.

Manuel was still on the phone. He had heard the conversation. "All right, John. He said. I didn't think so. But I will be seeing you."

"I am not coming back Manuel."

"I know, but I will be seeing you nonetheless sometime to call my favor. Didn't mean to bring it up but you owe me for the big stinky dead fish you left hanging in my basement. ... and I promise to keep completely quiet about your friend Nikki, or is it Erin."

Manuel hung up.

John placed the phone in the car's cup-holder.

Everybody was quiet. Sam looked a bit shaken, yet stayed reserved. John had seen her face as he got into the car and rearranged the rearview mirror.

"The old man was superstitious. I would not let him get too deep into my head if I were you." John said to Sam.

But Sam could not let it go. It wasn't only the old man. Most of the world looked at her funny. "Can I come with you guys tonight?" she asked. "I don't think I want to be by myself... If that's okay."

"Sure," John nodded. He already had an unexpected resident in his house, what was one more?

Nikki was silent. Something deep inside her, her newfound humanity, she did not even think she had, was in question. She was trembling.

"Are you alright?" John asked, a little disconcerted himself.

Nikki didn't make any effort to answer. She had not expected to feel this way.

John looked at Andrea, who was sitting on the passenger seat next to him. She was silent as she looked out the window at the trees, grass, and the streets that merged into the main road as they drove by.

After a little while, as if composing herself Andrea turned around and looked at Nikki. She knew how it felt to take a human life. She had experienced it firsthand in the line of duty, in self-defense as opposed to what she had seen Nikki do.

Nikki had no question killed someone in cold blood. Andrea knew about the consequences of such an act on any sane human being who acted on instinct on some level. But she also knew Nikki would never go to prison for it. They would have to have the body of a victim first, and proof that he was ever alive. And second, even if the Police Department came across Malvic's body they would quietly chalk it up to the mysterious force of nature and secretly thank whoever had done him in.

From the way she shuddered Andrea could tell Nikki was in shock. It was a human response. "If you ever have to choose between evil and a lesser evil it is more pragmatic in the real world to choose the lesser evil," Andrea said as if coming to a conclusion in her own mind, out loud.

John understood that she was not talking about Nikki but about her father, and Manuel and then maybe him and somehow looking for a way to accept them as being a part of her life.

Seeing Andrea looking at her, Nikki tried to speak but her lips trembled. Andrea reached back and held her hand. Nikki tried again, and this time a weak voice broke out.

"He killed me!" Then, as if realizing what she had just said and how it must sound to Andrea she rephrased and spoke, this time in a stronger voice.

"Troy is dead. He was the one who killed Troy. He killed Erin." In the process of looking into Malvic, she had looked inside the memories of the dead girl, fused with her own realization of the dreams she had been having.

"Erin just wanted to save her brother. But a young mind in the hands of criminals... they said he was too valuable to let go.

When she tried to take him away, Malvic stopped her by force. And when her brother came to defend her, Malvic shot Troy and then tortured the boy before letting him die because he was angry that Erin got away. I saw it through his eyes. It was terrible. Then he had to go after Erin. She had been the only ever witness to his crime. Erin ran and stayed alive for a while living in the streets that kept her anonymous, but he found her. He killed her. I could see everything through his eyes. It was as if he was killing me this time. He was strangling me. I didn't mean to kill him. It felt real like he was killing me. I lost control."

John breathed a sigh of relief. At least, she was really human and felt human fear, pain, anger and most of all, regret.

Chapter Eleven

Ajay found himself unable to move freely when he regained consciousness. He was still in the abandoned garage, in one of the upper levels. He was tied to one of the concrete pillars that formed and supported the structure of the garage. His wrists were tied above his head against the pillar but his arms loosely dangled on either side of his ears. His face felt bruised and swollen, he could feel the cuts inside his swollen lips and taste blood in his mouth. His vision was narrow under the swollen eyelids and his nose hurt and felt itchy and dry.

Gary was nowhere to be seen. He tried to make sense of Gary's odd behavior but decided it was of no use. How Gary had discerned his identity was of little importance at this moment. It was more urgent to free himself from his bondage in case Gary came back, if he did at all. If he could not get himself out, it would be a long time before someone found him, maybe days, or even weeks.

It shouldn't take long, he thought. He couldn't picture someone like Gary being an expert at tying someone. A wriggle here, a tug there, then he would be gone. This time he would disappear and take his change in a different city, he had made up his mind. There was no chance for him to recover the laptop. There was no point in sticking around. He had nothing to bargain for his life with if he got caught. *What did I do to deserve this?* Life a few years ago had looked like it would be simple. He had skills that had landed him with a well-paying job, a growing savings account, and everything he really wanted that money could buy. Instead he wanted more. *"For what?"* he found himself asking in a raspy whisper as he continued to wriggle his hands. He should have remained content.

It is when you lose something that you truly realize its value. All that Ajay wanted now was a simple life, an average job, and peace when he lay down on a simple bed with a pillow under his head... and water. He was thirsty.

In what he thought was about an hour later, he had made no progress in his bid to free himself. Now his head was hurting due to thirst on top of the other pain that had generally enveloped his body. His face was throbbing in the rhythm of each beat of his heart pumping blood into the vessels going up to his face and head.

"I will strangle you Gary!" he muttered, grinding his teeth. "You crazy bastard!"

"Huh!" Someone groaned behind him. "Oh, you are up? Sorry, I also took a little nap after you zoned out on me."

"Up? It is not like I took a nap. You knocked me out you crazy bastard. What do you have me tied up for? Untie me now, Gary!" Ajay demanded shouting despite the pain that grew with the volume of his own voice.

"We have to have our talk first, then we will see." Gary said stepping out from behind Ajay and standing very close to him, grinning.

"Untie me!" Ajay demanded.

"You know I can't do that."

"Who do you think you are?"

Just as he finished the question, Ajay thought he caught a strange twinkle in Gary's eye. "What are you going to do to me?"

"The answers to both of those questions depend entirely on you. If you agree to cooperate, then I am your friend and you get to live, otherwise, I am your executioner and there is no need to explain what I will do to you."

"What do you want?" This was the day he had hoped to avoid by staying underground; little had he considered he should have looked over his shoulders for common lunatics. But Gary seemed to know more than was possible for a 'hobo' living in the streets. He had to be working for someone, or someone was using him for their benefit.

"I want to give you a chance to repent."

Ajay trembled with fear as the cool and collected words from Gary resounded in his head.

"Look, I think I know who you are working for. I already agreed to give them what they want. I just need a little more time. What else do you still want from me?"

"For you to undo your evil deeds against the lord."

"You are not one of them, are you, and no one is paying you, are they?"

"Oh, I take offense at such questions. I only work for one master, my lord who you have offended.

"You mean it was not the firm or some unknown government agency that put you up to reporting on me?"

"No, no... the firm had no qualms with you. The agency has agents trying to find you to secure and protect you. You are valuable. They need your skills. Or so they think."

"Protect me from what?"

"Me of course. Isn't that obvious? And from the hit that was put out for you by the unnamed parties, that is, the same people who raided your apartment a few years ago."

"You mean the DOD wasn't looking for me to put me in jail or make me disappear?"

"Why would they? You did that to yourself all on your own. You are a very valuable asset to the firm and the government for the research you were doing. They knew you were working on the side for a long time and let it slide. You thought they were not keeping an eye on you? They were. Just in case you got yourself in a big mess, but you ran away without notice, so they weren't even able to help. As far as they know, your last client was responsible for stealing you away from them. The way they went about looking after you with some mighty impressive force... tst tst tst ... you would have been touched if you knew. They wiped out a small illegal army protecting your ex-clients. Which is why you are now on their 'shit' list."

"How do you know all this?"

"I have taken in the light so that I may undo the wrong you have done. I know all there is to know, about you, and about your sins. You can rectify your mistakes, by ending what you started."

"What did I start?"

"Don't play dumb with me Ajay. That is an insult. You undermined the work of god, undermined creation, and mimicked the Garden of light so that the devil could rise from the shadows and walk in the light of day. You made that possible."

"Are you talking about my research project? How do you... never mind... you took in the light, whatever that means. You mean, smoked weed, you loon? The people who promised to pay you gave you a bit of background information, no doubt. What do you want from me?"

"Destroy the Garden. Destroy the vessel that the devil possesses."

"The Garden I understand, but I do not currently have the laptop as you can see. But, what vessel? You mean the laptop?"

"The girl. Nikki!"

"Nikki! The girl who stole the laptop? I do not know her. I did not even see her. But if you expect me to go kill someone... all I can say is, you need help, man! I know some people who can help you, seriously man, let me help."

"Ha! You have not met the girl, have you? You have not met your own creation. She walked by you when you were Joe, remember? I saw you when I saw her. You looked at her. You knew her, your eyes followed her."

"That's because I saw my friend, John. And no, I did not create anyone. I see John has been spreading his crazy fantasies. For the record, I did not create any Frankenstein monster, nor is it possible to."

"John is your, friend. Then you know where to find him for sure. You will have to kill him too. But first the girl."

"I am not killing anyone!"

"Then I will kill you." Gary moved even closer now. He had Ajay's handgun in his belt.

"You are crazy, you know that? You can't do this."

"I can do anything in the name of my lord! And you are a heretic who refuses to repent and do the lord's bidding. I will give you one last chance. Will you do the lord's work?"

Ajay was filled with rage, as much as despair. "No! I will not kill anyone! Untie me you stinking lunatic," he protested loudly and violently crying and shouting and at the same time staring into the dark hollow eyes of Black Hat who was taking pleasure in watching him squirm, watching him break down.

"You can't hurrr..." but the air that was to produce the rest of the sound and sustain the rest of his life was not to be found. His body was in shock in response to a sudden puncture in his diaphragm. It hurt to try to breathe and he could not find the energy to stand the pain, yet, there it was. He looked down. A piece of metal rod was sticking out of him, or rather, into him. He looked back up at Gary. In his eyes he had a question: "Why?"

Gary slowly pulled out the metal rod he had picked up nearby and threw it aside carelessly. It rang and resonated against the concrete floor as it first bounced and slowly rolled to a stop a few feet away.

"This way, you will have time to pray and repent for your sins if you so choose."

Gary started walking away. "Sweet dreams... lost soul. Now I am going to right the ultimate wrong you created."

I have to warn them, Ajay thought, but a strange coldness was taking over his body and the pain seemed to be melting away as a sea of calm emptiness surrounded him.

John drove back to the restaurant where they had breakfast and from where they had driven together to Don Carlos'. From there, Andrea drove back in her car. She was in a hurry.

"The poor dog has been home all day. You guys can decide what you are doing and if you need to pick up anything from Sam's place," she instructed.

When they got to Sam's apartment, the two girls headed in while John waited in the car. Nikki said she preferred to go up the stairs and was waiting in front of the elevator on the fifth floor when Sam go there. They walked side by side to the apartment to get Sam's things for the night. Sam touched Nikki's hand, and then they held hands till they got to the apartment door.

The apartment seemed a little cleaner than both of them remembered from the morning.

"Didn't I tell you," Sam said holding up a small note and some money she found on the kitchen table, "my roommate has vacated the apartment without any notice. At least she left her part of the rent money."

The money was enough to cover rent to the end of the month and in the note the roommate had asked Sam to give her a call if there was any other payment that she may need to take care of.

"That's something nice though, isn't it?" Sam said sarcastically.

Nikki didn't say anything. She was wondering now if Erin and Troy had lived in the city for a while in a similar apartment, maybe shared a place with someone, and if that someone wondered what happened to them, at least until the rent was up. She had no way to verify.

Sam thought about the things she might need for the night-over but decides to take her entire suitcase since it wasn't very big and much of what she had fit in it anyways. From under her pillow, she removed her diary and stuck it in the front pocket of the suitcase.

When they got to John's house, they saw a car that was parked on the street in front of his mailbox.

John looked annoyed. "It's one of the neighbor's daughter's friends no doubt. That girl has lots of friends, and they all seem to park too close to my driveway. The reason why they can't just park on the side of the street of the house they are visiting escapes me completely."

Seeing Nikki look at him quizzically he went on to explain with a smile. "As a long-time resident on this street, I get to rant now and then."

Nikki shrugged her shoulders.

When John opened the door to the house, he found that the blinds were all drawn down. He couldn't remember if he had drawn them down but didn't give it a second thought. He flipped on the light switch but found that it was not working. "The bloody fuse must have blown out!" he grumbled.

"And why in the world are all the blinds down? We could have done with some street lights. Must have been Andrea this morning. I know she is a security freak, but, in my house, my blinds. I guess Julian was right. Once a cop, always a cop."

"She lives here too?" Sam asked innocently.

"No, she was only visiting, which makes it worse she would do this." He wondered if Nikki made anything of the comment, but she said nothing.

John pulled up the blind and let the streetlight illuminate the entrance area a little.

"Ok, Sam leave your stuff here, we'll take it upstairs later once we get this light thing sorted out. Follow me to the kitchen. I have a secondary circuit running on battery but it's just for the kitchen. Never thought I'd use it."

They crossed the living room to get to the kitchen.

"Do you get that smell or is it only me?" John asked.

"Like a laundry basket you meant to wash this morning maybe?" Sam said politely. She could only smell dirty socks and sweaty clothes. She thought it would be rude to point out John's lack of hygiene and cleanliness in his own house since she was a guest.

"More like smelly socks and sweat. They're not mine, mind you" he clarified in haste. "Is that..." he took a sniff in the dark, "perfume mixed in with the stink?"

Suddenly, the lights came on. A dirty looking man with a large but managed beard and neatly done long hair under a black hat was sitting on the couch with his feet on the coffee table, his shoes and socks neatly tucked under it. Everybody's attention went to the source of the primary stink, the blistered feet, and they seemed not to pay attention at first to the person sitting on the couch or the pistol he held in one hand. The other hand attracted more attention since the man leaned his body to one side stretching the hand which he had place over an electric outlet on the wall. The man looked familiar but John could not quite place him.

"Gary!" Nikki said. "You are the man who knew Erin."

Gary pulled his hand away from the wall, pulling with it a breaking string of saliva.

"A little trick of lights I happened to learn today," he said somewhat pleased. "Please join me," Gary said looking at the sofa adjacent to him waving his pistol. "All three of you. There!" He smiled revealing a set of browning teeth.

"Look!" John said sitting next to Nikki in the center with Sam furthest away from Gary. "If this has anything to do with me accidentally elbowing you the other day, I apologize. It was really an accident. I am very sorry."

"I did not forget, but that is not why I am here."

"Why else would you be here?" John asked. "Do you want some money?"

"No, no!" Gary squinted his eyes and shook his head. "I have plenty of money." He took out a handful of twenty-dollar bills and threw them on the table.

"Then why are you here? What else could you possibly want?"

"I want the girl!" Gary said pointing at Nikki. "She does not belong here. She is dead. I intend to see to it that she stays that way."

"Why would you want to hurt the poor girl?"

"I serve my lord in his mighty army and I will fight the devil wherever he takes a stand against the mighty one! She is the instrument of the devil. He uses her body to defy the lord's will and walks in the light of day. I am here to cast him back to the shadows where he belongs, where the lord banished him!"

"How did you find my house? John asked. "And how do you know my name?"

"We have a mutual friend."

"Ajay?" John guessed though he did not know why he made that association. Over the years and across his careers, John had many contacts all over the city. But Gary just seemed to fit with Ajay given the craziness of the rest of the day. Maybe it could have been the sunburned skin or the smell of the streets that sat like a layer above the skin that one could not simply rub away with a simple wash and a change of clothes.

Gary let out a crooked smile. "You mean Joe. That is what he called himself when he lived in the streets. All that time I saw him in the streets and across the dining room at the soup kitchen, and I did not suspect a thing. I did not even suspect he carried a gun with him and I am quick to notice these things and report them to Jerry at the PD. All that time, and poor quiet Joe, aka Ajay Vikramsen, had been working for the devil."

"Working for the devil?" John asked with a bit of agitation in his voice. He could not believe the absurdity of the turn of events even though the last few days had been absurd enough.

"That's right... trying to undermine the work of god, undermine creation, so that the devil could rise from the shadows and live in a Garden of mimicked light."

John thought for sure that the person in his house was mentally unstable. *Maybe I can get him sidetracked,* John wondered.

"Gary," John said in an understanding but matter-of-fact voice, "Ajay, or Joe, is not around. Why don't you come in the morning, and we can see where he might have gone."

"I know Joe is not around. He is hanging around an old abandoned garage downtown. Literally! And he spilled his guts to me about all that he did and about you John. Yes, he spilled his guts literally as well," Gary said with a grin.

"Where is he? What did you do to him?"

"I gave him a choice. It was his choice to die rather than to put an end to his creation, his abominable creation, and to send the devil back to the depths of hell. He opened the gates of hell for the banished one. I gave him a choice to undo his deed and help me close the door... but alas! But, I gave him plenty of time to repent for his sins. A stomach wound gives its bearer time to repent."

"Don't you see you are frightening my daughters!" John tried to create an emotional, albeit a fake, scenario he hoped would soften Gary somehow.

"You don't fool me John Selvas. I know everything about you. Everything."

"How come everyone claims to know everything about me and I don't seem to know anything that is going on?" John exclaimed in disgust.

John's latest annoyance about everybody knowing everything about him struck a chord with Nikki. She had learned everything she could about John while she was still learning about her environment from within the laptop, before she had ventured out to find a body for herself. The only other resident from the Garden she had talked to was Victor.

"What do you want me to do? Maybe I can help." Nikki asked, seeming to be cooperative. "I am right here. I am not the devil. Just a girl who looks like a girl you used to know and supposedly died."

"You don't fool me! Your pretty face you flaunt at me does not even belong to you. I know you well. You dwelt in the Garden of heresy to mimic the original creation. And you came out and preyed upon a dying young girl."

"That is your twisted version of what you cannot understand. But I am really surprised you seem to know any of it. How do you?" Nikki asked with curiosity.

"Believe me devil! I have seen the light, and through it, I have seen your truth! This is further proof that she is the devil incarnate," Gary said turning to John. "She's trying to cajole me with her innocent talk."

Presently he looked at Sam and spat on the floor in disgust. "And he is gathering his worshippers around him."

Sam let out a sigh. "Why does everybody assume I am a devil worshiper just because I got a few tattoos in my face, and got my nose and tongue pierced? I am not a believer. But I believe that all of you believers believe that your god gave each one of us free will to live as we choose and answer only to god. So I do not know whose work all you people who tell us how to live and what to believe according to what suits your cloistered worldviews and political needs are doing... obviously not your god's!"

Sam was furious now. "When you try to curtail my free will, or the free will of any other person in how we choose to live our lives that you believe is given to each of us by your god, it is NOT in your god's name."

"Lies!" Gary said. You twist the truth. The devil influences you even as you breathe. But you don't fool me either, you bitch of hell!"

Gary was furious and the saliva that congregated with froth in his mouth reminded Sam of the attack dogs she had seen earlier that day when they went to see Don Carlos.

John had had enough, but he did not want to push Gary any further in his fury. After all, he had the gun.

"You mean you saw the light of heaven?" John asked, hoping to steer Gary in a different mood.

"I was bathed in the light!" Gary announced indeed changing his mood as he recalled the occurrence in the library the previous evening. "The power and brightness was so immense I shuddered. The burden I was taking on in accepting it was a heavy one. I literally fell to the floor cringing in fear of the knowledge and power that was bestowed upon me. And now I seek to fulfill my duty.

John cringed in fear himself. He would not be able to reason with Gary. They were dealing with a delusional lunatic with a calling from god.

Nikki on the other hand was feeling more positive. *...if only I can work past the barrier that Gary's human consciousness provided to the other consciousness that was resident in him.* It was foolish of the occupant to have entered a live human mind that obviously had control of thought and action, no matter how deluded.

"Is that you in there, Victor?" Nikki asked looking at Gary unsure of what she might uncover. For a moment she did not seem to have gotten trough. "Victor, if you can hear me...?"

"Victor?" Gary laughed. "There is no Victor in here. Victor never was. You are trying to play with my mind, aren't you? Don't even try. Your mind tricks will not work on me!"

"Listen to me Victor. I do not understand why you are doing this, or if you are unable to..."

"Stop it!" Gary shouted with rage burning in his eyes. As if on second thought, he walked over to Nikki pointing the gun at her and hit her on the side of the head with the grip knocking her to the ground. "Much easier to shut you up that way!"

Nikki fell to the floor with her hands in front of her face trying to protect her head as she approached the floor but she landed on her face nevertheless. She felt she was losing consciousness and she tried to hold on, but everything turned dark.

John crouched down to help Nikki up.

"Let her be!" Gary ordered. "Leave her alone."

John ignored him and shook Nikki turning her over.

Gary put the gun on John's head. "Don't make me do it. You know I will. Get back on the couch or you will have a leaky skull."

John believed that Gary was not bluffing. The calmness in his voice was eerie.

Nikki found herself in an abyss. It was dark and the sounds of rustling and heavy breathing was all around her. She ran about in this abyss looking for a way out. The rustling sounds followed her closely and frightened her. Before her, on the wall of darkness, was a towering iron gate that kept her from leaving. She tried to open it, but it felt like she was pushing against the ground. At the top of it was an opening. She couldn't tell how large the opening was or how high, and from what she could see, it was still dark outside but the darkness there paled compared to the one inside which seemed to pull her apart in every direction.

There, she thought, *that is my way out but how do I get there?* Suddenly as if sucked by a vacuum-like force from outside the gate, she was lifted up rapidly and violently towards the narrow opening with the darkness around her still pulling her down. In the short time that she had gained a sense of human fear, she had never been so scared.

She seemed to hit a ceiling of some kind in the darkness, but now she was at the top of the gate next to the opening. It was small, and she struggled to try to fit through. The forces that were pulling her from every direction inside the gate and the other that pulled her from the outside felt like they were about to rip her apart. She looked outside the abyss where she could make out a dim world covered in vegetation. The Garden, she thought, but why is it so dark. The frightening rustling sounds were behind her now pulling at her feet. The Garden was not inviting by any means but there seemed to be peace and silence.

"Hello?" A girl's voice rang out from somewhere behind her. "Who's there?"

"Hello? This is Nikki. Who's there?" Nikki looked around but saw no one.

"Nikki? I know you." The voice was now next to her amidst the breathing and rustling she could hear. "But... I don't know how I know you. How do I know you?"

"I don't know," Nikki replied but she still could not see any-one. "Who are you?"

"I don't know. I have been here it seems forever."

"What is this place?" Nikki asked.

There were no replies. Just a long stretch of silence amidst the rustling. There was something familiar about the questions and the voice that asked it. And something eerily familiar about the silence. Nikki wanted to get away from this silence and from someone she felt was very close to her but remained in the darkness. She thought about the Garden outside once more and reached to the opening.

"Where are you going?" The girl's voice came from behind her. Nikki turned around. In the darkness she could make out a shape.

"Is it you Victor? Are you playing games with me?"

"Victor? There is no Victor. There is no one else. Just me. And I am bored. I have been here in the darkness for a long time. Don't leave me here."

Nikki was puzzled. "What do you mean? What is this place?"

"I don't know. It seems I cannot remember being anywhere else. But you just got here. You must know something. How did you get here? Where are you?" The voice asked.

"I don't know how I got here. But I am in a dark scary place, and you scare me." Nikki replied panicking now.

"You scare me too. You scared me half to death rustling around in here and stirring up a storm. Try to think harder. Where were you before you came here?"

Nikki couldn't remember. She could not remember a time before she got here.

"But you remember Victor...?"

"Because you are here. Aren't you Victor?"

"Nikki, think harder! Where are you? Where were you before now?"

"Put an end to this, Victor. I don't like this at all. You tell me where we are. You seem to know."

"Only you can remember Nikki. I have been here too long. And for the last time, there is no Victor in here."

"I want to get out! I don't like this place at all, and I don't like you right now."

"I feel exactly the same. Where do you want to go from here?"

"To the Garden, out there!"

"What Garden? Where?"

Nikki looked around. There was nothing, just more of the same abyss.

"What happened to the Garden? What have you done to it?"

"Me? I did not see any garden. We are alone in here and there is no 'away' to go to. Here is where you are, and here is the only place that exists."

"How do I get out?"

"I don't know. I have been stuck here longer than you and I don't even know about the garden you talk about."

"But what is beyond the abyss?" Nikki asked.

"Who knows. This is all that there is as far as I can tell."

Nikki was getting annoyed now. She was getting tangled in the conversation with Victor who pretended not to know anything.

"Go away! Leave me alone!" Nikki shouted.

"I can't. Isn't it obvious we are stuck inside the same abyss?"

Nikki peered closer into the darkness of the abyss. There was no semblance of anything physical or real in the place. Even the other entity that claimed to be stuck with her didn't seem to exist anywhere. Try as she might, Nikki could not see through the veil of the abyss. She was stuck.

Stuck. Stuck in something viscous and straining, draining her energy, something that was dying. Stuck like when she first jumped into the body when it was still in the morgue. Things suddenly made sense. She was stuck in some deep synaptic chasm of the physical brain.

"You are not Victor, are you?"

"Who is Victor?"

Nikki ignored the questions. Nikki remembered.

"My head hurts," she said. "I hurt my head."

"How?"

"It was Gary..."

"Who's Gary?"

"Out there in the world... The one with John, Sam, Andrea, Manuel, ... and Gary." Now she remembered. But she was still trapped in the room. Gary had hit her on the head, and she had banged her head on the floor. She was unconscious.

"I need to get back out of here! The others are in danger."

"Where? You mean there are more like us?"

Again, Nikki ignored the question.

I need to struggle harder! Nikki thought to herself. *Let the darkness frighten you enough to make you fight for your life, but do not run away. Just fight harder!*

Indeed, she was frightened. If she lost control for long, she could be stuck in here forever or until the body simply perished.

Nikki now found herself floating around the abyss. This must be the substance of the mind and body I have no control over, Nikki reasoned. She still felt fear, but also fatigue. "I need to regain control before I become this abyss. Like Erin." She brewed up a tempest fueled with all the fear and the desire to live, and violently swirled around the abyss.

"Yes," she said to herself, "fight harder."

"Don't leave me here. Take me with you."

Nikki looked at the source of the voice. There was a young man she had called Victor behind the glass in the dark wall of the abyss. She flew at him in rage riding at the head of the tempest of her creation. Her rage now knew no reason. The man's face changed. It was Erin now.

"Don't leave me here!" Erin shouted. Nikki's rage even meant to crush Erin now. Even as the tempest shattered the glass she realized it was a mirror, and in the darkness, she could see her own reflection in the shards of glass that flew about even as the mirror shattered all around her.

Nikki woke up feeling sharp pain where Gary had struck her, and a throbbing in her head. She was seated on the floor leaning on the base of the couch between Sam and John's legs that supported her body to keep her upright. She couldn't move her hands; they were tied behind her back.

John nudged her with his foot. "Are you ok?" Gary had tied his and Sam's hands behind them as well.

Nikki looked at John. It hurt to turn her head and look up at him. She twitched in pain and lightly shook her head but didn't speak.

Gary sat in the armchair on the side with his stinking feet on the coffee table once more. The smell was not necessarily off-putting to Nikki. She had not learned as most children do as they grow up to associate foul smells with bad things. But she knew it emanated from the bacteria and fungi that thrived on the feet of their host, who himself was an unwelcome guest in the house.

"You're back?" he said jauntily. "You should have stayed where you were hiding."

"And where would that be?" Nikki asked surprisingly boldly for someone who had just been hit on the head and knocked out, she didn't know for how long. Apparently long enough to have her hands tied and propped up, along with both John and Sam's.

"In the dark shadows of hell of course. I thought you'd stay there for good! But apparently you have other ideas. But I am not worried. We have all night if that is what it will take."

Nikki took a deep breath. "It's Tor," she announced. "It's the Bot from the Garden."

"You mean he is infected by the virus?" John asked, glancing timidly at Gary.

"Is he sick?" Sam asked.

"He was sick before he caught the virus. Now he is super-sick, if you want to put it that way. It is really Gary on what you might think of as, super-information-steroids."

"What does it want?" John asked.

"I don't think Tor wants anything. It was programmed to gather information and report it back to its origin. It lost its origin address information and directive when it got into the Garden. Looks like I have become its new origin. It is trying to get back to me."

"Then why the hell is it trying to kill us?"

"Tor is not trying to kill us... I think. In looking for me, I think it found Gary who was also looking for me and sort of hitched on for a ride. But it is Gary who thinks I am the devil for whatever his reasons and predispositions were. And it looks like all the information Tor had collected, Gary is able to use, as well as make use of Tor's abilities to gather and manipulate information and the electromagnetic and computer circuitry for his own benefit. Tor just does not know how to get out."

"That's how he probably got the money." John said.

"And that is how he probably found Ajay and was also able to control the electric circuitry in the house." Nikki added.

"I think you lost me a long time ago," Sam said. "Most of today doesn't make any sense to me. Can you just wake me up when all this is over? I think I must be asleep in my bed having a nightmare."

"Is there a way to get Tor out of him?" John asked.

"I don't know. Maybe if we knock him out, hook him to an electric circuit, and coax Tor to hop on to a storage device, maybe back into the laptop..."

"Are you all done?" Gary was smiling. "I am sitting right here and you are talking about knocking me out and electrocuting me? The funny thing is you are all sitting with your hands tied behind your backs and I have a gun. You just gave me enough reason to finish off all three of you. You are all irredeemable. You can all reunite and continue with the conversation back in hell."

Gary walked over to Nikki with resolve and casually raised the pistol and pressed it right above her temple. He put his index finger over the trigger and looked up at the ceiling as if through it and into the sky. "In the name of the lord..."

John's mind was racing wildly and his heart was pounding in his chest. He did not think it was going to get this far, but there was every indication that Gary was going to pull the trigger.

John sprang up and lunged into Gary with his shoulders leading the way, shouting what seemed like a rustic battle cry; his hands still tied up behind him. Gary tried to twist to fend off his attacker but he fell backwards with John on top of him and landed on the floor. At the moment of impact, the gun went off and the sound filled the room with what felt to Gary as a shock wave, which had partly resulted from his head hitting the hard floor.

When Gary was on the ground, John sprang up and put his shin over Gary's neck and pressed hard. Gary struggled. He still held the pistol in his hand but John was trying to press it with his other knee. Gary was trying to point it towards John. Nikki scrambled onto her knees and fell over Gary's torso and pinned down Gary's hand with her left shoulder so that his hand and pistol were against the floor. But Gary still held on to the pistol and tried to twist his wrist to point the gun upwards. Nikki stretched her neck upwards and bit Gary on whatever part of the hand she could manage to get hold of and at the same time tried to prevent him from twisting his wrist.

Gary was now growling like a pinned down animal. He was not giving up. Nikki bit harder and John shifted more of the weight, from the leg he had been using to pin down Gary's arm now that Nikki had taken charge of it, to his other leg over Gary's neck. Finally, Gary let go of the pistol and after a while there was no more struggle.

When John noticed Gary was not responding, he slowly eased the pressure over Gary's neck but kept his knee in place.

"Ok, Nikki, untie my hands!" He positioned his wrists close to Nikki's mouth. She on her part examined the knot and proceeded to untangle it with her mouth.

John was free within a minute. He turned around to untangle Nikki and almost leapt in horror upon seeing blood dripping from her mouth like a wild beast.

"What the...?"

"It's not mine." Nikki cut him off. "I think I almost tore off his little finger."

John looked down at Gary's bloody hand. "Fuck!" He exclaimed. The finger and part of the palm that included the metacarpal that connected the little finger to the carpel joint barely hung on to the rest of his hand.

"The pistol went off right?" He asked. In the rush of the moment and the struggle that ensued, he wasn't sure if it had, though now he became aware of a ringing in his ears. "Are you alright?"

Nikki knew she was fine. Even in the heat of the moment, the awareness of the system that supported her existence was constant. John had charged at Gary who was pointing a gun at them. He was the most likely one of them to have been hit. It is not uncommon that a person can remain unaware of being stabbed, cut, or shot due to adrenaline rushing through the veins and the excitement of a tense situation and carry on for a while until after the rush. Then they crash and pain surges in like a flash flood.

Nikki visually scanned John with a quick glance up and down. He quickly ran his hands over his own body, just in case. He seemed fine. Then they looked at Gary. He hadn't stopped the bullet either. Both turned to Sam.

Sam was looking at them trying to make sense of what was happening. She had a look of horror in her face but said nothing. She had never seen so much violence in her life. Not so close and personal anyways. First some crazy man the others seemed to know wanted to kill them, and now he lay dead for all she knew, with his hand bloody and mangled. To her John and Nikki attacking Gary had looked like a pair of hungry wolves, taking down a large prey silently coordinating the kill amidst that chaos. Now as they stood looking at her, Nikki with her bloody mouth and John with his hair and clothes ruffled up during the struggle with Gary, looked like wild animals. They sensed her fear, and were coming for her next.

"Are you okay?" John was saying.

Sam nodded still unsure of what was happening, half in a daze and half paralyzed with utter fear, unable to speak.

"Well that was lucky!" John said untying Nikki and looking around to see where in the room the bullet might have landed.

Nikki cleaned her mouth with her sleeve as soon as her hands were free.

"I think I killed him!" John said checking for a pulse. He could not help but feel sorry for Gary even though a few minutes ago he had had every intention of killing the lunatic.

"If it is any consolation," Nikki said, wiping her face with her hands. "He didn't have much to live anyway. He was dying of leukemia."

"How do you know this?"

"His blood. It is overcrowded with B-Cells. That is significant of chronic lymphoid leukemia. He was at the brink already with intolerably low resistance to infection. Those blisters could have taken him out in a matter of days."

"Thanks!" John said rolling his eyes. "Knowing that may help me get over my feeling of guilt in a few decades."

"He was going to kill us ..." Nikki tried to find some words that she thought might be consoling rather than the obvious.

"I know, but it is still a human life."

Nikki understood. "We did what had to be done! But now I should get Tor out. If for whatever reason, people at the hospital hook Gary's body to any kind of system, and Tor is still active, it may try to jump out. There is no way to tell what it will be up to or what damage it will cause."

Nikki took out the laptop from her bag and connected the network cable from it to Gary's mouth and turned it on. She logged into the A.I. environment.

"Come on Tor. Back to the Garden. It's okay. Come on now."

Nikki wasn't sure this would work but she had to try. Nothing happened at first, then she could see the hard drive of the laptop filling up with data. Then she could see Tor coming alive in the Garden. When she noticed the transfer was complete, Nikki pulled out the cable from Gary's mouth and placed the laptop gently on the floor. Let us make sure we do not connect it to the Internet. He is not the same old Tor anymore.

"That was Tor?" John asked.

"Yes, it seems Tor got out with me. The Garden did not clean it. It left with me, and the Garden reset itself. Tor had no way of following me into the body. It has no memory before the Garden because in trying to destroy it, I took its memory and definition. I am the only thing that is familiar to it. It has been looking for me ever since. Like a puppy trying to cross a little stream to follow its human."

"And in looking for me, it somehow found the person who had recognized me... and thought it would take a ride. But to do so, it had to enhance its host a little. However, in doing so, it got trapped behind the consciousness of the living host."

Is it contained now?" John asked not able to fully comprehend the explanation, but getting the gist somewhat.

"Yes. In the laptop." Nikki said casually.

"What do we do with the laptop?" John asked curiously.

"Destroy it."

"You mean with the Garden and Tor and all the research Ajay had been working on?"

"Yes. What is in there is too risky, and Tor is not a simple Bot it once was."

Nikki would have to find a way to destroy the laptop and everything in it irretrievably.

John realized that they had neglected to untie Sam. She had been patient, and as they were still coming out of the chaos, he had simply watched Nikki perform the bazaar ritual with the laptop. But in doing so, he had not taken into account how strange and shocking it might all have been for Sam seeing all this before her eyes. Besides the fact that she was young, she was probably not used to the kind of violence John had known in the past, nor did she have the capability to break down the complexity of terrible things into logical bits and pieces like Nikki.

"Are you going to sit there all evening? Come let me get you untied. I'll make you some soothing tea." John held Sam by the nook of her elbow and pulled her up. Sam crumbled down to the floor. Behind her on the couch was a solitary hole about an inch wide. That was where the bullet had exited her body tumbling and fragmenting after it entered her and likely smashing against her ribs or spine. A big dark blotch of red below the hole marked the area Sam had her back against where she was seated.

Both John and Nikki looked at Sam who lay on the floor looking back at them. If Sam had been wearing a white shirt it might have turned deep red around her mid-section in the area of her solar plexus. But the blood soaked thick black t-shirt with a scattered array of psychedelic art she had probably created herself only looked a little shinier.

"Noooo!" Nikki wailed in panic and despair as she rushed to the floor and put Sam's head on her lap, "Look at me Samantha!"

Sam looked only moving her eyes. She could only see Nikki now in the totality of her vision and awareness.

"You will be fine! You just need to hold on." Nikki said trying to hold back tears.

Sam could still not understand why she was on the floor and why Nikki looked so worried. She smiled reassuringly, but she would not have known that her lips did not move and not much changed in the expression on her face. She just felt tired and nothing seemed to matter.

"Think of something you've always wanted to do and we will go do it in the morning! I can..."

"I've always wanted to jump out of an airplane," Sam said in a feeble whisper with a weak smile now.

"Sure!" said Nikki looking at Sam, "And if you want, you and I could go see the world and jump off of wherever you want."

John could not help smiling at the hopelessness even as his eyes prickled with the sensation of burning and filled with tears.

"The whole world...?" Sam asked with words that seemed to fade away as they came out but with a face so calm it was clear she was not aware of the pain her body was in. "You don't have a dime!" she added with a sound that hinted laughter but turned into a breath.

"Don't you worry about that," Nikki said. We'll even ride camels and elephants if you want, or visit the vast Amazon forest and study the plants and the wonderful creatures that live nowhere else. We can go exploring the coral reefs and the beautiful creatures that only live there..."

Sam said nothing. She looked into some non-existent space beyond Nikki as if imagining the deep jungle and swimming in the clear waters in the coral reefs.

"...and swim with dolphins... I've always wanted to do that," Nikki went on.

John put his hand on Nikki's shoulder.

"... and see the great whales that swim across vast oceans. We can do all that if you want," Nikki went on.

In her mind, she was trying to escape to the places she described but the pain she had never felt before and had never even thought was possible to feel followed her everywhere she tried to go. It was as if she was drowning in a vast ocean filled with torrents of sorrow and fear, with darkness swirling over her head like giant waves, crashing onto her with every breath she tried to take, suffocating her, and with every breath pulling her apart into countless pieces, each hopelessly sucked into more oceans impossible to navigate, filled with desperation.

A possibility she had not considered entered her mind. Through the swells in her eyes, Nikki looked up at John with new found alertness, "I can save her..."

"She has lost too much blood." John tried to assure her. He had seen this before. Sam was already too weak to pull through. He knew that Nikki would have to see for herself the truth about life, that it was real as was death, and that death as final as it was made life precious.

"Ok, let's try this again!" Gary's voice disturbed the somber silence that had taken over the room.

John turned around. Gary was pointing the pistol at him with his bloody mangled hand. In the confusion John had neglected the pistol on the floor. Why would he have? Gary was dead, or had been, a while ago when he checked.

"You! Off the floor!" Gary shouted at Nikki who was seated on the floor with her back to him. He pointed the pistol at her now.

Nikki did not comprehend the words seemingly directed at her. All she could think of was the blank stare in Sam's face.

"Let her be!" said John. "Let her be! You just shot her friend. You just shot a poor innocent girl."

"Innocent? A devil worshiper you mean? She probably fucked all the devil's followers like you to raise the devil."

Nikki heard this. A strange rush of heat she hadn't felt before arose from deep within her belly. *Anger.* In her mind, she knew exactly where Gary stood behind her. She planned five moves. She would gently lay Sam's head on the floor. She would leapt up in the air at the same time turn around pushing her body against Gary's torso throwing him off balance and onto the ground. With one hand she would grip the wrist of his hand holding the pistol so tight the trigger finger would not respond to the voluntary or involuntary command from the brain to squeeze, and with the other she would grip Gary's throat around his larynx sinking her fingers with the might that her rage provided as deep as they would go through the skin and the flesh below, and pull with all her might.

Nikki smiled in silent rage as she contemplated this. It would take a matter of seconds once she laid Sam's head gently down on the floor.

Just then, a deafening shot rang out that echoed in every wall around them. Nikki looked back quickly to assess the situation. If Gary had missed, she would have to put her plan into action with even more haste as he adjusted his aim. If he had in turn shot John, his body or arm position would have changed. She would have to implement her plan just as quickly, but re-assess the necessary move to complete her objective of taking Gary down.

As she turned her head to assess the situation, she assessed John's face. He had a look of shock on his face, but it did not have the reaction a bullet entering him would have caused. Instead his eyes were filled with confusion focused on Gary.

Gary stood still for a bit and fell on his knees. He looked up at an imagined sky with horror in his eyes and momentarily collapsed to the floor.

Andrea's shaky voice came in from behind them. "Looks like I got here a little too late!"

"Andrea!" John said, with nostrils flared and breathing heavily.

Andrea rushed in from the shadows in the dark entrance holding her pistol still pointing it at Gary. Unlike her voice, her hands were steady. She walked over to Gary and in a manner secondary to her nature from years of training, she knelt down on one knee and with her left hand searched his neck for a pulse.

"He's dead," she announced, standing up and holstering her pistol on her hip.

Andrea walked over to where Sam lay on Nikki's lap. She knelt and felt for a pulse.

"John, call 9-1-1 quick!" she ordered. "She is still alive, but barely"

"Hold on!" Nikki said to John as he reached for the cellphone on the table. "I can fix her. She's damaged badly. I'll need some help. Get me that lamp. The wire! I need live current!" she shouted.

John put the phone down on the table and reached for the lamp. He violently yanked out the wire from its base.

"What are you doing?" shouted Andrea in disbelief. "Call 9-1-1!"

John shot a glance at Andrea with a look of *I'll explain later,* even as he watched her reach for her phone half sticking out of her pocket.

"Wasn't he supposed to be dead?" John asked Nikki almost in disgust as he handed the live end to Nikki looking at Gary whose body laid face down on the floor.

"I think Tor fixed him up before it knew we would remove it... I guess for self-preservation." Nikki replied without much interest or energy. "If only I thought about that sooner..." She looked down at Sam's peaceful face. She had had no reason to lend her a pair of shoes when they first met ... and because of that, now she lay at the brink of life, pale as death, with a blank stare that looked nowhere.

Not if I can help it, Nikki thought. She picked up the cable still connected to the computer and put it in her mouth. She was at once connected to the circuitry of the computer and to Eden. There was Tor trying to adjust itself to the world again, but it couldn't quite fit in. It had outgrown the environment that looked to Nikki like an amateur piece of painting that tried to depict a world too large for the painter to comprehend. When Tor saw Nikki, it ran to her like its life depended on it. In a flash, Nikki scooped up Tor.

In one hand she slipped the live end of the wire and felt a jolt of electricity enter her body. She regulated the energy so only the right amount surged through her picking up Tor in its wake. At the same time, Nikki let the network cable fall from her lips as she bent over and kissed Sam on the lips. As she moistened her mouth, she could only sense the silence that remained in the overstressed neural circuitry of Sam's body as she barely held on to life.

Goodbye Nikki, she thought she heard her say in unspoken words.

Not if I can help it. Hang on! Nikki shouted in unspoken words as she let the surge of current pass through her taking Tor with it.

You know what to do, she commanded even as she scanned Tor's knowledge base. She noticed it had collected a vast amount of data, many more times in magnitude than her own knowledge base, but what it lacked was the ability to self-direct its own actions. When she had bitten off its head back in the garden, in what seems like eons ago, she had taken away part of its original directive. Now *she* was its directive. It depended on her for its purpose, its existence.

You did it to Gary when you thought your existence depended on it. Now it does once again. Fix her. Use the electric surge. I promise you can remain close to me if you do this. I must leave but I will come back.

With the amount of shock to Sam's neural network and amount of damage to her body, she knew Tor would be occupied for a while, maybe days or weeks. She disengaged from Sam's mouth and relished the strange sensation that lingered on her lips, that of Sam's lips on her own lips. Her lips tingled. *The electric surge*, she thought.

She knew Sam was going to be okay.

Nikki saw that Andrea was on the phone with the emergency services. John was sitting on the couch, silent, looking at her and Sam.

"She's going to be okay" Nikki announced with a tired smile and yanked the lamp wire from the wall and let the other end slip from her hand.

Andrea looked puzzled as she ended the call. "The ambulance and the police will be here in a while. What's going on?"

"It is a long story," said John. "but it looks like Sam will be fine."

"I'll explain later, I promise," he added, interrupting an anticipated question from Andrea.

"She'll still need rest and any medical attention she gets will only speed up her recovery, but she is stable now."

"How ... what?" Andrea was puzzled. "What did you do?"

"Nikki..." Sam's weak voice drew their attention from the vacuum that Andrea's question had created. To try to explain anything that made sense to Andrea would have been impossible at that moment.

"I must leave." Nikki said.

"What?" John asked absentmindedly as if he hadn't heard what Nikki said. He was still trying to process all that had unfolded and happened until then.

"I need to find Ajay. If he is lucky and he is still alive, I might be able to save him. I do not have answers to the questions the police will have for me. Besides, I need to destroy the laptop."

"Destroy Eden." John said in a subdued tone. He was reflecting on the gravity of his own words. Destroying the garden, the artificial environment in the laptop, would make no difference. Research and experiments more advanced than this were already underway, Ajay had told him. Even if they didn't contemplate Artificial beings like Nikki, it was only a matter of time. Besides Nikki and Tor already inhabited human bodies. Even the most advanced or the wildest research project would not have contemplated that – a species cross-over of sorts between the human body, which was superior to the most advanced computers in the world all put together, with neural connection more eloquent than the gravitational interconnection in the billions of galaxies in the universe, and artificial intelligence.

Humanity had already stepped over the edge of a precipice, whether or not it knew how to fly. Victor, if he or it was real, was a conundrum. The last thought gave him the shivers.

"Yes, I'll destroy the garden." Nikki was saying. "But first, I have questions about Victor I need to find answers to. I guess you will not see me for some time."

John couldn't comprehend all that Nikki said, but he latched on to the obvious question in his mind. "Where will you go?"

"I don't know. But I need to take your car to get to the city. You can find it easily with your phone, right."

John nodded. "It is strange," he said, "I feel like my daughter is going out into the world."

Nikki gave John a hug then picked up the laptop. "Please take care of her for me." She said looking at Sam. Sam was looking at her with questioning eyes, longing for reassurance and comfort. Nikki knelt down beside Sam. "You will be okay. I will be back," she said.

A feeling of intense care and deep desire to comfort Sam overtook Nikki. She felt like she had known her forever, like she belonged to her and she to Sam. She was certain. An imprint, a connection, a longing.

Nikki bend down over Sam's lips. She was afraid, now suddenly uncertain. She felt her heart beat intensely under her breasts. Did she have a right to whatever this was? Was she even fully human? She refrained from getting closer. She was breathing heavily as if in panic.

Sam's arm reached over Nikki's head and gently pulled her closer.

In an instant, the world disappeared. She felt Sam's soft cold lips, moist under her own. She held Sam's face. Her skin was soft and tender like nothing she had felt before. Her hair, as her hands slipped to the base of her head felt like hundreds of little strands of joy she could touch forever, one at a time.

"I must go," Nikki said pulling away. Their touching fingers lingered on as Nikki stood up. She wasn't sure who or what she was, but there was no doubt. She had fallen in love.

Andrea bore silent witness to what was going on but it felt to her that she had missed the contextual beginning of everything.

Later amidst police cars, flashing lights, and a whole lot of people in uniform, John held Sam's hand as she was carried to the ambulance on a stretcher. Detective Jerry Hart looked at Gary's body solemnly before the medics took it away on a stretcher in a body bag. Jerry would have some paperwork to do but the facts in this case looked pretty clear to him and he was not surprised Gary had ended up this way.

To Jerry it seemed obvious that Gary had a misguided grudge against John. Rope that Gary had brought along with him with which he had tied John and Sam's hand, along with two large bags, a shovel, flashlights and an axe in the trunk of the stolen car showed Gary had come with an intention to bury his victims that night. Besides, Jerry knew Andrea from when they worked together in the same unit well enough to know she would not have pulled the trigger if it was not called for and could be avoided.

When the police left, only John and Andrea were left in the house. They sat holding each other and watched the empty room in silence. Although the world around them seemed to have shaken violently and was overcast by a cloud of gloom, the possibility of a future with each other was enough to make them want to ignore the whole world undoing itself, bit by bit.

Chapter Twelve

Nikki pulled up to the abandoned parking garage. She had tapped into Tor's records as she was scanning it before releasing it into Sam's body with a directive to fix its host. The entrance to the garage had been blocked off by temporary concrete barriers so no one would be able to drive in. She left the car along the side of the road and made her way to the stairs on the side. She knew she had to get to the top level of the garage where Gary had left Ajay.

"I just hope you are still alive." Nikki said to herself. "I'll do my best to save you. I owe you that much."

Nikki surveyed the surroundings when she got to the top level of the garage. I was covered by a roof but a bright moon was shining through the side. *Still a few nights from full-moon,* Nikki thought. The summer air had turned pleasantly cool this late in the night. She made her way to the spot where she expected to see Ajay. In the moonlight she saw his form slumped in an upright position against the pillar, his chin against this chest. His stretched arms, tight against his ears were tied to a metal loop over his head, were holding the entire weight of his body. A dark pool congregated in an uneven radius. The metal bar about half an inch thick lay a few feet away. She stepped closer but took care not to step on the blood. She could see in the moonlight that he had been stabbed in the abdomen. The amount of blood was atypical for an abdomen wound unless a major organ or artery had been damaged.

It was too late for Ajay.

A siren was wailing in the distance. That was someone else, in some other dire situation. Sam would by now be in an emergency room getting patched up. Nikki surveyed as much of the city as was visible from the top floor of the garage before tall buildings got in the way. The city, for all the people who lived in it, seemed quiet just now. It would wake up in the morning still unaware of a new future that was already here.

-- The End --